The War Across the Stars

the Stars

© Alex Pennington
27 August 2007

THE WAR ACROSS THE STARS
By Alex K. Pennington

Prologue

We were watching, waiting in the cold, harsh weather of Marzoc. Nevin was to my right. Our fingers were on the triggers, despite them being numbed by the cold. Admiral Cope was in our scopes. We could have fired but instead we held our fire. We followed orders and waited.

The man in charge of the entire UED fleet marched from his gunship toward a larger tent in the center of the camp. Admiral Cope entered the central command tent. Robert followed him in. We waited for the explosion. It didn't come.

Alex Pennington

Part I
The Vorgian War

Alex Pennington

Chapter 1
The Start of a War

"All right boys" Colonel Miller said, "Our unstable relationship with the Vorgians is crumbling. War is imminent. That is why we need to prepare you for action," he continued. "I want you all here at 1200 hours."

"Yes sir," we responded.

We were excited. Our first action… Most of us didn't know what we were getting into. Nevin Poffinbarger was my closest friend. He stood beside me as we listened to the large man who stood before us. We left the briefing chambers and went to the mess hall.

It was mostly quiet in the mess hall. We were thinking of what it would be like, and the adventures to be had. Our team of five civilians and a former Navy pilot were an odd bunch to send into a war, especially as special ops. But the government had a plan. In fact, it was an extremely successful plan.

Ryan Dunkelman was bound to be our squad leader. He was nearly twenty-eight revolutions old and had combat experience as a squadron leader. He apparently had also survived a crash deep in enemy territory. He had thin layer of stubble around his mouth, despite the shaven preference of the military. His hair was a light shade of brown.

Philip Fergensen was a smart man from a wealthy family. He was only a revolution younger than Ryan, but he was a bit larger. For a smart guy, he had plenty of muscle. His hair was exceptionally short, as he preferred the buzz cut to anything longer.

Max Pippin was basically an idiot. He had no respect for Col. Miller and was always making jokes. Most of us didn't much care for him. His dark blonde hair was the longest out of our squad and he commonly stood around with his mouth in a crooked smile. He was the youngest out of our group at a mere twenty revolutions, but that was no excuse for his behavior. I doubt he had any idea what was in store for him.

Robert Washington was an odd character that always gave me a strange feeling. He seemed like the type that enjoys killing. The kind of person who would become a serial killer if it weren't for the military. But I guess you would expect to find one or two like that in the armed forces. The military makes a great way to keep them in line and put them to good use. I could only hope they'd keep Robert in line. At least men of his type were usually good in combat.

Finally, there was Nevin who sat beside me while we ate. He had jet-black hair that was about as long as mine. We both shared the same carefully trimmed hairstyle, but with varying color. Nevin was twenty-four revolutions old, which was the same age as me. We had attended school together when we were younger, and both had families in Ebony, Euphola. My parents and sister still lived there. I hoped that I would get to see them again soon.

Five minutes before 1200 hours, we went to our lockers and grabbed our SR-4's. The base, located on the military stronghold of Euphola, wasn't all too large. We could quickly move from place to place without concern for being late, though I thought we should try being early. We walked the short way to the briefing chambers.

When we arrived, Colonel Miller was there. He was a large, round man, about forty revolutions old.

"Hello boys," he bellowed as we walked in.

"Hello sir!" we replied.

"Ross, you need to work on your aim. We're gettin' too close to the real deal and it's one of the worst here!"

"I'm sorry sir! I'll work on it," I told him. If only we knew how skilled I would become.

Within a few minutes the rest of the squad arrived in the briefing chambers.

"All right! Attendance!" Colonel Miller boomed. "Fergensen!"

"Here."

"Dunkelman."

"Here sir."

"Washington"

"Uh… here."

"Poffinbarger"

"Present sir"

"Pippin"

"Right here"

"And Ross."

"Here sir!" I returned.

I wondered why we had to do attendance with only six men, but I knew not to question my superior… especially over something so petty.

"All right then, we are all here! Let's head out

to the targets."

It looked dark outside… Perhaps it was another fierce Eupholan electric storm. While Euphola wasn't the origin of our people, it had quickly built up a reputation for military superiority during its early colonization. It had been centuries since the first colony ship arrived, but Euphola now represented the pinnacle of Elonian colonization. Though with a threat of a fierce storm on the horizon, I had to prepare myself for anything.

"Ready boys!" Colonel Miller shouted.

"Yes sir," we responded, though even together we weren't as loud as him.

We prepared ourselves for the 'Run, Shoot, and Take Cover' drill that generally characterized our afternoons.

"Go!" Miller's voice shot though the air.

Nevin and myself were the two fastest people in the squad. We jetted ahead of the others by about five meters and gaining. When Nevin reached the cover point, he leaped clear over it and somersaulted on the ground. I climbed over the one-meter rock slowing me down. By the time I was on the other side he was nearly five meters ahead, with Washington on the rock.

I knew I had to win. I had to get better. I was twenty meters away from where we take the shot. Washington fell over after crossing the rock. Max Pippin still had not reached the rock. Miller was not happy with him.

"PIPPIN! Too slow, get the lead out!"

"You should try..."

Alex Pennington

"WHAT DID YOU JUST SAY!" Miller roared.

"I'm sorry, sir" Pippin said.

"Drop down and give me one hundred push-ups! NOW! You have one minute!" Miller screamed.

By this time, Nevin, Washington, and I were all aiming at the target and it just started a heavy downpour.

Then three shots rang out. Two of the once blowing balloons burst. Only my round soared beyond the balloon without the satisfying pop. In seconds, the other two were on their feet heading to the cover point. I fired again. This time I hit. I was shocked, considering two shots was a new record for me. This might be my chance. I knew I was faster than Washington and with Nevin it'd be luck.

I was gaining on them both. Then Washington saved the day. In an unexpected move, he tackled Nevin and took both Nevin and himself to the ground. I passed the two who were still getting back up. I started to climb over the rock. Pippin was just climbing over it for the first time. I pulled myself over, filled with determination. I had done it. This was my first win. It was also my first placing higher than fifth.

"First to cover is James Ross!" Miller exclaimed.

Nevin repeated his leap again and landed in second.

"Second to safety is Nevin Poffinbarger!" Miller announced.

No sooner had he finished the sentence,

Robert landed behind cover.

"Third place goes to Robert Washington!" he bellowed.

Ryan Dunkelman and Phillip Fergensen took forth and fifth. Max Pippin took last. What a surprise.

"Alright boys, good job all of you, except Pippin. Everyone give me fifty, Pippin you do a hundred, understand?" he explained.

"Understood," we answered.

We began our push-ups. Pippin looked exhausted already. I focused and performed my set as quick as I could. I finally finished third. I heard Pippin softly counting to himself "Fifty-four… fifty-five… fifty-six..." Miller thought he was taking too long.

"Pippin! Faster boy! For every thirty seconds you waste that's thirty more."

When Max finally finished, having been forced into a larger than average push-up count, Nevin opened up conversation with me.

"Good job James" Nevin said. "That your first time winning?"

"What do you think?" I replied.

"Sorry," he said back.

"With a record of five firsts in a row, you aren't easy to beat," I admit.

"Yeah, I know, but I'm surprised Ryan wasn't closer to the top. He has a longer win streak than me. He may not be the fastest, but he sure knows what he's doin'," Nevin said.

"Attention! It's time for the next session!

Alex Pennington

Remember, we are making you soldiers!" Miller boomed.

I could tell Max wanted to go in, away from the rain. He always avoided anything tough. Fortunately, he kept his thoughts to himself, rather than telling Miller and getting yelled at again.

"Alright. There are balloons set up way down range. Your goal is to shoot all five in a row... with one shot. There are twenty lines of balloons. If you fail to shoot all five with one bullet, you must move on to the next line and try again. You all have to share the twenty lines. If you run out, and not all of you have completed the objective, all of you fail. You must depend on each other. Remember that!" Miller explained. "You all understand?"

"Yes sir!"

"GO!" he yelled.

We all ran toward our shooting position. It wasn't far, and this time we were a team, rather than competitors. We all fired. Ryan hit all five. Nevin hit four and had to move on to another row. Another volley. Nevin and Philip were done. I had only hit a total of three balloons. One the first shot, and two the second. We shot again. It was hard to nail the balloons with the strong winds. Washington finished next. I hit four, surprising myself.

"Gah..." I mumbled to myself as I moved to the next position.

Max fired and missed completely. At least he could reuse the row. In this challenge, it seemed that hitting zero was better than one through four.

I shot again. *Pop, pop, pop, pop, pop.* All

five balloons burst as my bullet tore through them.

"Yes!" I cheered.

"Don't get too excited, James," Robert said. "Max won't make it. We'll lose anyway."

At this point, there was only one row left. He had to either miss completely, or hit all five.

"C'mon Max! You can do it," I yelled.

He fired another total miss.

"Boo!" Washington jeered.

"Hey!" Miller called. "Quiet!"

Pippin's finger slowly pulled the trigger. The bullet soared from the rifle into all five balloons.

"Ye-ah!" Max yelled. "Woot! Ye-haw!" he continued.

"Great job, Max," I told him.

I may not have liked him, but he actually pulled through. I had been worried my success would be wasted by his failure.

"All right boys, lap the complex eight times. I'll see you inside," Miller said.

I looked up to see a flash of lightning. The ground was mud and we were soaked. We were all faster than Max, and lapped him several times.

When we finished we entered the building. I was exhausted and cold. Miller was hunched over on a bench watching a news alert. His face showed grim surprise and disgust.

"And we're back. During a meeting on the Elonian planet of Delacrose, Vorgian official Rigel Korth shot all three Elonian delegates. It came as no surprise to the Vorgian government. Most information remains classified. The three representatives who were left dead were Brandon Mᶜlure, Mason Neely, and Garreth Johnston. Four of the building's guards were severely wounded. Chancellor Valedez and the Senate have ruled that this matter must be taken to war. Troops are preparing as we speak. The first target is expected to be Enphuerzo, but all solid information remains classified. Many people look at this as our opportunity to seek vengeance on the Vorgian people for what happened ten revolutions ago," the anchor said in an alarmed tone.

Max finally came creeping through the door and noticed us staring at the news.

"Hey fella's... what's up?" he asked.

"The war has started with the Vorgians. They intentionally murdered three of our delegates on Delacrose. Four of the guards are now receiving medical treatment," Miller told him.

"Oh... Wow..." Max said, shocked.

"I knew it was only a matter of time before those darn Vorgians started this up," Miller revealed. "Be prepared for a call any day now. It'll come."

He was right. Only a week later we received a call for the Rangers to go to Enphuerzo.

"Boys... The time has come. We're sending you to Enphuerzo to destroy the ground based power generator of the *Fargo* space station. It is used to recycle power from the station and recharge major systems, such as shields and energy weapon batteries. Spies have reported that it is in the Aruvia Desert," Miller instructed.

"Sir!" Washington said. "It's not there. The

spies must have found a decoy."

"What do you mean?" Miller asked.

"It is in the Pombo Jungle."

"That's not what our intel tells us! And we trust our spies to do their job!" Miller growled. "You will be going to the Aruvia Desert. GO! Your transport will be outside." Miller yelled.

We went to our lockers first. I grabbed my pack, SR-4 and all my ammunition. Then I picked up my Hopkins-81 pistol and put it at my side. Nevin preferred the H-44 to the H-81 due to it's light weight and high caliber.

Our first action… it was so close. Sometimes I wish it had never come. We went outside and boarded the transport. We were ready.

"Hello, my name is Bob Jenkins. I'm going to be your pilot. Enjoy the ride."

The man was incredibly thin and pale. He looked nervous and unprofessional. Immediately I grew concerned he was as new as we were.

We sat back and felt ourselves rise off the ground. We rose higher and higher until we entered the Eupholan atmosphere. As I looked out the window, the view was awe-inspiring. The rain was pouring down onto trees and plains. Then, I thought about the mission. I immediately became nervous. I felt my body tense up.

"Hey Rob," I said.

"What James?"

"Why are we going to Enphuerzo first? It's the furthest planet from Euphola," I told him.

"That space station… *Fargo*… is very big and

strong. If we take it out first, Vorgian morale will drop. Particularly since if this ever came down to a last stand, it would be a great help in such an endeavor. I don't know if the Elonians... erm... *we*, can even beat it."

"So it could end the war quickly?" I asked.

"Yeah, or it could strengthen their resolve... who knows, maybe it's a trap," Robert suggested.

Then we were interrupted. "Oh... um... Hi. That Miller guy. Oh... Ahh... He wants to talk. Um. With you," Bob Jenkins stuttered.

"Alright, let's hear the colonel," Ryan said.

"Hello? Come in! Are you there?" Miller was saying.

"We're here sir," Ryan said.

"Good! You have two hours to destroy the objective before Admiral Dixon arrives with his fleet. Don't fail him. Dunkelman, You're in charge. Complete the mission and we will *officially* promote you to sergeant."

"Roger that sir," Ryan said.

"Over and out," Miller concluded.

"Um... S'cuse me," Jenkins squeaked. "We are about to warp. It could get messy on the other end."

Then we heard the three coordinate points being dialed in. I'd never warped before, so I didn't know what to expect. Civilian craft only used Ultradrive for FTL transportation between planets.

I looked out the window and saw a blue light surrounding our ship. It began to fade. Then I saw Enphuerzo. We had been nowhere near Enphuerzo just moments ago, and yet in less than a second we had traversed the immense distance between the two worlds. It was incredible.

Our ship began to quickly descend toward the planet. Suddenly, I felt the entire ship shake.

"We have a problem!" I heard come from the helm.

"What happened?" Philip Fergensen asked.

"Ahh… Ahhh… We're getting shot at. We have been spotted by *Fargo*. This wasn't in the plan. We have been hit. Shields are at twenty percent. We need twenty-five percent shields on this ship to make it to the surface. That is, without it getting a little warm," Jenkins said.

Ryan ran to the controls, in the helm. We began to go faster.

"What are you doing?" Jenkins asked.

"Trying not to get killed!" Ryan said back. "Oh… Oh… Oh, good idea! Have you ever piloted one of these transports?"

"Nope, just Interceptors. Quite a difference," Ryan told us.

"That's just grand," Jenkins murmured.

We continued to descend rapidly. Through the window I could see laser blasts pass by, narrowly missing our transport. It was only a matter of time before they secured a missile lock.

We started going through the atmosphere, a warm glow appearing around the shields.

"Shields are at twelve percent," Ryan said as we went deeper into the atmosphere.

It was eating away our shields, which needed

to remain active due to what appeared to be multiple design flaws with the new transport.

"Seven percent!" he called.

I climbed up into a small glass dome. It was located in the center of the ship. Multiple missiles were approaching our transport. Fortunately, we were out of range of *Fargo*, but enemy interceptors were in the air. I slipped down the ladder just enough to call out to Ryan.

"Guys! Missiles at six o'clock. Ryan, speed up," I yelled.

"If we go much faster, we'll burn up what is left of our shields," he announced.

Then, the ship shook violently. I held on tightly to the ladder in the center.

"Looks like Warp Drive is down!" Ryan exclaimed.

Chapter 2
The Base Strike

I could feel the ship getting hotter.

"Shields are at zero percent!" It's gonna get awfully hot in here, Ryan called.

"I kinda figured that one out Ryan!" Nevin said.

The heat was quickly draining my energy. Finally we burst out of the dangerous portion of the atmosphere, into the air that the people below breathe. It slowly began cool.

"Phew!" Ryan sighed. "That was close."

I started to climb down the ladder when I saw something with the corner of my eye. I turned my head and saw two VDF-74 interceptors coming for us fast.

"We have company!" I announced. "They're opening fire!"

"This can't be happening!" Jenkins uttered.

"Well it is!" I responded.

"We're all gonna DIE!" Jenkins screamed in fright.

"Well… I'm trying to avoid that!" Ryan shouted back.

The ship shook again and began to fall downward. The already rough ride quickly felt as if everything had gone wrong. A steady alarm activated in the helm, only adding to the chaos.

"Guys! I'm losing control," Ryan told us. "Engines are down!"

"Please don't get us killed," Philip said.

Alex Pennington

I climbed back up the ladder. Suddenly cannon fire shattered the window dome. I simply let go of the ladder to avoid a bullet through the brain. Pieces of the shattered window fell to the floor below.

"Ow... What was that?" Max grunted when some of the pieces cut his arm.

"We're still falling!" Ryan said from the helm. "About a minute before impact!"

"Everyone to the back of the ship, I've pulled up as far as I can!" Ryan said as he came running out of the helm.

"Here it comes!" Nevin warned as we all held onto anything in the back to support us.

A loud crunching sound filled the air. We saw fire in the front of the ship. I closed my eyes as the front of the ship came closer. The crunching grew louder.

"Aaaaaaaaaaaaaaaaaaah!" Jenkins screamed in terror.

The crunching stopped. It felt like we had stopped sliding across the ground. I opened my eyes. It was bad.

"Guys?" I said as I looked around what was left of the ship.

The front was terribly smashed, forced together like an accordion. I couldn't even see where the ladder was.

"I'm okay," I heard Ryan say.

"Help me... Am I okay?" Jenkins asked.

"Ooooooh... you're dead..." Max said mockingly.

"I-I-I am?" Jenkins questioned.

"No, Max is kidding," Nevin said.

"You guys are off subject again," I said.

"Let's look for a way out," Ryan ordered.

"The door was up front," Philip said.

"There isn't an up front anymore," Nevin pointed out.

"So we are trapped in the burning wreckage of a transport ship on an enemy planet?" Max asked.

"Yeah, pretty much," Nevin answered.

"Maybe we can shoot a hole through the wall. This transport seems to fall short of standards in almost every aspect, maybe it has poor armor too," I suggested.

"Yeah," Ryan agreed.

He took out his H-81 and shot the wall eight times. No penetration.

"Maybe our SR-4's would work better," Nevin added.

"Worth a try," Ryan said. "All right. Everyone see that the spot I hit?" Ryan asked.

"Yep," Philip said.

"Ready," Ryan called. "Fire!"

All shots hit their mark.

"Yes!" Max yelled. "We punched a hole straight through the wall."

"Hold on…" I said. "What do we do with a couple centimeter hole?"

"Oh…" Max sighed. "Not much."

"Well, it sounded good," Nevin admitted.

"We all have a couple grenades," Ryan said.

"In an area this small, I think the explosion would kill us," Phillip pointed out.

Alex Pennington

"True," Max agreed.

"What if the explosion was on the other side of the wall?" I asked.

"How could we do that, James?" Ryan inquired.

"I'm not sure, but I think we'd survive," I answered.

"I really don't like the sound of that," Jenkins whispered from the corner.

"Oh, well. Would you rather live out your slow starvation with us in a tiny space of burning transport!?" Max exclaimed.

"N-n-no," Jenkins said.

"Oh!" I said. "Our SR-4's did get a hole through the wall. So if we put enough together, we can slip the grenade through the hole."

"Great plan," Ryan told us.

"The fragmentation would surely incapacitate one of us," Philip warned.

"We're not using frags," Ryan countered. "We've got concussion for this op, purely explosive force."

Within three minutes we had fired a decent ring of holes. Then we started to connect them into the larger hole. It took a lot of ammo but we had brought plenty. Then, only twenty minutes after the crash, we were nearly free.

"All right Max, start it and push it through the hole. Okay?" Ryan instructed.

"Understood," Max said.

He pulled the pin, then tried to put it through the hole. As he pushed it in however, it stuck in place.

"Guys! Help! It's not going through!" he yelled frantically.

Ryan ran over and kicked the grenade with all his strength. It was barely enough, but it fell through.

Ryan leaped backward, trying to distance himself from the explosion. Then we heard it explode, blowing down the wall of the battered transport.

"Yes!" Max called out. "We need to hurry. Dixon's gonna be here and need that generator down," Ryan instructed.

Luckily for us we had crashed near the Aruvia Desert. We took off running, dragging Jenkins with us.

"Guys," Robert said. "It's not going to be here!"

"What makes you so sure?" Max asked.

"I had a friend who was Vorgian. He worked for the government, told me some things he probably shouldn't have," Robert answered.

"Right," Max said doubtfully.

"I guess it's worth a try," Ryan decided.

"Fine…" Max whined.

We redirected toward the Pombo Jungle, which was not too far off from the Aruvia, despite fairly sizable differences in weather. The desert was hot and running only made it worse. Jenkins, being a poorly trained pilot, quickly grew too tired to keep up. In response, Phil actually ended up half-dragging the man along.

"This is nonsense!" Jenkins complained. "We

should stop and take a break."

"No," Phil replied.

By the time we reached the perimeter of the Pombo Jungle we were exhausted. Without warning Max collapsed.

"Max!" Nevin called.

"I'm okay," Max moaned. "Just a little tired."

"Um… O-kay," Nevin told him.

"How much time do we have?" I asked.

"Looks like we have about forty-five minutes," Ryan said.

"Wow. That was a long run," Nevin pointed out. "Rob, you better be right."

"We should have done this sooner!" Jenkins advised.

We waited for about five minutes before we continued. The jungle's plants and trees cast shadows onto the ground. They caused the jungle to appear dark and gloomy.

"We've got to be close," Ryan said as he pushed through some shrubbery.

Then, I heard gunfire. We all dropped to the ground. Phil pulled Jenkins down; otherwise he probably would have just stood there to die. The shots were obviously from an automatic weapon.

"Keep low," Ryan whispered.

"Understood," Nevin said back.

We saw leaves getting shot off trees and dirt splashing up as gunshots hit. We were looking around through our scopes for the gunman. I heard one shot. The machine gun stopped.

"Bull's eye," Ryan said quietly. "Let's go."

The War Across the Stars

We stood up and attached our SR-4's to our packs and pulled out our handguns. It would be close quarters combat once we were inside the complex. We ran over to the structure, a dead body leaned over the sandbag machine gun nest on top of it. Then, we were directly in front of an iron door with a code lock.

"Any ideas?" I asked.

"We have two grenades each and enough Eupholium to blow up the whole base," Ryan said.

"Let's save the Eupholium for the mission itself," Nevin advised.

"I'll try to hack into the system to open the door," Philip said.

"Go for it," Ryan approved.

After about two minutes of waiting Philip finally found something.

"Guys, I didn't open it yet, but I managed to pull up a map of all of the guards' stations," Phil told us.

"Phil, you're a genius," Max said in awe.

"W-w-w-why do we care where the guards are?" Jenkins wondered aloud.

"Dude… It's obvious man," Max said slowly.

"Max! Is this some kind of joke to you?" Ryan questioned.

Max merely stared back at him silently.

We finally looked at the map displayed on a small screen above the keypad.

"All right," Ryan said. "We go in and there is a split in two directions. Then some guards along each symmetrical path," Ryan observed.

"What's symmetrical mean?" Max questioned.

"You serious?"

"Yeah, I am."

"It means the same on each side," Ryan informed him, shaking his head in dismay.

"Okay," Max said.

"Anyway, let's look here. It keeps going on each side. They each have a door that leads into a small hall and the command room, which has guards everywhere," Ryan continued.

"But look," I said. The halls keep going past the side doors. Each end has a power generator!" I realized.

"We should split into two groups and go down each hall," Ryan said.

"Right," Phil agreed.

"I'll take Jenkins," Robert called.

"I'll go with them," Philip added.

"No. Just me and Jenkins," Robert told him.

"Why?" Nevin asked.

"I'd like to get to know him better," Robert retorted.

"I did it!" Phil announced as the door began to rise.

"Let's go. And Rob, I dunno what's wrong with you... but I trust you," Ryan said as he passed two of the four Eupholium charges to Robert.

We walked in and split up. Ryan, Philip, Nevin, Max, and myself took off down the left hall. Robert and Jenkins went down the other.

"Kinda strange that Robert *wants* to work with Jenkins," Max said.

"I agree, but we need to stay focused," Ryan told us.

We then saw the first pair of guards. We approached slowly, hoping not to catch their attention before killing them. Then, we opened fire with our pistols. There were five of us and only two of them. And since we had the first shots, they were easily defeated. My shots connected… but they weren't the first. I wasn't responsible for the kill.

We continued down the hall and saw more guards, this time aware of our presence. We all started shooting and rapidly downed both guards. We needed to move fast, in case the gunfire caught the attention of anyone else.

"Good job guys," Ryan congratulated. "Anyone hurt?"

"Nope, I'm fine," Max said.

"All right. Let's go."

We continued down the hall, all the way to the door to the command room.

"Max!" Ryan called. "You stay here and make sure no one comes out from here," Ryan said as he pointed at the door to the side hall.

"Okay," Max agreed.

The rest of us took off down the hall to the generator room. It had a large door, similar to the one at the entrance to the complex.

"Get it open ASAP, Phil," Ryan said.

"Working on it. Won't be long," Phil responded.

I held my H-81 tightly as I repeatedly looked around the hall.

"I'm in… Done!" Philip said.

The door opened, revealing a large machine. We proceeded cautiously into the room.

"Where are those guards who are supposed to be here?" Nevin asked cautiously.

"I don't know," I murmured in response.

Ryan crouched down and began prepping the Eupholium charges. I looked around the room for some clue as to where the guards were.

"What if they are just waiting to ambush us?" I asked nervously.

"That would be unfortunate. Let's keep our guard up," Philip told us.

"The Eupholium's ready!" Ryan announced.

"Great. Let's go," Nevin suggested.

We took off down the hall, moving as fast as we could to escape before the blast. The Eupolium was on a timer and I didn't want to be in that building when it reached zero.

"MAX!" Ryan called. "Four minutes 'till this place blows."

"Oh…" Max responded. "I should start running." "Great idea Max… Way to go," I said to him as I ran by.

Chapter 3
A Battle to Remember

We kept running down the hall until we reached the intersection that Robert went down.

"Where do you think Rob is?" Max asked.

"He may still be setting up," I suggested.

Then, we ran out of the building and hid in the bushes near the base. Suddenly, Robert came running out of the building. He was alone.

"Where's Jenkins?" Ryan asked.

"Dead…" Robert answered. "He was shot in the head a few times."

"Ouch," Max replied. "That had to hurt."

"Max! I can't believe you even placed in the competition to be on the Rangers," Nevin said.

"Did you get the Eupholium set up!?" Ryan yelled.

"No. There were too many of them. I was just setting it up when they came in the room," Robert explained.

"Then they shot Jenkins and I surrendered. They took me down the hall. I kicked the guard that had my weapons and they spilled to the floor. I grabbed my pistol and took out the other guard. Then, I took off out the door," Robert finished.

"Gah! I knew I should have sent someone else with you. Did the base think you were alone?" Ryan questioned.

"I think they know that there were more of us.

"I sure hope not," Nevin said.

"That's not too big a deal at this point," Phil

said in his deep voice.

"I agree," I said. "Surely they can't disarm the Eupholium in time, even if they find it."

"James is right. Let's go. If that Eupholium blows, I don't even want to be this close," Ryan warned. We took off, tearing through the jungle.

It was not long before a powerful explosion shook the ground. I looked back and saw some trees light up in flame. Then, a second explosion filled the air.

"Outstanding!" Phil cheered. "I didn't even think about how the first explosion would set off the other Eupholium charges."

"Phew, I guess it worked out then," Robert said nervously. "Sorry for the scare there, Ryan."

I looked back to see the entire facility destroyed, flame spewing from the gray ruins of the building.

"Seven minutes 'till Dixon arrives to destroy *Fargo*," Ryan announced.

"Just in time…" Nevin added.

We continued through the jungle and then burst out into the desert. Leaving the shade of the trees, I felt the temperature noticeably rise.

"Without our transport, how do we get off the planet?" Nevin asked.

"Call Dixon," I said.

"Our transport had our only form of communication," Ryan informed us.

"So… we're trapped," Max sighed.

"I bet a Vorgian base would have some sort of emergency escape vessel," Philip said.

"That's all fine and dandy, but we just blew the base to smithereens!" Max added.

We took off through the desert for any signs of another base. We ran for an exhausting twenty minutes until we found a lightly guarded Vorgian Transport outside of a small Cecrete structure, similar to the one we had just destroyed. There were several soldiers meandering around the ship. It appeared to be some sort of border patrol outpost, perhaps guarding the perimeter of a higher order facility.

"All right…" Ryan whispered as we dropped to the sand.

Ryan then pointed silently at various guards, then at one of us.

"Fire!"

All of the soldiers dropped to the ground as Ryan, Phil and Robert unleashed rounds at their targets. We ran over to the transport.

"Get ready," Ryan said.

We pulled out our pistols and approached the door. Ryan knocked on the door of the transport, hoping the pilot would mistake him as one of the guards. The door slid open and we moved in. Ryan took the shot. He removed the body, and then took the controls.

"Let's get outta' here," Max said.

We rose high into the air and began to see *Fargo* battling Dixon's fleet. At first, the ride was relaxing, bearing with it a satisfying feeling of completion. I had not only survived, but so far wasn't directly responsible for any kills. I was still innocent. Though I knew in war, it was only a matter of time before that innocence was lost.

Suddenly, three Vorgian Avenger-class Battleships warped onto the battlefield.

"Uh-Oh…" Nevin said. "This will be a battle to remember."

"Yeah… If we survive!" Max pointed out.

At the head of the Elonian fleet we could see the *Concordia*, the massive flagship of Dixon's fleet. It was a memorable sight as its main batteries hailed fire onto the enemy. As we neared the *Concordia*'s landing bay, Ryan tried to contact Dixon.

"Come in… This is Ryan Dunkelman of the Elonian Rangers, he announced.

"Please send identification codes," Dixon's voice boomed. "You're showing up as a Vorgian ship."

"Sending now…" Ryan told him.

"Codes approved," the COM officer informed us. "Gates to the main hangar are open."

Our transport flew through the open gates into the primary hangar bay. Then, the hangar shook, bouncing our transport as we landed.

"I'm alive!" Max exclaimed.

"For now," Nevin responded, referencing Max's earlier comment.

"Let's get to the bridge," Ryan suggested.

We ran out of the hangar bay, and then ran for the bridge. We made our way through the metallic halls of the ship, passing several crewmen along the way. It was not long before we were far enough inside the ship that it became easy to forget that there was a battle going on around us. We climbed several staircases as we made our way to the elevated bridge. When we arrived on the CIC floor, we moved quickly toward the large metal bulkhead that led to the bridge. It opened with a quick tap of the nearby panel.

"Are you Dunkelman?" Admiral Dixon asked, turning away from the view port.

"Yes sir!" Ryan said as we all saluted.

"Good to see you alive," he told Ryan. "Fire a salvo of Pyro Rockets at *Fargo*."

"Yes sir!" the weapons officer said.

A stream of twenty Pyro Incendiary Rockets shot from the front of the ship. They crashed into *Fargo*, erupting into flame after penetrating the station's hull. The flame ignited several nearby VDF-74 fighters. *Fargo* was running on reserve power now, which would quickly lead to its demise.

"Captain Chambers!" Dixon called.

"Ready a nuke."

"Understood, sir," Chambers said. He entered a code into the weapons system. "Sir? What's our target?"

"The furthest Avenger… There," he said, pointing at the holographic TRIAD display.

"Target locked." Dixon gazed out the window toward the battleships.

"Chambers… Fire the nuke."

"I love nukes!" Max exclaimed. "You know, the big plumes."

"Get out of here!" Dixon yelled at Max, his face showing quite clearly that he wouldn't put up with Max's behavior.

"Yes… Sir…" Max said as he left the bridge.

The sight of him finally being punished for his immaturity brought a bit of satisfaction to me.

The nuke launched out of the bow of the dreadnaught. It hurtled toward the enemy battleship.

"Expected impact, five seconds," the weapons officer announced. "Four…three…two…one…"

The missile exploded inside the Avenger, after just narrowly piercing its armored hull. The explosion blew off the first quarter of the ship, exposing it to the vacuum of space. The remainder of the ship began to break apart due to the extensive damage to the bow.

"Wow…" Nevin remarked. "I've never seen a ship blow up."

"I've only seen it in simulations and recorded battles. Never right in front of me…" Philip said.

Then the COM link opened and we heard voices.

"Help!" All turrets are down. We've lost the warp drive. We're gonna d—" the voice said as the transmission stopped.

"Sir," one of the officers said. "We just lost the *Voyager.*

"Understood, Roberts" Dixon said, seemingly unfazed. "Another salvo of Pyros," he ordered.

"Understood, sir," the weapons officer said.

I watched out the window as laser shots and rockets flew about, amidst autocannons and missiles crossing paths.

"It's really incredible, isn't it?" I asked.

"Yeah," Nevin agreed.

Then the COM link opened and an

authoritative voice came over it.

"This is the *Comanche*. Neutron Bullet is fully charged and ready to fire."

"Target the station," Dixon ordered.

I watched in awe as a blue streak flew from the bow of a ship and slammed into the space station. It was much faster than the rockets that were still being exchanged.

"Sir!" the weapons officer called.

"We've exhausted over half of our Pyro Rockets."

"All right… Give 'em a round of Seismic Rockets," Dixon told him.

"Right away sir."

"Commander McNary…" Dixon said as he turned to the commander. "Give me a status report."

"Understood," Commander McNary said while she put the data on-screen.

"Thirteen percent shields, sir. We still have an amazing ninety-six percent hull integrity. Warp and Ultra drives are up, and sub-light engines are fully operational. As for fleet-wise, we've lost several ships," she explained.

"Which ones?" Dixon requested.

"We've lost *Voyager*, *Theta*, *Intrepid*, and the *Blackened Bruise*."

"Did Captain Braizer survive? Anyone brave enough to name their ship the *Blackened Bruise* is respected in my fleet," Dixon said.

"So far we can't be sure, sir," Commander McNary informed him.

"Understood Commander," he uttered quietly.

"Hey!" Philip said, pointing at a small Vorgian frigate. "It's headed right for us!"

"Oh no... I think you're right!" Ryan announced. "Admiral! We need to target that frigate over there. I believe it is trying to ram us."

Dixon glanced down at the TRIAD display.

"That does appear to be its intention," Dixon said in an alarmed tone.

His usually expressionless face showed faint signs of worry. I was terrified.

"If it hits our ship, will we take enough damage to blow up?" I asked.

"Not even close..." Phil said knowingly. "However it could easily destroy a portion around where it hits. And possibly additional damage if the bulkheads aren't sealed off around the impact area."

"Let's hope it doesn't hit here..." Robert told us quietly.

"Agreed," Nevin, Philip, and I said in unison. Then, Ryan walked back over to us.

"He's aiming all of our turrets on it. We have to destroy it before it impacts us," he informed us.

"Sir! It's closing on us. Impact to engines in ten seconds," McNary announced.

"Redirect all power to the engines! NOW!" Admiral Dixon commanded.

"Powering engines, sir," the nav officer said.

"Hurry," Dixon ordered as he looked toward his navigation officer.

The *Concordia* began to crawl forward.

"Engines at maximum," McNary announced. "Not fast enough, sir. Two seconds before—"

The ship shook and sparks shot out of some of the equipment. There was a crunching sound, and then a massive explosion. It caused the ship to shake again. Nevin and I both fell to the floor.

"Sir…" Commander McNary began. "Sub-light engines and warp drive are down."

As I stared out at the battle, the mushroom-bulb at the top of *Fargo* showed clear signs of extensive damage. Large breaches in its hull began to appear as the surface fractured.

"This is our chance," Dixon boomed, seemingly recovered from the impact already. "Ready a Mark II Seismic Rocket."

"Yes sir!" the weapons officer announced.

The COM opened again with another transmission.

"Sir… this is the *Appomattox*. We have lost all shields and hull integrity is low. Permission to jump?" the captain explained.

"Permission granted Captain Rebik," Dixon accepted.

I knew a ship was about to jump, so I looked around the fleet. Then the familiar blue light surrounded one of the destroyers and then it was gone.

"Firing Mark II Seismic Rocket sir," the weapons officer announced.

A long blue and white rocket pushed out of the bow of the *Concordia*. The rocket launched forward, slower than most rockets, and far slower than the Neutron Bullet had been. Point defense beams flashed around the rocket to no avail. As it impacted, a massive blue wave blasted out of the bulb, breaking it open. Without sides, the peak of the bulb lifted away from the rest of the broken station.

"How exactly do those rockets work?" I asked Philip.

"They are composed of extremely dense Hentronium with a seismic charge inside. Upon impact, inertia causes the unstable charge to hit the Hentronium with enough force to set it off."

"Right… That's great," Nevin said, obviously confused.

"Okay," I respond, "How about Ultradrive?" I asked curiously, trying to distract myself from the gnawing fear of the *Concordia* exploding like the great station *Fargo*.

"It works by putting us out of phase in a dimension where everything is exponentially smaller. Ships that were around us would not be in the alternate dimension, unless they too enter Ultraspace. As we travel at normal speed, the distance that must be traveled is vastly decreased. As soon as we drop out of Ultraspace we will remain at our relative location in our dimension. Essentially, this reduces the total distance a ship must travel, as opposed to attempting to boost the speed with which it does so," Philip explained.

"I see…" I said, somewhat confused by the technical jargon.

Suddenly we heard a tremendous explosion. I hurried closer to the window. Where I once saw *Fargo*, I now saw nothing but rubble left of the station.

"Sir, *Fargo* has been destroyed. Mission complete," Commander McNary announced. "Remaining Vorgians are jumping."

"Good work crew," Dixon congratulated. "That's it for us, we just have to sit back and let the Marines do their job."

"Sir! Final damage report is eighteen percent shields and gaining. Hull integrity remains about eighty-seven percent. That frigate took its toll on the engines. Ultradrive is still online, though," Commander McNary informed the crew.

"That's good," Dixon approved. "Set us into standard orbit."

"Yes, sir" McNary said.

She moved over to the COM console and opened a link with the ships in the fleet.

"We have won. For now just set into standard orbit and await further instructions," she announced.

With the battle over, we were asked to leave the bridge, and were escorted by a guard to a relatively small room with a few naval cots. It wasn't the most comfortable place, but it felt secure compared to the hustle and bustle of the bridge. We waited on board the *Concordia*, mostly in that room, for at least a day. Then Admiral Dixon walked in with news.

"Hello, Dunkelman," he said as he stepped into our room.

"Welcome, sir!" Ryan responded as we all saluted.

"At ease," Dixon ordered calmly. "We have our jump drive back online."

"Se-weet!" Max exclaimed.

"Careful soldier," Dixon warned.

"Ok…" Max whined.

"Do you need anything else, sir?" Nevin asked.

"Actually, I do." Dixon answered. "Two things to be precise."

"Cool!" Max said. "There are two!"

"Soldier!" Dixon growled.

Max simply shrugged.

"Anyway…" Dixon continued. "Our shipyards above Euphola have just launched our new super-weapon. It is called the *Enforcer*. It is so large, it doesn't fit into any of our current ship classes."

"Wow," I murmured in amazement.

"Yes, 'wow' is right. It is nearly two and a half times longer than my dreadnaught. Plus, since dreadnaught is our highest class, many people think we should make one more class. But more importantly, the *Enforcer* is going to Hothonos. Spies report that two avengers and about eight frigates jumped in after Enphuerzo. We will be testing the *Enforcer* there. It will have two back up ships to accompany it. The *Lone Wolf*, which is a destroyer, and the frigate, *Sandy Shore*. I personally don't like the idea. However, the Senate has voted forty-eight to twelve that we test it there," Dixon lectured. "And if *you* are any indication… the Senate doesn't always make decisions I like," he continued, revealing his distaste for the Ranger program.

"Understood, sir," Ryan said strongly.

"What else is there?" Philip asked curiously,

obviously having enjoyed the last speech, despite the Admiral's underlying resentment.

"The other news is that the Rangers, Beta Squad, and the Lambda Raiders are going on a joint mission to Sontonos. You will be meeting them in four hours."

"Aren't the Lambda Raiders the squad with the Laser rifles?" Philip asked.

"Oh, and isn't their a pair of twins in that group?" Nevin asked.

"Yes to both of those," Dixon answered. "The Lambda Raiders are led by Master Sergeant Deborah Pinkip. Master Sergeant Dylan Johnston commands the Beta Squad. He is the son of the Elonian delegate Gareth Johnston. The same one who was killed on Delacrose several days ago."

"All right," I said happily. "I'm ready to work with someone with a motive like that."

"Yeah," Max said. "A tough dude, with a 'tude."

"I'm just gong to ignore you this time," Dixon grunted. "Meet Airman Wanda Xavier in the primary hangar bay in three and a half hours. She'll pilot you over to the *Liberator*. From there you will jump to Sontonos. Yes, you will have a small fleet with you. A total of three ships. Once cruiser, one destroyer, and a frigate. You will be on the cruiser. The rest will be explained there. Good luck," Dixon finished.

"Yes, sir," Ryan said as he saluted.

The admiral walked out of the room and went down the hall to the right. We waited in our room for about three hours. Then after grabbing our belongings, we headed toward the main hangar bay. We arrived several minutes early, so we just sat around.

"This'll be great," Max said.

"Yeah," Nevin said.

"All of those ship names confused me though," Max mumbled.

"I'll explain," Ryan offered. "The smallest ship is a corvette, however that excludes fighters, transports, scouts, and other small ships. Then, from smallest to largest the ships are: frigate, destroyer, cruiser, battleship, and our biggest is the dreadnaught."

"Nice," Nevin sighed. "Any particular reason you decided to memorize all that?"

"I was in the Navy for five revolutions as a pilot. I was stationed on the *Hope*. Then I was shot down on a ground run. I managed to capture a Vorgian sniper rifle and made it home. I practiced in my spare time for a while. Then, they thought I was so good with it that they decided to put me in the new Special Forces team. And now look, I am in charge of a crucial group of snipers," Ryan concluded.

Chapter 4
Assault on Sontonos

By this time, we were soaring through space towards the *Liberator*. Much to my dismay, it was the same style of transport as the one we used on Enphuerzo. The transports were small, so each team used a separate vessel. I greatly preferred the Corsair dropships that we had used prior to these new transports.

"I wonder what this Dylan fella's like," Max stated.

"But more importantly..." Robert stated, "I wonder what the mission is."

"One minute before arrival on the *Liberator*," our pilot, Wanda, informed us.

I saw a large ship with five laser turrets and two railguns. As we neared it, the ship appeared to grow larger. The transport turned and we cruised into the hangar bay. I climbed up the ladder and looked back through the window. I saw two more transports coming behind us.

"I'm ready to meet the teams we're gonna work with," Nevin said thoughtfully. "I mean, these are big names we're talkin' about."

Next, we touched down on the floor of the hangar bay. As we plainly walked out to the transport, we saw the landed Beta Squad marching out of their transport.

"Wow...they march..." Max said semi-thoughtfully.

Alex Pennington

"Ryan Dunkelman," Master Sergeant Dylan Johnston called. "Nice to meet you."

"Same here Master Sergeant."

"Do you have any important intel for us?" Francis Gonyon, one of the Beta Squad, asked.

"I'd assume nothing you don't already know," Phillip said to Francis.

"Aah, Phil, it's good to see you again, man. I didn't figure you'd have anything."

I smiled slightly, impressed that Phil personally knew one of the Beta Squad. The six-man team was one of the most renowned special ops teams in the Elonian Empire.

"Let's go find what this raid is all about," Sergeant Deborah Pinkip said as she and the Lambda Raiders approached us.

"I concur with Sergeant Pinkip," Johnston agreed as we gathered together and began walking to the bridge, where we began introducing the teams.

"Hello, I'm Corporal Carl Hays," a tall soldier greeted.

"I'm Joseph Hays," said a slightly taller soldier who looked like Carl. Their only difference appeared to be a few centimeters in height, Joseph's hair was darker, and Carl wore glasses.

"Mikel Eric," an average sized soldier stated plainly, clearly not big on introductions.

"Hi, I'm Maria Clause," the shortest member of the Lambda Raiders introduced herself.

"That's my team," Sergeant Pinkip announced.

"Alright, team, now it's your turn," Ryan told

us.

After our introductions, Sergeant Johnston said, "OK, then, Gonyon! You can start."

"Yes sir," Gonyon said back, "I am Francis Gonyon. I'm the tech expert. Give me a technical snafu and I'll fix it or reprogram it to do whatever we want," he explained.

"I'm Steven Roland," a man with very short black hair said.

"Scott Keys," a particularly strong-looking man announced with a scowl on his face.

"And I'm Benjamin Butler," a short, stocky, bald soldier said.

His build indicated he was from Delacrose, the largest planet in the Jerico system.

Then, we opened the door and walked into the bridge.

"Hello..." a man with the captain's insignia emblazoned on his shoulder announced, "I'm Captain Palmer."

"We are ready for the mission," Johnston said.

"Good" Captain Palmer said quietly. "We all should know Rigel Korth correct?"

"Yes sir!" Sergeant Pinkip acknowledged.

"Your mission is to assassinate him and do as much damage to his military complex as possible. He has been terribly hard to keep track of, but we know he will be there. He was promoted all the way to Colonel after his stunt back on Delacrose. Though for all we know, he may have held the rank prior, and it just wasn't public."

"Ahh... that fool!" Sergeant Johnston uttered

angrily. "I will personally remove him from existence!"

"Furthermore..." Captain Palmer began. "Francis Gonyon, co-inventor of the Absolute Zero Gun will be using his gun in combat today. Gonyon would you like to explain it?"

"Yes sir," Gonyon accepted. "The A-Z gun is slow to fire, but it has devastating results... on anything. It fires a super cooled projectile that upon impact fills a square half-meter area with ultra cooled mist. That entire event occurs under a second after its launch. The mist, near instantly, freezes anything it touches to absolute zero. This causes all molecules to essentially stop moving. In that state they are extremely easy to break. So, with that in mind a bullet is launched zero point one two five seconds after the A-Z shot. The bullet then hits the target shattering the entire area that was ultra cooled," Gonyon explained.

"Ha, ha! I should have expected something ingenious like that." Phillip exclaimed.

"Yeah, but let's use an example. If we were to shoot the wall of a building, depending on the thickness, we could theoretically punch a hole clean through. Imagine the effect on massed infantry. A drawback however, is that it takes about fifteen point eight seven two seconds to cool the next round. Which means the user will definitely need escort, and that in its current form, has little chance of becoming standard soldier armament. The super cooled bullet is made of dense Hentronium. The mist is stored in a capsule held at two hundred degrees to help avoid the mist destroying the bullet. As long as the mist is in the packet its effects are essentially neutralized. Once the trigger is pulled, the first bullet passes through the tip, and a weak force field bursts the packet. The mist then leaks out of the capsule and spreads out over its half-meter radius. I have one of the two currently existing A-Z guns. The other one is at a classified testing facility," Francis concluded.

"All right…" Palmer sighed. "Now you all know how that thing works. I think it's about time you get to see it work," Palmer said.

Several of us nodded silently.

"In about five minutes we jump. When possible try to use the correct tactics for this. Have the quiet lasers in front, snipers picking off the enemies from the back and the assault rifles providing cover for the snipers in case of attack."

"We know the rules sir, I'm ready for the mission," Sergeant Johnston announced, seemingly bothered by being instructed on ground tactics by a naval officer.

"In that case, head on down to the hangar bay. We'll want you on the transport and ready to launch as soon as we arrive at Sontonos, Sergeant. So be ready." Palmer instructed.

"Yes sir," Johnston called out.

We then hurried down the hall, all the way back to the hangar bay. We all reentered the transports and sat down.

Then the *Liberator*'s intercom came on and we heard Palmer's voice, "All crew at battle stations, Palmer out!"

Then we all prepared to jump. Although we were unable to see, I could tell we jumped. Then, there was an explosion, coming from within the ship.

The intercom came on again, "Repair Team B, please report to Hall D, Deck 7. We landed right on top of a Vorgian Fighter Squadron," Palmer's voice commanded.

"That sounds bad," Robert said to us.

"Let's get outta here," Airman Xavier said.

We began to lift. A voice came over the transport's COM.

"This is Phifer," a deep voice said. "The bay is open. Let's roll."

"All right," Wanda responded.

We began to drift toward the now open gateway. We then began to rapidly pick up speed.

I climbed up the ladder. What I saw froze me with terror. There were four Vorgian Cruisers, and seven Frigates, three Corvettes, six Destroyers, and two Avenger-Class Battleships. It would take more than three ships to take on that fleet.

Then, the COM link opened. "This is Palmer. The *Liberator* has sustained heavy damage to its shield. We are already at forty-four percent. Make this quick."

"What's happening, James?" Max asked.

"There are over twenty ships out there!" I groaned.

"Oh shoot!" Ryan said in an alarmed voice.

"That is not good," Philip sighed.

"What did we expect? It's a Vorgian planet!" Robert pointed out.

We had nearly made it to the atmosphere. I looked port of the ship. Then I saw one of the orbital laser defense turrets. It had turned toward us and soon opened fire. Beams of bright red light passed by our transport. We began our entry into the atmosphere. One laser turret had concentrated on the Lambda Raiders' transport, forcing them to sway side to side to try to avoid the onslaught. Then a singular beam passed through the transport, causing the oxygen to quickly begin escaping into space.

"We are halfway through the atmosphere," Wanda announced.

The laser turret finally stopped its assault, having fallen out of range. About two minutes later we broke through the dangerous portion of the atmosphere into the air. As we descended we saw a large building, several AA guns stationed on top. As I feared, they opened fire. Explosions from the AA shells erupted around our transport, one of them shattering the window on the other transport. Then, the COM link opened with their craft.

"This is Timms," the voice said, "We have taken heavy—" I heard an explosion from beside our transport. An AA shell had collided with the helm of his transport, likely killing him instantly.

I looked toward the side to see the door open up and Sergeant Pinkip leap out. Mikel Eric, Carl Hays, and Maria Clause followed her. However, I did not see Joseph Hays. Their transport had begun to descend at a near vertical angle.

"We are unable to regain connection with the Lambda Raiders," Wanda informed us.

I watched their damaged transport get pummeled with AA shots, ripping it apart.

"Most of them jumped out," I said.

"Most?" Ryan questioned.

"I never saw Joseph Hays jump," I answered.

"Those who jumped are probably dead by now," the pilot said.

"That is unless they had parachutes. But most of these transports don't have parachutes. That could ruin the whole mission," Ryan shouted.

Then, yet another explosion irrupted beside us. It shook our transport causing Max to fall over. Despite all the explosions, the transport had taken minimal hull damage.

"Shields are at four percent," Wanda yelled. "Another blow like that and we'll be toast."

"I hope you are kidding me," Max said.

"Not if it's direct!" Airman Xavier replied.

The waves of explosions were relentless. Suddenly, the transport took a sharp turn to starboard. An explosion popped right where our transport had been.

"Come on..." Robert grunted.

Once more the COM link opened. "This is Palmer! We're gettin' pummeled out here! Shields have been down and most weapons are offline. The *Heart of Gold* is gone! Hull integrity is sixty-two percent! The *East Wind* has positioned itself directly in front of us. It'll only last so long!"

"Understood, sir," Wanda responded.

"I don't think they are going to make it." Ryan sighed.

"Thirty seconds before we can land!" Wanda called out, hope in her voice.

"Yes! Land!" Nevin said excitedly.

"Solid ground awaits us!" Max sang.

"Finally," Philip said.

We plummeted towards the ground and then began to slow down. Soon, we were arcing into a horizontal position. Then we were only two meters above the ground. We were so close. The vehicle slowed to a stop and landed on the tropical shores of Sontonos.

"We're here! You are all free to go," Wanda reported.

"Let's scream it loose!" Max exclaimed. "Sorry."

"Right..." Ryan said as he exited the transport.

As I looked back, I saw the Beta Squad transport coming in; by the time our entire team was out, they had landed.

Wanda stuck her head out of the cockpit into the main compartment. Despite the fact she was unable to see us, she still yelled out that another COM had come in from Palmer.

"He sent a detachment of ten Marines planetside," Wanda continued. "He wants ya to look out for 'em."

"Understood," Ryan said.

He pulled out his desert camo Marine style hat and plopped it on his head. I then watched as he detached his SR-4 from his pack and made sure it was loaded.

"Let's go, team," Ryan ordered.

"Yes... Sir?" Nevin said, still trying to decide if Ryan's rank dictated the honorific.

We hurried along the beach. Philip pulled out his data pad and it projected a 3-D image of the local terrain approximately four decimeters off the pad. Its standard blue holo light flickered as we observed the map.

"So, if we head due east along this beach we would end up at Rigel's base in about thirty minutes," Philip said as he carefully examined it.

"Correct," Ryan said observantly.

"Maybe ol' Korthy won't be there," Robert suggested playfully.

"Korthy?" Max sputtered. "That sounds like one of my silly nicknames. Copy Cat!" Max accused.

"His name is Rigel Korth, and it doesn't really matter. Let's just focus on the task at hand," I interjected.

"Stu–" Max began.

"Max," I quickly cut him off. "There's no need to say anything."

"Ok, so we just head down the beach as quickly as possible... All right?" Ryan asked.

"You bet!" Nevin said excitedly.

"Sergeant?" Ryan questioned.

"Yes... I understand the plan," Sergeant Johnston said quietly. "Team," Sergeant Johnston then bellowed. "We've been quiet so far. Let's go make some noise!"

"Yes sir!" his troops sounded.

"Lets do a full charge straight there. We'll cut down that time. Rangers... you better keep up,"

Johnston warned us.

   "Done deal," Ryan said.

Chapter 5
The Danger Zone

We were now halfway down the trail, running at an incredible pace. We had encountered no resistance. At this rate, we were only a few minutes from Rigel's complex. We came closer and closer, still without any signs of the Marines or the Lambda Raiders.

Then, we trotted up to the top of a hill and looked down to see the R.K. Military Complex. The words were stamped on the side in dark red letters. The complex was the deep gray of hardened Cecrete 7, the second strongest when it comes to Cecrete. The strongest was Cecrete 10, which the Vorgians likely have no access to. It was recently invented on the Elonian planet, Benbos, located on the far border of the empire. The problem, the Vorgian Revolution, granted free rights to Sontonos, Hothonos, Vorga, and Enphuerzo, but essentially dismantled any trade between Vorgian and Elonian planets. They formed the Vorgian Empire and since then have had very little positive contact with us. So basically, no trade with the Vorgians, means no Cecrete 10.

"James, Nevin... flank this complex on the right side here," Ryan instructed.

"Butler... Roland... you go with them to provide cover fire in case they need it," Sergeant Johnston ordered.

"Yes sir..." Butler muttered.

We stealthily crept along the edge of the base.

We kept our distance at about twenty meters as we looked down into the round pit in which the complex was placed. Once we were in our position, I stuck my hand up in the three-fingered OK signal to show we were ready. I slowly popped my head over the rock that hid us. I saw Ryan doing the same signal.

"Nevin…" I whispered. "Take aim."

We both took aim at the two guards. My heart began to race. When I took this shot, I would, for the first time, take the life of an enemy. I feared it might change me, and make me someone I wasn't. I inhaled slowly. The guard stood there, gun slung before him, casually talking to the other sentry.

Then four shots rang out and four guards dropped. With the guards down, I watched as Ryan and Dylan ran across the field toward the complex. I began to push myself off the ground, when I heard an unfamiliar voice.

"Put your weapons down."

We slowly turned around to see a Vorgian Officer with five guards. Two of them looked like Vorgian SAS, or Superior Armed Soldiers. They were the best soldiers the Vorgians had. There were only about four hundred of them in the entire system of Jerico.

"I'm Lieutenant Trevor Davis. You will all be coming with me."

All of us except Steven Roland slowly put our weapons down.

"I won't surrender to you!" Roland proclaimed.

"Fire…" Lt. Davis utter calmly.

Several assault rifles opened fire. I watched, shocked, as his body fell seemingly in slow motion. An ally killed right beside me, mere moments after I had taken my first life. Steven's body hit the ground with a light thump, his final breath having been drawn.

"Yeah, we'll surrender," Nevin sighed.

"Rise!" Lt. Davis ordered.

We slowly stood up, carefully keeping our arms raised.

"Remove your side arms!"

We pulled off our side arms and carefully put them down. I turned my head back and saw Ryan's team crawling through a small hole in the door of the complex.

"Let's go," Lt. Davis said sternly.

We began walking to the base with SAS and other soldiers all around us. One of the soldiers carried our weapons. Soon, we arrived at the door of the complex. Lt. Davis gazed at the hole with a perplexed look."

"That's odd," he murmured.

"Sir, someone has probably infiltrated the base," one of the soldiers said.

"Really?" Lt. Davis said sarcastically. "Sound a Level Four security alert," he ordered.

"Yes Sir!"

One of the SAS hurried to the door panel and keyed in a code. Soon an alarm began to blare.

"Let's get you to the brig..." Lt. Davis told us.

What remained of the damaged door slid upward, allowing us entry.

"Go!" he bellowed.

We slowly walked through the doorway. I saw dents and pockmarks in the walls. Several Vorgian weapons were scattered on the floor. We continued down the hall and turned, revealing a ring of black scorch around the hall about one meter long.

"Looks like some grenades went off in here, "I whispered to Nevin.

"Ours?" he asked.

"I'd say so..." I responded.

Then, a Vorgian soldier came running down the hall.

"Help! Help! They're right back there," the soldier cried.

"Quiet," Lt. Davis ordered.

The soldier was unarmed and looked tired.

"Grab a weapon," Lt. Davis ordered the soldier. "There's plenty around here!"

The soldier moaned, but walked over and picked up a nearby pistol from a dead body.

"Let's go…" Davis said.

We continued down the hall, seeing obvious signs of an engagement. I looked ahead at Benjamin Butler. He was short, likely from the high–gravity planet of Delacrose. He was bald, but he had a thin mustache.

"Where are ya takin' us?" Butler asked.

"I've already answered that!" Lt. Davis yelled. "You're going to the brig."

After about three more minutes of walking we heard gunfire. It was mostly automatic assault weapons, but there were some pistol shots.

"Stop!" Lt. Davis commanded.

He turned and entered a code to the small door that we were standing by.

"We mustn't be engaged," Davis informed us.

We turned left and went through the door. The entire base was made of deep gray Cecrete 7. Only dim, flickering lights on the ceiling lighted the halls. The hall was thin, only wide enough for two people shoulder to shoulder, to walk through at a time. Nevin and I were beside each other. Both of the SAS were in front of us. The tired soldier walked behind us with another soldier to his right. Behind them Lt. Davis was walking down the middle of the hall with two more soldiers directly following him.

One of the lights behind us flickered, sparked, and while making a popping sound, went out. The hall ahead turned both left and right, leaving me unaware of where we would go. When we arrived at the intersection, the SAS turned right.

"Won't this lead us to where we heard gunfire?" Nevin asked quietly.

"I would think that it would," I sighed.

I looked up to see stairs. We slowly approached them. It seemed quite obvious that the stairs were our destination. Within thirty seconds we had reached the stairwell. As we walked up the stairs, it seemed that there was gunfire below us, likely the same team as before.

"Is that Dunkelman's team?" Butler asked from in front of us.

He walked behind the two SAS. He was wide enough he didn't have someone by his side.

"Probably…" I said.

Then a loud explosion roared from below us. I then heard a voice cheer. Anything after that was too quiet to hear through the walls. All of the sounds had been muffled. I listened closely, hoping to hear something to tell me who it was. But I was unable to hear anything. Soon, the straight path began to slant downward. Ahead I saw a door, which we slowly approached. One of the SAS entered a code on the door. It slid away and we walked through the open doorway. It was a large room with four cells on each side. They were each about three meters tall, with energy bars connecting the ceiling to the floor. The space between was far too small to squeeze through.

"Open cells Epsilon, Digamma and Zeta," Lt. Davis bellowed.

"Yes, sir!" one of the SAS boomed.

He hurried over to a central panel. He punched in several buttons and the energy bars faded away on three cells. Nevin looked back and saw the door behind us close. We all were escorted to separate cells. Then once we were all in, the bars materialized in front of us.

Lt. Davis turned and left with his soldiers. As he left, one of the SAS twirled around and assumed a guard-post position.

We waited for nearly two hours, with no sign of a way out. I began to think about my family. There was a fear that I wouldn't see them again. I needed a way out. I had to survive.

I could hear Butler eating his granola bar in the cell beside me. That gave me an idea. I thought about it for a while then decided it likely would fail. I wished Philip were there to tell me its chances of success. The control panel was attached to its post by a 45-degree angle. Despite the fact that it seemed impossible, I pondered the idea for what had to be at least thirty minutes. In that time I came up with several alternatives, none of which seemed promising. Surprisingly, they hadn't noticed my battle knife. That meant I had a granola bar, a knife, two boots, and my ID tags, which could be thrown with any effect.

That was when things began to fall together. I could clearly see the guard. If I could get his attention with my ID tags, perhaps he would come closer. Then, if he's close enough I'll stab him through the bars, if not, I can try nailing his head with a boot. However, my aim wasn't the best, so I might miss. But I was willing to take the risk.

I unclasped my tags from around my neck and slid them through the energy bars.

"Huh…" the SAS said as he noticed movement.

He came closer. My heart rate soared. He reached down and swiped them up. He was just out of reach; I threw my boot with all my strength. It crashed into his stomach and he bent over. I readied my other boot and gave it a toss. Luckily he was just raising his head and it nailed him square in the nose. He fell back moaning, but he was SAS. So I didn't think he was done. I carefully reached through the energy bars, knife in hand. Then, I plunged it through his boot and into his foot. He screamed in pain.

"Whappening?" I heard Nevin ask from his cell.

I pulled out my knife as the SAS tried to pull himself away with his arms. His assault rifle sat on the floor beside him I pulled in my arm and stuck my bootless foot through the glowing bars. If I were to get too close it would burn right through my leg. My leg was shaky but it came closer and closer. My toes could barely reach it. I lowered my toes and touched the back of the gun.

I carefully eased it closer, though it was a struggle. The SAS was still in pain, but it appeared that he was going to try and get the rifle as well. He began pulling himself back toward the rifle. I finally scooted close enough for my heel to slide the gun close. It was within reach now. I pulled my leg back and reached my hand out. I grabbed the gun's handle and jerked it through the gap of the bars. I pulled it up to my shoulder and sprayed a burst of bullets into the SAS. He fell over silent. Somehow, killing him had been easier than the last man. Perhaps it was him being the second, or perhaps it was the real and direct threat he posed to my own life.

"He's done!" I called out.

"Who?" Nevin questioned.

"The sentry!" I called back.

Butler was closer to the panel. He had a view of the direct side of the panel.

"Ben!" I yelled.

"What?" he asked.

"Throw your boots at the panel," I answered.

"Why?"

"Maybe it will shut off at least one of our cells!"

"I'll try…" he said. "But I don't think it will work."

I saw a boot fly out of the cell toward the panel. It hit. Nothing happened. Then, there was another, it too successfully hit the panel. The energy directly across from my cell flickered then faded.

"Aaah!" I screamed angrily.

"Now what?" Nevin asked.

"I don't know..." I mumbled.

We waited around silently, my mind feeling beaten from the failure. But then a risky idea came to mind.

"Guys… I'm gonna shoot the control panel."

"What!" Nevin said in an alarmed tone. "We could break it and these bars would be here forever!"

"Or… it could shut them all down," I reasoned.

I took aim squeezed the trigger and a stream of bullets roared into the control panel. It began to emit sparks as the bullets ripped through its thin metal casing. Loud pops and crackles filled the air, along with the noise of the assault weapon.

Then, as a bullet hit something vital, flames spewed out of the bullet holes. I stopped my assault with six rounds left in the gun. I stared at the energy bars for what seemed like a minute, but I knew was much shorter. Then, they flickered and faded.

"Yes!" I exclaimed happily, "Oh, yes!"

"Freedom," Nevin sighed.

We all hurried out of the cells into the main

room. "We need to find the armory," I ordered.

We ran towards the door and then noticed something... it was closed.

"Oh curses!" Nevin sighed loudly.

Once again, I found myself wishing Philip was nearby. Then, the door began to slide away and right in front of us were two SAS, with no weapons other than a pair of holstered pistols. They looked surprised to see us instead of their friend. I fired three shots into one of their stomachs turned up and put three more into the second one's head. The assault weapon was empty. Nevin walked through the door while Benjamin and I recovered our belongings. Once we had our boots back on we rushed out the door. We stole the two pistols, and then proceeded down the hall.

"If we aren't fast enough they may close the other door," I announced.

We hurried to the intersection and looked left. The door was closed but there was still the other path that we hadn't been down.

"Lets try this route," I said.

So we took off down the alternate path. It was dark, with most of the lights flickering. When we made it to the end of the hall, we found that the door was open. We looked around. On the wall was an arrow that said, *Armory*. We went down the hall the arrow said and found a large opening, likely a blast door.

Through the opening was a large, open area that had a small side door. It was open and we could hear voices. We slowly approached the doorway.

Alex Pennington

They sounded relaxed, likely unaware of our escape. I peeked my head around the corner. Three Vorgians sat around a table eating. They didn't have any weapons on them, but the armory was full of them. Finding some wouldn't be hard.

"Let's act like one of them," I whispered as I pulled my head back.

"OK", Nevin said.

We walked in casually and headed toward a large divider that was packed with weapons on both sides.

"Hey there," one of the Vorgians said in a friendly tone.

"Hi…" I said nervously.

We slipped behind the divider. They couldn't see us, so we stopped and thought about our next move. There was a row of Vorgian assault rifles along the divider. On the wall there were rocket launchers and rockets as well as some shotguns. On the far wall, burst rifles were lined up neatly. I grabbed some additional rounds for my new assault rifle.

"Go grab some of those burst rifles," I whispered.

Ben and Nevin rushed to the wall. They each scooped one up and ran back to my position. We all popped out from around the corner and opened fire. All three of the soldiers fell limply in their chairs.

"That went well…" I said.

"Agreed," Nevin responded.

"Now… let's find our stuff," Ben suggested.

"Right, good plan," I told him.

The War Across the Stars

We scoured the armory for a couple of minutes, before Nevin said, "Found 'em!"

We rushed over to see two SR-4's, one AR-27, two H-81 pistols, one H-44 pistol, and six grenades. They were carelessly lying in a pile as if the person who carried them had just dropped them. We all grabbed our weapons. Nevin and I hooked our SR-4s to our packs and put our side arms back in their holsters. We kept the automatic weapons in our arms. I took as much ammo as I could find, and stored it in my pack. There was a row of laser rifles stored along the right side of the divider. They were tempting but four weapons would be heavy.

Then, the alarm that had stopped shortly after our arrival in the prison cell, resumed once more.

"Oh frik!" Nevin blurted.

"Let's guard that door, we can try to hold them off," I said.

"How do you know they will come here?" Ben asked.

"That's how!" I said pointing at a camera positioned in the top corner of the room.

It was right next to the door, with its view targeted right on the table adorned with the bodies of freshly killed guards.

Chapter 6
Tronadan

We had held off waves of Vorgian troops for nearly fifteen minutes by this point, though the flow continued. Ben had been shot in the arm and now rested in the corner underneath the shattered camera. I pulled back into the armory and reloaded. I only had twelve more rounds with me other than the forty-five in its clip. I soon emptied the clip and popped the remaining rounds in. Then, a grenade flew in the room with us. Nevin and I ran back behind the divider. Then we heard the explosion, fragmentation bouncing across the room.

"Aah..." we heard Ben Butler cry out.

"Are you okay?" I asked.

There was a five second pause.

"No…" Ben muttered.

"You're alive!" Nevin said joyfully.

We ran back out from behind the divider. I fired the final rounds at an SAS and watched him fall. As I backpedaled I threw the assault weapon and hit an incoming Vorgian. I quickly pulled myself back behind the divider for cover. Nevin was fighting alone now, so I had to hurry. I was on the right side so I grabbed a laser rifle. The L-10's battery was at one hundred percent charge. I ran back to the battle and fired beams of light into my foes. The rays of concentrated photons left large burns on them. The battery in the L-10 was old technology, leftover from the Vorgian Revolution. It had significantly less power than the modern L-101's in use by the Elonian

Military. As a result, my stolen L-10 fell to forty-four percent battery power before long.

Then, three Vorgian SAS armed with L-10's charged in the room. Nevin ducked and put his burst rifle in front of his face. A laser beam punched into the weapon, melting critical parts and leaving it useless. However, the beam did not penetrate the entire weapon. Nevin stood up, tried to shoot, and nothing happened. I managed to take out one of the SAS though another one took a shot at Ben, striking him in the hand.

I returned fire, hitting the SAS in the face. Nevin had managed to grab an assault rifle and push forward. Some of the Vorgians were retreating down the hall, though plenty more were coming. I grabbed onto one of the last surviving Vorgians in the room.

"What's the code to this door?"

"I won't tell you, "he said.

"Oh yeah?" I questioned as I pointed my L-10 at his face.

"Fine… its 1-2-6-1…" he reluctantly said.

"Go!" I screamed as I let go of him.

He quickly went toward the oncoming Vorgians. I entered the code into the control panel for the blast door and it began to close. Several bullets flew by my head as it descended, until at last, the blast door sealed. Nevin let his arms rest, dropping them to his sides. I looked around, nervous of the possibility of more Vorgians. Nevin and I returned to the armory quickly.

"They're are probably going to reopen the doors soon," Nevin told me.

"I know."

"Let's get some launchers," I suggested. "Grab some Sparkers." I ordered, referring to the nickname given to the rockets.

Sparky Industries, a massive weapons industry based out of the Elonian planet of Elphera initially produced them, though their simple design soon became commonplace on both sides of the conflict.

We ran over to the rocket launchers and both grabbed one. Then we grabbed some rockets labeled with big white letters spelling "Sparky Industries." We quickly moved back to the transition room between the armory and the blast door. We each aimed the one-barreled rocket tubes toward the door.

The door began to slide open. Nevin and I unleashed the first volley of rockets through the opening. The waves of Vorgians flew backward as the impact of the two rockets erupted with explosive force. Inside the tube the second rockets slid into place. The second volley soared out of the tubes. Then, the Vorgians opened fire. Bullets pinged off the wall behind us as we reversed. I fired the last of three rockets at the Vorgian assault.

We pulled back into the armory and entered the code.

"1...2...6...1..." I murmured as I punched in the numbers.

The door closed and I began sliding three more Sparkers in the tube.

"Ben...it's gonna be OK," I told him.

"I doubt it. This mission has had more snags than just about any I've ever been on," he groaned.

With our launchers pointed at the small doorway, Nevin and I decided to alternate fire. The door opened. I fired first. Shortly after Nevin fired. The close proximity of the explosions rocked the room. More Vorgians approached. I launched a second Sparker. The rocket soared for a little less than a second before colliding with a Vorgian soldier. The following fireball was enough to clear the doorway again.

Suddenly, the Vorgian assault ceased, many turning and retreating backward, as if something greater had caught their attention. Then, much to my surprise, Robert appeared in the doorway that the Vorgians had been pushing for.

"James, Nevin. Phew. I've distracted them, let's get the heck out of here," he said intensely.

"Um... OK..." I agreed. I grabbed a fully charged L-10 and made sure I had all of my weapons. I set down the heavy rocket launcher and looked at Robert.

"Ready," I said.

"Me too!" Nevin cheered.

We burst out off the room. Nevin waved his new rifle around frantically. Then he brought it up to his face and peered through the scope. The hall was desolate now.

"I don't see anything... We really are clear," he said.

"I know," Robert stated matter-of-factually. "As I said, I distracted them."

"How?" I inquired.

"Not important. What matters is that we have

a chance to get out of here in one piece," he retorted. "I'll explain later."

We quickly ran through the tunnels. Robert seemed to know where he was going in the facility. He also knew the code that we had attained from the Vorgian.

"C'mon, keep moving. We won't be clear for much longer," Robert said, a hint of concern splashed over his face.

We listened and hurried down the hall. Up ahead I saw a blast door, like the one by the armory. Rob quickly entered the code. The blast door began to open. I saw what appeared to be the base's hangar.

"Rob what are we doing?" I asked.

"Yeah…I'm not likin' the looks of it," Ben moaned.

"We're done here Butler," Robert said, swinging around and drawing his H-81.

Four consecutive bangs rang out as Rob shot Ben in the head. Ben fell backward onto the floor, blood splattered across the wall and doorway.

"Hey!" I called out as I pulled the L-10 to my shoulder. "Calm…down…" I continued carefully.

Rob turned his surprisingly steady hand toward my head.

"Did you really think that Jenkins was killed by the Vorgians? Did you think that I wanted to 'get to know him?' Well, I didn't. I shot him and told my friends back at the base that you were there. Friends I had served with for years, and known for even longer! You killed them… and now it's my turn!" Robert bellowed angrily.

"Robert? What are you doing? We trusted you! You are one of… You were one of us," I told him.

"I was never one of you," Robert announced. "From the moment that the original Rangers were killed on Konori I was ready! Korth appointed me as his infiltrator. My goal was to capture the A-Z Gun... and yes we already knew about your secret project. Right now it and Francis Gonyon are on their way to Tronadan, Robert explained fiercely.

"Are you serious?" Nevin questioned.

Robert turned the H-81 and pointed it at Nevin. I held my finger tight on the trigger of the L-10.

"Oh, and by the way, that malfunction of the original Ranger's transport… the one that killed them all and laid the groundwork for the Senate's pathetic shooting competition… That was no accident. We were responsible for that as well. Your people have underestimated us! It was all part of our plan… Now… its time for you to die!" Robert roared.

Then in one swift move I pointed the L-10 at his leg and pulled its trigger. It left a large scorch on his leg and completely burned away the green and black pant leg covering his knee. He crumpled over on to the floor and pulled the trigger of his H-81. The bullet flew by Nevin's shoulder.

"Let's get out of here!" I said.

"Shouldn't we kill him?"

"I can't…" I said solemnly, knowing that I should.

"You're right…we've served with him for so

long now it seems," Nevin sighed. "But still…"

I pointed my gun back at him again. I paused, considering the consequences and benefits. I had killed people already that day. Soldiers. But I hadn't killed someone I knew. Someone who despite his militant and unusual behaviors, I cared about as a friend. I couldn't do it. I lowered the laser.

We turned and ran back down the hall as fast as we could. Within minutes we burst out of the front door. We could have crawled through the hole left by the A-Z gun, but decided to just open it. On the ground were several dead Vorgians.

"Where's the rest of the team?" I asked not expecting an answer.

"I don't kn—" Nevin began.

"Right here!" Sergeant Pinkip answered.

All of the Lambda Raiders except Joseph Hays stood in front of us, walking in from either side of the doorway.

"Hi…" I said wearily.

"Where's Joseph?" Nevin asked.

"He was hit with the photon beam that burned through our transport. He died before the transport even hit the ground. We parachuted out of the transport. Timms was killed by the blast," his brother answered.

"Let's go find Beta Squad," Sergeant Pinkip ordered.

As we headed back toward our transport we explained what we learned, including Robert. We traveled much slower this time than the first time. Sergeant Pinkip was more relaxed than the strict

The War Across the Stars

Sergeant Johnston.

After about thirty minutes of walking down the sandy beach we began to hear small bursts of gunfire.

"Hurry! They may need help," I said.

I had been leading the group since the Raiders hadn't been to the transport yet. But then Nevin, who was faster, zoomed ahead. I held my trigger tightly, ready to fire at the first sign of the enemy. We started up a hill. Our transport was parked nearby. I reach the top, right after Nevin. We looked down in the small valley we saw the transport and the rest of the Rangers. Scott Keys was the only member of the Beta squad in sight. Then I saw the Vorgians had surrounded half of the round valley. I sat down my L-10, pulled out my SR-4 and took aim. Nevin followed my lead and did the same. The Lambda Raiders hurried down to the battlefield before shooting, to avoid giving away our position. My first shot hit an SAS. My second hit sand. My third hit a tree. But then I hit a Vorgian in the head and he fell over.

Philip appeared to be working on the transport's engine. Ryan was shooting his H-81 into the waves of Vorgians. Max occasionally stuck his pistol out of the transport and fired a couple of shots. Then he would pull back his hand and head and hide. The battle raged for another minute, then the Vorgian's stopped coming. My SR-4 only had five of the thirty rounds that I had taken to Sontonos. I clipped it back on my small backpack and scooped up my stolen L-10. Nevin and I charged down toward the transport at full speed.

"James! Nev!" Ryan shouted. "'Bout time, we were worried about you."

"We were in prison," I told him.

"We have bad news," Ryan said.

"So do we," I said.

"Robert's a Vorgian", we said together.

"We'll discuss it later, I have a feeling the Vorgians aren't giving up," Ryan announced as he tightened his sweaty grip on the H-81.

No sooner had he said that, the Vorgians began to come over the hill once more. We opened fire, but they were pushing us back. Suddenly, we heard a long burst of assault weapons fire. A hole was torn through the Vorgian line and seven Marines rushed through. They continued to spray the Vorgian line with bullets.

"It's Staff Sergeant Lawrence," Ryan called.

"Yes it is!" one of the soldiers announced as he released another burst of rounds.

Several Vorgians began to tumble down the gently sloping hill. Staff Sergeant Lawrence hurried down to the transport.

"How much longer, Phil?" Max yelled down from within the transport.

"About four minutes!" Phil answered.

We continued to fight for nearly two minutes, bullets pounding the ground around us, as well as several dinging off of the transport. That is when I noticed a deep, but faint rumbling in the distance.

"What's that?" I asked Lawrence.

I looked over at him. He was a mid-sized man

with a thin, wispy mustache. His hair came down to his glasses, though it was mostly covered by his desert camo hat,which was much like Ryan's. He didn't respond to my question.

Nearly thirty Vorgians lay dead on the ground.

"Almost done!" Phil called.

"Good!" Ryan returned. "Keep it up!"

We fired several more shots into the line.

"Done!" Philip yelled excitedly. "At least I believe it is now functional!"

"Get in!" Ryan ordered.

Everyone started to dash toward the two transports. I managed to get on behind Nevin. Ryan was right behind me. I heard an explosion and looked back out of the transport. A Vorgian Preston-Class Tank was rolling over the mound. Then, an SAS threw a grenade toward our transport. The Marine who had earlier announced their arrival caught it and tried to get it away from the transport. He pulled back his arm and was midway through throwing it when it exploded. He flew forward from the impact and landed in the sand.

Staff Sergeant Lawrence was the last person who was still outside the transport. As he was getting on he turned and saw his second in command, sprawled out and bloodied, in the sand.

"No! Zihark!" he screamed.

Then, a Vorgian sniper shot him through the stomach and he fell. Scott Keys reached out and pulled Lawrence's limp body inside. The doors of the two transports closed. Then, the two ships began to rise off the ground. I heard a terrible whistling as a high-explosive tank shell whooshed by our transport.

"That 'un woulda hurt!" Wanda called from up front.

We continued out ascent and were soon out of the effective range of the Preston Tank.

"So James? What happened down there?" Ryan asked.

I told him about our capture, Lt Davis, the prison, our escape, the armory, and finally Robert.

"You did good...very good" Ryan said. "Due to the fact I'm Sergeant and I need an X.O. I'm promoting you to Corporal for your efforts and successful escape."

"Thank you," I accepted, feeling honored that he would pick me.

"Thank *you*," Ryan said back to me. "For performing well down there."

"Where's Beta Squad Sir?" I asked respectfully.

"I'll explain..." Ryan offered. "We sniped the guards and pushed forward. Gonyon used the A-Z Gun to put a hole in their door. We went in and continued the process. In fact, he even shot a Vorgian's head with the A-Z Gun. It was interesting... Then it took a turn for the worse. The alarms started and those SAS started showing up everywhere. Thanks to the A-Z Gun we managed to infiltrate his command center. That's when Robert went sinister. I had my gun pointed at Korth's head. Johnston had his pointed at the guards. Robert turned off the lights and activated the fire valves and put some water in the room. In the darkness, Robert,

The War Across the Stars

Rigel Korth, and the SAS all escaped. By the time the lights came back on, they were gone, and Johnston was soaked. He wasn't very happy. Then we hurried out to try and find them. We made it to the front door and turned. He had escaped through it. We all ran outside and then Robert ran right back in, pushing through us before we realized it was him," Ryan explained.

"Wow…" I replied.

"We tried to shoot," Ryan said. "But only took out some SAS. When we went back inside the building, Robert stood there, just down the hall, with his H-81 pointed at us. He fired once, hit Johnston's arm, and slipped behind the corner. Dylan did some serious screaming and then barreled down the hall. About then, more Vorgians than I took the time to count, came out in place of Robert. That made us run. As we scrambled back up the hill, Francis Gonyon was shot in the leg and fell over. Plus, I have no idea what happened to Johnston," Ryan concluded.

I began pondering where Francis was.

"What about the A-Z?" I asked.

"Probably in Vorgian hands…" Ryan sighed. "Oh yeah… probably right were it doesn't belong."

We began to leave the atmosphere of Sontonos.

"Fella's… we have a major problem!" Wanda informed us in her Elpheran accent.

"What might that be?" Ryan asked.

"Only rubble remains... Sensors show there is quite a bit."

Once again I climbed up the central ladder. In

the distance I could see the Vorgian Fleet. Several Frigates, Cruisers, Destroyers, and the two Avenger Class Battleships representing all that was left of the Vorgian defense. However, that was far more than enough to destroy our transport. I slid back down the ladder and heard the COM crackle on.

"This is Captain Palmer… Are you there?"

"Yessir!" Airman Xavier said happily.

"We warped back to the fleet at Enphuerzo, which by the way, is mostly controlled by us. The Marines are doing their job. On a grimmer note, the Sontonos warp beacon was destroyed during the battle. That means the only way to get back is via Ultradrive. Your orders are to warp here ASAP," Palmer ordered.

Then, an unfamiliar voice came over the COM.

"We are under fire from the laser satellites! Shields are terribly low! We have…" the COM produced a string of static. "…Drive," The COM suddenly spat out.

"Wah? Repeat last transmission," Wanda requested.

"Warp…down… need to… quickly!" the voice said in between static.

"Sir?" Wanda said as she resumed communication with Captain Palmer.

"Yes?" Palmer asked. "Our warp drive is out and I think that the Raiders just lost theirs."

"Curses…" Palmer answered. "Attempt landing on Tronadan. Wait there for rescue."

"Understood sir!" Wanda exclaimed, as she

pulled hard on the controls.

I felt the ship lurch to the side and ahead I could see Tronadan, the habitable moon of Sontonos.

"Um… whappening?" Max asked.

"We can't warp and these new transports don't use Ultradrive." Ryan explained. "We'll be forced to await rescue on the moon over there."

"Oh… Why don't they just warp in and pick us up then?" Max questioned.

"Do you ever listen?" I yelled at him. "The warp beacon was destroyed!"

"Who… how am I s'posed to know how that silly thing works? "

"We do!" Nevin, Ryan, Phil, and I said.

"Oh…" Max mumbled.

"And I'll gladly explain it," Phil said excitedly.

"Oh no," Nevin said. "Not again."

"Alright, let's begin," Phil stated, ignoring Nevin's comments. "There are eleven… correction… ten warp beacons in the Jerico System, one at each planet. It produces a field around it large enough to encompass multiple dreadnaughts. This field prevents ships from warping on top of each other. Now this only registers recently warped ships. A flaw in the current system is if a ship travels through normal space over the Beacon, such as those fighters, the field will not detect it. It was designed primarily for warping in fleets. That way every ship in the fleet has it's own place to appear after a warp," Phil explained.

"Make sense?"

"Oh… what?" Max asked. "Do you need me to repeat that?" Phil asked.

"Oh! Um… I get it. Yeah, that's it. No, no repeating needed," Max said, obviously unaware of how it really works.

"Ok," Phil said.

"We're 'bout to land on Tronadan!" Wanda called. "We're going through its atmosphere now."

I remembered that Tronadan had much less atmosphere than most planets and was barely habitable. It was only after one and half revolutions of terraforming that the first colony began to look like a city. Four hundred and fifty days of terraforming just to get a hot, volcanic moon as a place for people to live. Currently, only fifty thousand people even live there. I only knew of two cities, Tronadan City and York. I didn't know of or expect any military bases.

"Almost thar!" the airman exclaimed. "This atmosphere didn't take near as much shielding as most planets. 'Course it's not really a planet," she babbled.

Then we felt the transport lurch as the resistance of the upper atmosphere gave way to the troposphere. I wondered why it hadn't done that on Enphuerzo or Sontonos. I assumed it was due to the damage to our transport's engine. Soon the transport was easing toward the dark brown ground. It was a cracked, dry land, as Tronadan received little rain and relied on shipments of additional water to survive.

We heard a soft bump as we touched down on the ground. The transport's door opened and Ryan stepped out. I followed him and watched as the other transport landed. We looked up as we heard the roar of an atmospheric dropship. That is when we saw a Vorgian Wildcat dropship soaring by. Surely it couldn't be Gonyon, since he was coming from Sontonos.

"James…get in!" Ryan screamed as he hopped back into the transport.

I quickly followed, unsure of Ryan's intent. Ryan barked some orders at Wanda and the transport began to lift. I was somewhat worried about what his plan may be. The transport's only defense, or offense as I feared he would make it, was an L-101 scaled twice as large as normal mounted on the front. The transport turned and sped the same direction as the dropship.

"Full speed!" Ryan ordered.

"Yessirree!" Airman Xavier called out.

Since the transport was designed for space it would naturally be faster than the atmospheric drop ship, likely enough to catch up. Whether or not that was a good thing I had yet to find out. The dropship likely had missile pods and a chin-mounted minigun. Fortunately though, the minigun would probably be fixed into position, making it only a forward defense weapon. It should be useless on a target behind the dropship.

"Target their port engine," Ryan commanded.

"Yepperdo!" Wanda exclaimed.

Beams of laser shot from the bow of our transport. In an instant they impacted, melting the engine. The dropship wobbled as its pilot tried to keep it steady. I could see the warm blue-orange thrust decrease on the two starboard engines.

"They're re-stabilizing!" Philip said as he looked out the cockpit's window with Ryan and Wanda.

"Go for the aft-starboard engine," Ryan said.

Another column of light shot from the transport in a split second. The engine sizzled as the impact melted it. The thrust weakened to nothing as power to the engine cut off completely. The remaining starboard engine powered back to full to equalize with the port engine.

"Try and contact them, " Ryan said.

"Okay," Wanda agreed, surprisingly not adding anything unnecessary. The COM crackled to life and Ryan stated his demand.

"Land your ship immediately or we will disable it. Our sights are set at your next engine," he said nudging Wanda.

"Okay, I see," Wanda whispered as she aimed the laser at the engine.

"It is in your best interest to land."

Nothing came over the COM. Suddenly, the dropship's engines pointed down and the dropship began to hover in place. Our transport zoomed past, our pilot unable to react in time.

"We overshot it!" Phil announced.

"Pull this back around Airman!" Ryan ordered.

"Jus' call me Wanda!" she replied, immediately pulling hard on the controls.

The transport's shields began to take minigun

fire. That was followed by several missile impacts, shaking the ship.

"Engine systems are only thirty-two percent operational!" Wanda yelled.

The transport jerked violently as another pair of missiles hit. Finally the transport swung around and approached the oncoming dropship.

"Controls are functioning at twenty-five percent standard response time! I feel like I'm flyin' a slug!" Wanda yelled.

Our transport fired again, melting a hole in the dropship's window.

Wanda began to pull back hard on the controls. We were heading straight for the dropship. Bullets bounced off our shields. Another laser burst melted the dropship's front-port engine. It began to spiral as it became limited to one side propulsion. Then I realized we were seconds away from impact, getting way too close to the enemy. With the last burst taking out the engine, the tail end of the dropship swung around. It crashed into the bottom of our ship ripping off our L-101 laser defense system.

"There go our shields!" Wanda exclaimed.

As my mind raced at the thought of what just happened, I climbed up the ladder. I saw the dropship spinning as it descended. Then one of the engines exploded. The flames soon enveloped the entire dropship.

"That was close," Philip said as he slowly shook his head.

"But it worked," Ryan pointed out.

"Had that been one of our Corsair Dropships,

we'd be dead now," Phil said.

"And that's why I'm glad to be technologically superior," Ryan responded. "More importantly though, let's head back to the other transport. If the A-Z Gun is in Vorgian hands… we need to take it back."

After about four minutes, we arrived back at the location that the other transport had been waiting. Due to extensive damage to the engines, the return trip was slower. The ship slowly descended toward the cracked surface of Tronadan. I heard a light thud, as we hit the ground.

"Everyone outside!" Ryan ordered.

We all stepped out onto the ground.

"According to James, Gonyon will be taken here," Ryan said. I smiled briefly, happy that I helped. "So we're gonna get him back."

"Oh…we are?" Max asked.

"Yes Max, we are."

Scott Keys shook his assault rifle in his arms. "I'm ready," he commented.

"We'll split into two groups. I'll lead one and Deborah can lead the other," Ryan instructed.

Pinkip merely nodded in agreement, seemingly willing to let Ryan give some commands despite her rank.

"Then, we'll search the sky for one of their transports. Do not engage civilian craft. Understood, team?"

"Yeah," we answered.

"Okay," Ryan said.

Then, we divided into groups. Nevin and I

were with Ryan, so were Mikel and Carl. I could see sadness in Carl's eyes at the loss of his brother, yet through it all he fought on. Then I thought of what we've been through. I've stood beside two of our men as they were killed, and despite the fact I barely new Steven or Ben it still bothered me. I should have done more. I shook my head to clear my thoughts.

Ryan was on his way back to Wanda's transport. I hurried to catch up with Nevin. We then hopped on and prepared for anything. I could see the other transport departing in another direction as we left the ground.

"Now make sure you don't shoot their ship. Okay Wanda?" Ryan said.

"Uh-huh. I get it *real* good," Wanda answered.

Minutes later we were in the air in search of Vorgian transports. Then the COM crackled on.

"We found our first target, they're landing now."

"Understood," Ryan said.

"Looky! Sensors see a real faint object nearby! It's not one of ours," Wanda explained.

"Get us there!" Ryan ordered.

"Kay, kay, I will," Wanda accepted.

"James… C'mere!" Ryan called.

I squeezed into the already cramped cabin.

"Keep your eyes open," Ryan said.

I looked around the sky in search of transports.

"Sir!" Wanda shouted. "Two additional ships just showed up."

"What are they?" Ryan questioned.

"Dropships, fully armed."

"Be careful," Ryan warned.

"They're 'proachin' our position!" Wanda announced.

"Take evasive action," Ryan commanded.

My eyes darted around looking for the hostiles.

"There!" I said, pointing at a Vorgian transport.

"I see 'em," Wanda said.

We began to turn in their direction. I noticed the dropships had opened fire. The transport rattled as several missiles impacted the shields.

"Shields at thirty percent!" Wanda said.

We were gaining on the transport, though it seemed to be descending toward the ground, as if to land.

"Twenty-one percent," Wanda updated.

We were less than a hundred meters over the ground. The Vorgian transport was heading toward a small, deep gray structure.

"Come on..." Ryan murmured as we sped toward the black-coated transport.

The Vorgian transport eased toward the ground. The door opened and several SAS came out. Then, I saw a now-familiar face, Lt. Davis.

"Sir," I said to Ryan. "That's Lieutenant Davis. The one I told you captured us."

"All right... If he thinks he can take our people, we'll take him."

Then I saw Francis Gonyon step out. He was

blindfolded and handcuffed. Behind him was an SAS holding the A-Z gun. Our transport was meters off the ground.

"Four percent shields!" Wanda said frightfully.

The transport door opened. Ryan unclipped his SR-4 and ran out first. Philip and I were right behind him. Ryan knelt on one knee and took aim. He fired. The Vorgian with the A-Z went down. Phil and I fired. Two more SAS hit the sand. My next shot hit Lt. Davis in the leg, but I was aiming for the SAS next to him. Lt. Davis fell to the ground clutching his wound. Finally the Vorgians realized our position and opened fire. Assault rifle rounds flew by. Ryan shot another round into the tallest Vorgian standing. I didn't even have a full clip left in my SR-4… Only three rounds.

We ran over to Francis. Ryan and I looked for the key. With a quick search we determined that the Vorgian who had the A-Z Gun had the key on his ammo belt. I unclipped it and ran over to Francis.

"Thank you," he responded as the metal clasp released his hands.

"You're welcome," I told him, "It was Ryan's idea."

Then a missile exploded beside us, bits of earth spattering over us.

"Get to the transport!" Ryan yelled.

We sped over to the transport. Though as I placed my first foot back onto the ship I looked back to see Davis still holding his leg as he appeared to put distance between himself and us.

"Ryan, if we're going to get Davis, we need to

do it now!" I called out, stepping back onto the ground.

"This here hunk of metal won't last much longer!" Wanda said.

"Okay then, get us out of here!" Ryan commanded.

"Ryan! Are we leaving Davis?" I asked again.

"Prex it James!" Ryan cursed. "Let's get him, hold up Wanda!"

Together, Ryan and I tore across the ground, more bits flying up all the while, and seized Davis from the ground. He put up a slight fight, but we managed to drag him back and tossed him into the transport. Without another thought Ryan took his head and slammed it against the metal door as the transport lifted skyward. The ship shook again, hit by yet another enemy barrage.

"Hold on!" Wanda said as the transport lurched forward with a sudden burst of acceleration.

Then the COM came on, "This is Sergeant Pinkip, we captured several high ranking officers," Pinkip announced. "We have some... information... What happened," The COM continued resuming its static.

"Their COM system must've been damaged," Phil commented.

"Hostiles are turnin' 'round," Wanda said.

Chapter 7
Rescue and Rest

"We're approaching Pinkip's transport," Wanda told us. "Visual!" Wanda reached down turned on the COM. "We have a visual. Ready to land!"

"Understood," the COM responded.

We quickly descended due to our landing thrusters on the belly of the transport being damaged. Our landing was hard and loud.

"Now we wait," Ryan commented.

Four long minutes passed as we waited for the COM to tell us that our ride home had arrived. Then it came.

"This is Captain Graham of the *Comanche*… Come in."

"This is Sergeant Dunkelman," Ryan began, "We've been awaiting your arrival.

"As expected, Sergeant," Graham announced.

"We're on our way sir!" Ryan informed the Captain.

"Good. We need you on board ASAP. We only have seven cruisers. This may be a rough fight."

"Understood sir," Ryan acknowledged. "We're en route, ETA is… eight minutes."

"Very good, Graham out," he concluded.

We continued to ascend into space. Soon the battle was visible, Elonian and Vorgian vessels waging war in orbit of Sontonos.

"I'm detecting hostile fighters 'hind us,"

Wanda said.

"Sir!" Ryan said as he activated the COM, "This is Sergeant Dunkelman, we have enemy fighters on our six! Requesting escort."

"It's yours, Sergeant," Graham responded. "Alpha One through Seven support those transports," he ordered over the fighters' COM.

"Yes sir!" Alpha One responded, his voice barely audible through Graham's open transmission with our transport.

An entire squadron broke away from the fight and came in our direction. Soon they had shot past us and proceeded to open fire on the Vorgian strike units.

"Keep it steady, we're almost there," Ryan said as we came ever closer to the cruiser. I recognized it from Enphuerzo, the word *Comanche* beautifully emblazoned on the side.

"Sir, open da gates," Wanda said cheerfully.

"Understood Airman."

The hangar gates slowly opened, and we soon passed through the energy barrier that kept the atmosphere inside the ship.

"We're in," Wanda announced.

"Acknowledged" Captain Graham said.

The second transport flew in behind us, slowed to a stop and landed.

"Let's go," Ryan ordered calmly as he exited the transport.

I followed closely behind.

The cruiser was well kept, it's walls were the shiny silver color of the Elonium-Jericonium alloy used in all new ships. Its lights were radiating bright light, yet not blinding. The air was cool but still comfortable compared to the tropical heat of Sontonos. In fact, the cool air was actually somewhat refreshing.

I soon found myself on the bridge of the *Comanche*. This room was slightly darker. Holopods and computer screens were scattered about the walls and desks.

"Sergeants," Graham said as he glanced over at Ryan and Deborah.

"Captain," they answered.

"I'll get back with you for debriefing in a moment," Graham said.

"Yes sir," Ryan responded.

"Sir Neutron Bullet at 90% charge," the Ops Officer informed the captain.

"Lieutenant Hill, prepare nuclear warheads Alpha and Beta," Graham returned."

"Uh…Yes sir," the Lt. hesitated.

I was surprised as well. Most cruisers only held about three nukes, activating two seemed like a desperate move. Even Heavy Cruisers, A subdivision of Cruisers, had as few as five nukes.

"Target the frigate over there with the Neutron Bullet…" Graham said as he pointed on the holographic TRIAD.

Tactical Reconnaissance Imaging And Detection, or TRIAD, served as the modern means of detecting just about anything. It was used both aboard ships and ground-based systems to by commanders to guide theirs troops and fleets through a battle of which the scale would otherwise be too large.

Though I was confused. The *Comanche*'s strongest weapon was the Neutron Bullet. Why would Graham target a frigate?

"Um… Yes sir," Hill accepted.

"Good… Now get a nuke locked on to both of those Avengers."

"Verifying targets… Done! The Neutron Bullet is armed. I'll get the nukes…" Hill said.

No one spoke for a few seconds.

"Alpha tube is locked on target. The tube is unsealed, Beta is seeking lock…" Hill said.

I waited, pondering Graham's next move.

"Locked… unsealing tube… done!" Hill continued.

"Sir, codes entered, targets locked, awaiting your command."

Graham closed his eyes in thought. He then pulled out a small command pod and entered several numbers.

"Fire the nukes, wait eight point four-three seconds after their launch and fire the Bullet" Graham ordered.

"Yes sir!" Lt. Hill said.

"Alpha is away… Beta is launched as well sir."

Seconds ticked by. Then the auto-fire, set exactly to Graham's specifications, fired the Neutron Bullet. It soared, a brilliant blue, quickly catching up to the nuclear warheads.

Near simultaneously the nukes and Neutron Bullet impacted their desired targets. Yet it was then I saw Graham's tactical genius. The two lead Vorgian ships both erupted with tremendous thunder. Not only that, but the Hentronium-cased Neutron Bullet ripped apart the outer hulls of three Vorgian frigates before coming to a halt as space junk. From the *Comanche*'s angle it had a clear path straight through several enemy ships. The impact was likely enough to disable all three ships. An entire third of the incoming Vorgian fleet was wiped out within twenty seconds.

"Perfect," Graham stated, "Let's see what they do now."

"That was incredible," Phil said in awe.

"Agreed," Ryan said.

"Super Cool!" Max exclaimed.

"Max, be quiet," Nevin countered.

Several Vorgian ships began turning around.

"Where are they going?" I asked.

"I would bet they're heading to the other side of the planet," Phil answered. "They'll use it as cover."

"Why not just warp?" Nevin asked.

"With the beacon destroyed, they'd have no quick way of coming back. I bet they have reinforcements inbound," Philip continued.

"How many?" Nevin asked.

"There is no way to know, but I would assume that they have enough to turn this fight."

Several ships curved out of view behind Sontonos.

"Power the engines!" Graham ordered. "Follow those ships."

"Yes sir!" The Nav Officer responded.

The cruiser began to accumulate speed. Graham reached out and activated the COM.

"Magnum Squadrons, Omicron through Sigma, target their engines."

Magnums were the fleet's heavy bombers, they were durable and well armed. Two light gauss Cannons mounted on either side of the cockpit and a torpedo launcher attached to the bottom made them a formidable foe. Once you add the chin mounted auto cannon, the Magnum was a well-rounded bomber.

"Interceptor Squadron Lambda, escort the Magnums."

"On it, sir," Lambda One replied.

The squadron streaked off toward the retreating Vorgians. Three Frigates had stayed in the fight to hold off our fleet, yet maybe six Vorgian ships had made it behind the planet to safety.

"How long before we get a clean shot at them?" Graham asked.

"Taking in to account their speed and ours, assuming that they hold steady…" the Nav Officer explained, "Our ETA should be about four minutes."

"I see…" Graham murmured thoughtfully. "Have the Neutron Bullet ready to fire."

"Yes sir," Lt. Hill returned.

The heavy cruiser steadily advanced toward the Vorgian fleet. Within minutes the *Comanche* and the rest of Graham's fleet had made it within firing range of the Vorgians.

"Target the nearest cruiser," Graham commanded.

"Yes, sir!" Lt. Hill responded as he entered the targeting solution. I waited nervously, pondering Phil's prediction. Seconds passed slowly.

"Fire!" Captain Graham ordered as nearly thirty silver orbs erupted in front of our fleet.

"Prex!" the TRIAD Officer muttered. "Twenty-eight Vorgian contacts."

"Get us back to Enphuerzo!" Graham ordered.

"Preparing coordinates, sir," his Nav Officer announced.

Activating the COM Graham said, "Fall back to Enphuerzo! We're done here."

A final rumble shook the *Comanche* and then only the steady hum of the engines remained. It was faint, barely audible, but within the expanse of space around Enphuerzo it could be heard.

"So Sergeants," Graham stated after about ten minutes of post-combat checks. "You said that you have a high profile Vorgian prisoner, correct?"

"Yes, sir," Ryan said crisply.

"Who?" Graham asked.

"James…. You met him, who was he?" Ryan inquired.

"Uh…" I stuttered, surprised to be asked. "Lieutenant Trevor Davis, sir," I told Graham.

"Thank you… Ross," he said, reading the name patch on my shirt. "I understand he is now in the brig… correct?" he questioned.

"Yep," Sergeant Pinkip acknowledged.

"Very well. We'll have him sent to a safe place ASAP, along with anyone else you may have captured. As for you, you'll be going back to

Euphola on the *Griffin*. It's an LRM frigate," Graham informed us.

"Thank you, sir," Ryan and Deborah said together.

"You'll debrief with Colonel Miller once you are on the surface. Pleasure working with you... Good luck!" Graham concluded as we exited the bridge.

Now we had to get to the hangar for a ride over to *Griffin*. We wandered back down the halls to the hangar. Once there, we looked for our transport, piloted once more by Airman Wanda Xavier.

"Hi Wanda," Max stated as we climbed on.

"Howdy ya'll," she responded. "Ride to the *Griffin*?" she asked.

"Yup" Ryan answered.

The ship began to rise and turn toward the gates. They slowly opened and our transport flew out, emerging into an ocean of darkness. We quickly approached the Long Range Missile Frigate. The ship was rather long for a Frigate. It had a wide extension on the back to house the engines and additional missile tubes. As we approached the hangar's gates, I noticed it was far smaller than the *Comanche*'s. Once we were inside, it became ever more apparent. Only two Carrier-Class shuttles were housed inside. There weren't any strike craft like fighters or bombers. In fact, there was barely room for our transport.

"Well... We're here," Wanda stated. "Y'all did good back there."

"Thanks..." Ryan sighed. "It coulda been

The War Across the Stars

better though."

"Whappened happened, Sarge," Wanda said softly. "Y'all did just fine."

"Right… Well let's just hope the Colonel thinks the same thing."

"Agreed," Nevin said.

We exited the transport and stepped out on the hangar's floor.

"Bye Wanda," I said thinking this would be the last time we would see the eccentric pilot.

"G'day!" she said back as her transport slowly lifted.

It turned around and exited the ship. Soon the gates closed behind her.

We walked around the cramped hangar and we arrived at the blast door that that was the primary exit. We waited quietly as it opened. Though soon Max broke the silence.

"That mission was coolio!" he commented.

I looked him straight in the face. His smile was wide and his hair was a sandy blonde. His eyes were a deep brown.

"Max… that mission was bad. We lost several of our best men. One of our finest revealed himself to be a traitor. There was nothing 'coolio' about it," I barked sternly.

"Whoa," Max's face went blank with surprise.

Then a soldier armed with only a holstered sidearm walked over to us.

"Corporal Gorman. I've been instructed to escort you to the mess hall by Commander Keller," the soldier said.

"Understood, Corporal, we're right behind you," Ryan said. We followed Cpl. Gorman down several halls and up a flight of stairs. It wasn't long before we had arrived at the mess hall.

"We should be jumping soon, thirty minutes after entering Euphola orbit you'll deploy to the surface via a Carrier. Till then, you wait here," Gorman told us.

"Alright… I understand Corporal," Ryan said.

We all approached a long table and sat down. However, Gorman waited at the door to the mess hall.

"Say… where's Sergeant Pinkip and her team?" Max asked.

"They… are debriefing elsewhere," Ryan told him.

"Obviously," Nevin said as he faked a cough.

"Hey!" Max said.

"Be quiet Max," I told him before he could complain about Nevin's comment.

Then, the ship-wide COM activated, "All hands prepare for jump."

The voice likely belonged to Commander Keller, but I didn't really know. Seconds passed. "Jump complete, we are in Euphola orbit."

"How do ya think the Colonel's doing?" Nevin asked.

"Probably being his old fat self," Max said.

Ryan glared at Max and suppressed protest to the comment.

"Yeah he's old and fat. A hero of the past," Nevin agreed, much to my surprise.

I, like Ryan, considered protest, but I decided

to follow the lead of my commanding officer and friend. So I sat silently, minutes dragging by before our return to Euphola.

Finally after what seemed like hours, Cpl. Gorman approached us.

"It's time", he announced, "If you would come with me, sir," Gorman continued to Ryan specifically.

"Absolutely, Corporal," Ryan accepted as we rose to our feet.

He then followed Cpl. Gorman back through the halls. We returned down the flight of stairs and into the hangar. We boarded the waiting Carrier Shuttle. Several other members of the crew joined us on board the shuttle. The last to board were two marines armed with AR-27D Carbines, which were shorter close quarter versions of the AR-27A.

However the AR-27A is often simply called the AR-27. The B model was recalled shortly after its issue by the military, after seemingly good test runs, they were soon found too prone to jamming in intense combat situations. The C model proved as an effective carbine but was soon bested by the current D model.

The shuttle door closed as the marines proceeded to the cockpit. They turned around and stood guard at the cockpit door.

"Commander… Carrier One, prepared for departure," the pilot's voice could be heard over the shuttle's COM.

"Carrier One you're cleared to go," a voice replied.

Our shuttle soon departed from the LRM frigate. It would take about ten minutes to get to the surface of Euphola from orbit. Carrier Shuttles were slower than the transports we had used before. They also required a parent ship to travel between planets due to its lack of Ultradrive or a Warp Drive. The Carrier did have high capacity; it could comfortably seat twenty-four people plus the pilot. Most large ships had Marines on board, the number depending on the class. An LRM Frigate like the *Griffin* probably only had about fifty marines on board, whereas a dreadnaught like the *Concordia* may have well over one thousand. No combat specific ships had sufficient troops for a full-scale invasion force. That role was specifically given to assault cruisers and heavy transport ships.

"We are coming in for landing," the pilot announced.

I assumed we'd be landing in Gibraltar, the capital of Euphola. As the shuttle door opened I knew I was right. Directly behind the loading ramp was a sign that said "GMC Landing Pad C5." The GMC, standing for Gibraltar Military Complex, was all I needed to place where we were. This was the largest military complex on Euphola. In fact, it was the largest in the Elonian Empire. We stood and exited the shuttle. The crewmen were right behind us. A pair of Marines left a nearby building and approached us.

"Sergeant Dunkelman?" the taller one asked.

"Yup and you?" Ryan answered.

"Sergeant Paulson," the marine responded.

The rank insignia patch on Paulson's shirt was the same as Ryan's, identifying them as equal rank.

"I'll be your escort to your flight. Once you take off, you should be at the Rangers' Complex within a few minutes," Paulson explained.

"Then let's get moving," Ryan suggested.

We followed Sgt. Paulson across the field and into a building. We walked straight down a hall despite multiple paths branching off. Military personnel bustled about the hallways. At the far end of the hall was another exit door. We continued down the hall and Sgt. Paulson opened the door. We went through the opening and saw the atmospheric transport that we would take.

"That's your ride," Paulson informed us.

"Thank you, Sergeant," Ryan said.

We approached the transport and climbed into our seats. Before long we were soaring well over Euphola's surface. I looked through the window, I could see for kilometers from the height. The ride was quiet, as most of the team was probably reflecting on the mission. I certainly did, as I spent nearly the entire trip replaying parts of it. My first kill… Roland's death… Robert's betrayal. It all seemed to be too much. But in the end, I knew I was a soldier now.

"Well we're here," the pilot announced over the transport's COM. As we came to a complete stop we stood and left the transport.

"Ahhh…" Nevin sighed. "A familiar building."

"It's a good sight, isn't it?" I agreed.

"Not here again!" Max exclaimed." "Fatso lives here!"

"Welcome boys—" Miller started to say from the door to the complex. "WHAT!" he bellowed. "Did you say 'Fatso'!?" he exclaimed.

"Oh prex, I hate this place," Max muttered as Colonel Frank Miller waddled toward him. Miller used to be in shape... ten revolutions ago. The original war, called the Vorgian War of Independence, was fought around three thousand days, or ten revolutions, ago. I was still a teenager then. The war lasted two hundred and seventy-five days, making it just under a revolution in length. The Vorgian colonies Vorga, Enphuerzo, Hothonos, and Sontonos decided to break away from the Elonian Empire, which at that time was the Elonian Republic. Despite the fact that our form of government didn't change, most Elonians began referring to the Republic as the Empire to instill fear into the Vorgians. Obviously it didn't do much, but the name stuck. Somehow, possibly because both sides had the same weapons and they had more determination, the Vorgian Rebels won the war. Over ten revolutions however, former top-of-the-line equipment became severely outdated. In fact, some Elonian pirate groups are better armed than present-day Vorgians. And this time, like last time, we have numbers. Our Capital Planet and homeworld, Eli, has nearly four billion people. Vorga, the Vorgian Capital, has just one billion. In addition, many of their colonies have less then four hundred million people.

"I might not be as trim as I used to be back in

the day, but Pippin… I! Am! Not! Fat!" Miller barked loud and slow.

"Hehehe..," Max chuckled, "You're right, you're not just fat….. you're obese!"

"Oh c'mon Max!" Ryan blurted, "Just be quiet."

"Thank you Dunkelman. Now Pippin I'm not done with you. Fifteen laps around the complex, yes, with the laser counter on. I'll know if you try to slip away. And as a side note, if you keep this up, I'll have you removed from the program," Miller said almost calmly.

It was strange for Miller, but I guess it's not every day that someone stood up for him while he's present. Yet, normal people aren't dumb enough to do stuff like that to his face, but Max isn't normal.

He ran off to start his laps, soon to regret his little stunt here. The complex was a fairly sizable building. Halls, rooms, and storage were the primary takers of space, but most of it was storage. There were at least a hundred SR-4's at the complex and well over five thousand rounds of sniper ammo. Then there were also targets, like balloons, dummies, and bull's-eyes. Then there were large fans for mimicking extreme weather conditions.

"As for you boys…" Miller said gently, "We'll debrief in my office."

Ryan, Nevin, Phil, and myself all jogged behind Miller as we entered the building. Colonel Miller took very long steps for his size.

Inside the building the halls were nice and warm. Constructed of Cecrete 10, the building itself was rather new. We moved into Miller's spacious office. We sat in the row of chairs facing Miller's desk. Behind his desk were two chairs, one of them already occupied.

"This is Colonel Terry McVane of the Intelligence Branch. He's gonna be listening in on our debriefing. "So… Let's begin," Miller instructed.

Ryan explained the events of the mission calmly. Miller's face became gradually solemn.

"Then we found out that Robert Washington was a Vorgian spy," Ryan told Miller.

"Ah-ha" Colonel McVane yelled, "Once again these bumbling recruits have failed. First they failed to effectively coordinate with the professionals at their disposal, then one of them turns out to be a spy!" McVane blurted.

"Colonel, settle down," Miller said gruffly.

"I have no need! My point is right there! So the Rangers, the finest snipers around are killed in a shuttle accident. We think we should just pull some civvies straight off the street to take their place!? Nonsense! Hosting a shooting contest was the best the Senate could do? Send some morons and tell the winners that they are to be the new Rangers! That's simply preposterous! They should have pulled our top men from the Marine Recon branch and put them there!"

"Now Terry…" Miller protested, "We tried, Recon wanted to keep their guys, and they have that right…especially in times of war."

"Oh… Is that so, Frank?!" McVane shouted again. "All about rights and regulations, huh? Well

Frank… with this evidence I'll have those civvies back home within a day! Except Dunkelman… he's actually a soldier," McVane added.

"Terry… I would like to request that…" Colonel Miller began.

"Frank, don't even ask. I'm leaving. I was here by my own request, not assignment."

He then stood up, strode to the door, and left the room. The office fell silent.

Finally, Miller spoke, "Sorry 'bout that boys. You've trained for nearly half a revolution. I'll do what I can to stop him from having you recalled," Miller said in an uncharacteristically soft tone.

"Thank you sir," Ryan and I said in unison. "You may proceed with the debriefing, Sergeant."

"Yes sir," Ryan accepted.

He resumed his explanation on our rescue by the *Comanche*.

"Well then… that wasn't good," Miller stated, "However… good job down there, Ross, we'll get your corporal insignia on by tomorrow."

"Thank you sir," I responded. The room once again filled with silence.

Then Miller looked at the floor, "Dismissed."

Chapter 8
Redeployment

Fifteen days slowly passed since Colonel McVane's outburst. Training had resumed… twice as hard as before. Colonel Miller had personally flown to Eli to protest McVane's claims to the Senate. He was back within a day and told us the Senate was undecided, yet they appear to want to keeps us… after all, it was their idea to host a sniping contest and have the winners fill the Ranger's place. I had tried out, hoping to achieve something. Then I ended up getting lucky and scored in the top five. Nevin had tried out with me. He was actually good, not just lucky. The Senate says they did it to start up a morale campaign; saying even common people can rise to extraordinary ranks. And just as they had hoped… they received over one hundred thousand new recruits Empire-wide within three days of the competition. People who wanted to "start ordinary, become extraordinary." My family was so proud when they learned that I was accepted. In fact, we even had a going away party with Nevin's family the day before we left for the training complex.

Now, I sat beside Ryan and Nevin in the briefing chambers.

"Vorga, we all know what it represents. It is the symbol that drives the Vorgians, their capital planet. Now… we must destroy it." Miller growled.

"We know that they're desperate, on Enphuerzo, one thousand Vorgian soldiers and nearly ten thousand civilians died in a series of nuclear suicide charges in the capitol buildings. They took with them forty-five hundred of our soldiers. The building had additional intel on defense and research labs on Vorga. Without that intel, this mission will be a bit more complicated. We want to keep as many labs intact as we can. Who knows what they may contain. Dixon will be taking forty-five ships, including the Enforcer, and for Pippin…. the Enforcer is the Juggernaut-class Super Weapons Platform," Colonel Miller explained.

"Finally," Max chuckled.

"You'll be aboard the assault cruiser, *Euphola's Sentinel*. You'll be going with Sigma Company and Alpha Company. Two hundred fifty marines each. These guys are good. For this mission, you'll be using specially crafted powered battle armor. Twenty-five of the top soldiers in each company will also wear powered armor. The armor will increase your speed, strength, and give you a tactical HUD to monitor your situation that includes who the ranking officer is, where your teammates are, and a twenty-meter motion tracker. It also can show marked objectives. There are neural interface programs being researched, but they have proved… uh, unsuccessful to say the least. So for this op you'll have to use the manual controls on the helmet. The techs will tell us things in detail later," Miller told us. "Now, the sub-machine guns you've been training with will be your secondary weapons. You'll still have your sidearm as well. The SMG will be equipped with a silencer. More top-of-the-line technology that suppresses the sound made by your weapon... also, very expensive," Miller pointed out.

You'll be going in using drop pods. There are about ten landing zones for the teams. Captain O'Connell's Sigma Company will be striking targets Alpha through Delta. You and his Second Squad, led by Sergeant Peterson, will hit targets Epsilon and Digamma. Captain Morrow and Alpha Company will take targets Iota through Zeta. You will be transferring the intel to this data chip," Miller said, holding up a small chip. "Fergensen, since I doubt anyone else in this group even knows how to translate encrypted data, I'll put you in charge of that."

"Yes sir!" Phil's deep voice bellowed.

"Dunkelman!" Miller said.

"Yes, sir?" Ryan responded, "I know you're good with Eupholium, blow the place as soon as you have the intel on the chip."

"Understood sir!" Ryan acknowledged.

"Once both objectives are secured and you've destroyed both labs you need to fall back to the L.Z. and several Corsair Heavy Assault Dropships will pick you up and transport you to our planetary foothold. Major Kohl's 2nd Battalion should have captured an area and established a base by then. If he doesn't... well we'll have a problem. However, I trust that he will. You boys have to do great to show Colonel McVane, and more importantly, the Senate, that you can handle the challenge of being the Rangers. To help prove that, we've decided to turn you into an all-purpose unit. Within a revolution you will be using SR's, AR's, SMG's, LMG's, heavy weapons, and more," Miller informed us.

"Wow, curve ball…" Nevin sighed.

"Yup," Phil agreed.

"You'll get on the shuttle for your ride to *Euphola's Sentinel* in half an hour. There you will get acquainted with 2nd Squad. So… good luck. Dismissed," Miller concluded.

The thirty minutes passed rapidly due to our anxiety of this raid to Vorga itself, the capital of the Vorgian Empire. Soon the base's COM announced that it was time. We grabbed our items; I had my SR-4, SMG-56, and H-81 with me. We ran out to the shuttle and hopped on. The Carrier-Class shuttle's engines fired up and soon we were on our way to the assault cruiser.

Ten minutes after our departure from Euphola, I could see *Euphola's Sentinel* in orbit. It was large for a cruiser, yet shorter than a battleship. I only saw two weapon batteries. There was also tons of small Elonium-Jericonium alloy plated circles, likely covering the drop tubes. There were hundreds of them lining the hull.

It wasn't long before we found ourselves in the massive hangar bay of *Euphola's Sentinel*. It had several Magnum Squadrons inside. In addition, there were five Carrier-Class Shuttles not counting ours, and seven Cavalier Heavy Lift Shuttles. Lining a far wall were nine Paladin Main Battle Tanks. They weren't very long, but they were fairly tall in design. A fusion cannon was positioned above the driver's cockpit. Its controls were simple allowing one well-trained person to aim the dual 100-millimeter cannons and drive. In the back was an armored compartment that could comfortably transport three people.

We walked for about a minute to get access to the door from our shuttle. Then a Marine armed with an AR-27D escorted us to a briefing room. There were several officers in the room. From the name patches it looked like Captain O'Connell and Captain Morrow were both present. The highest rank I could identify was a Major. One was called Kohl, while the other was Powell. Major Powell was a tall, thin man with dark hair. I assumed he was in charge of the battalion that Alpha and Sigma Companies belonged to.

We were then instructed to sit, so I sat down beside Ryan. Major Powell soon started the meeting. It ended up taking around twenty minutes, basically turning into a more detailed version of Miller's explanation. As we rose from our chairs I knew I was ready for this.

Our next stop was the techs in the armory. They would introduce us to our powered armor. We arrived in the armory minutes later.

"Hey!" a cheery man in a white uniform said. "You must be the Rangers."

"Yep," Ryan replied.

"Welcome, I'm Specialist Wheaton. I'm in charge of prepping your armor."

"All right," Ryan said.

"You will each be paired with me or one of my team. You will get some one-on-one time with one of us so you can get used to the armor and learn its systems. So... let's begin," Spc. Wheaton said happily.

As he said, we each were paired with one of his men. I was paired with Wheaton himself.

The armor was an onyx black with a clear, though partially tinted, visor. The face of the wearer was partially obscured, but you could still make out most of their features.

"You see," Wheaton said. "You could look at a grenade explosion without any blinding effects. That also works for other bright things, sunlight, normal lights, flood lights, you know."

"Yeah…" I said.

The visor was essentially a large square that wrapped around the front of my face. It stretched from just in front of one ear to just in front of the other. This served to reduce visibility obstructions. It spanned six centimeters above my eyes and four centimeters below.

"Now the armor is rather heavy, but with the extra strength provided by the suit's systems, you should be just fine," Wheaton said confidently.

The armor was mostly metal alloy, except at key joints where it was a softer flexible material. These parts were also a deep black, likely to avoid becoming perfect targets. It also had a pair of gauntlets. Most of the gauntlet was made of the flexible material. Only the back of the hand had the hard metal alloy plating.

I glanced over at Ryan's suit. It had a yellow stripe around each arm, just below the shoulder.

"What does that stripe mean?" I asked Specialist Wheaton.

"It shows that he is a squad leader," he answered.

"Oh…" I sighed.

"Here are your controls for the Heads Up Display," Wheaton said, pointing to a column of buttons beside the left side of my visor.

"Each one is a simple activate/de-activate button. On top engages additional visor tint, for situations that you know you'll be dealing with bright light. Below that is whether or not you want the motion tracker displayed on the bottom left of your visor. This final one is your primary tactical display. It shows a rough idea of the terrain around you. It also displays friend or foe locations. Objectives are displayed as a white orb. But that only covers twenty meters. Other friendlies in battle armor will have their name and rank superimposed on your visor to appear to be above their heads. That's only when you look at them though. All of that can be disabled with the bottom button I mentioned," Spc. Wheaton explained.

"Wow," I sighed, "That's a lot."

"So... let's get it put on you and we'll take you to the shooting range to get used to it," Wheaton offered.

He took me down a deck to the shooting range, the others following right behind me. It only took me about three hours to get used to the armor and its power. It was indeed rather simple. Max seemed to disagree though. He was still struggling after five hours had elapsed in the range. After about four hours of additional in-suit training we were escorted to our quarters where we would stay for the rest of the day. The raid on Vorga would be within the next few days. We had until then to practice.

Before long it was time… We stood in a room with drop pods lining the wall. Our armor was on. Sergeant Peterson held an LMG-97 firmly in his hands. It held one hundred and fifty rounds per belt and had an excellent rate of fire. The belt was held in a box that attached to the light machine gun. Thanks to the recoil dampener built into the gun its recoil was minimal, but apparently, in powered armor it was almost nonexistent.

"You are clear to enter the drop pods," Wheaton announced over the intercom.

I walked forward stepping into my assigned pod. Then I turned around and strapped the restraining belt around my waist.

"Sealing pods…" Wheaton said.

The opening in front me vanished as the metal plate sealed me in. I glanced over at a glowing red button beside the plate. It was the release button. It was for popping the metal seal off the pod after impact.

"Drop is in fifteen minutes," Spc. Wheaton murmured.

"Ten minutes," he said later.

"Five … we're jumping, be ready." Things started to get noisy as the two fleets clashed.

"Five... Four… Three… Two… One… Now!" he bellowed as a sudden jerk launched us from the tubes.

We descended toward our target with

increasing speed. Things hummed slightly and I began to decelerate. I must have hit the atmosphere. Each pod had a heat shield to avoid burning up during atmosphere entry. Then, an explosion erupted nearby. One of the pods must have been destroyed. My pod was vibrating maniacally. Suddenly, there was a thump and inertia put me down hard. Thanks to the restraint I had I kept my balance. I must have been on the surface. I heard bullets ping off my pod. I looked around my pod and decided it was time. I swapped my SR-4 with my SMG-56. Then I reached forward and slammed the red release button. Bullets zoomed by as the seal ejected.

I leaped out and darted for a rock. One of the Marines went down. I looked frantically around. I fired well-aimed bursts at several enemies, dropping them. Then I continued for some cover. I dove for the ground and slid behind cover. Then fire came from my side of the rock. The Vorgians had us surrounded. I hastily dealt with the Vorgians that I could see. More bullets pattered the ground around me. I searched the area. The closest Marine was Corporal Metternich. I dashed in his direction when a Vorgian Sparker rocket erupted on top of him. I noticed a machinegun position on a surrounding hillside. I blasted the position with the rest of my clip. Then I slapped forty more rounds into the SMG.

I saw a drop pod that was still closed, that meant either its contents were dead or it was Max. As I approached within twenty meters the words PSC Maxwell Pippin appeared over the pod.

"Great," I mumbled turning and silencing

another Vorgian.

Finally I saw a hole in the Vorgian blockade. I charged for it. My tactical display showed a friendly behind me. I turned my head back as I climbed the side of a five-meter cliff. It was Nevin Poffinbarger.

"Hurry Nevin!" I called.

"I'm coming James, hold on."

My head reached the top of the cliff and I pulled myself up. I crouched down to one knee and fired, several Vorgians dropped. I was getting better… I could feel it. My hit/miss ratio had improved dramatically since Enphuerzo.

Then, Nevin's head popped over the cliff and he pulled himself up. I scanned the area looking for our path to Epsilon.

"I think it's that way," Nevin said pointing straight ahead.

"Agreed," I answered as we charged in that direction.

As we ran, Ryan's voice came on the power armor's built-in COM link, "Rangers! Get to target Epsilon, I repeat, regroup at target Epsilon."

Nevin and I continued to run for two minutes. Then, our path narrowed because of two tall cliffs. The canyon descended about fifteen meters from ground level and it had a gradual decline. At the far end of the canyon were at least two machinegun positions. They were rather far away.

"Nevin…you see that?"

"Yup," he said.

I lay down to avoid detection.

"Lets surprise 'em," I ordered.

"Kay," he responded as he also lay down. I pulled out my SR-4 and took aim at the target on the left.

"You get the gunner on the right," I whispered.

He nodded and we both checked our targets.

"Now."

Two shots rang out. Both gunners fell over simultaneously. I swept the area with my Oracle Long Range Scope. The SR-4 worked well with many scopes. I had a 20x Oracle Long Range Scope, two-tier 6x/12x scope, and a three-tier 2x/5x/10x scope on my person, but often preferred the Oracle to any other.

"Looks clear..." I mumbled.

"I agree," Nevin said. We crawled forward several meters and then rose. We hurried through the canyon, halfway through, machine gun fire opened up. I jumped backwards and fell on my back. I dropped my SR-4 and whipped out my H-81. I saw the gunner hidden in a small cave. I popped off nine rounds as fast as I could and the gunfire ceased.

"Phew..." Nevin sighed as he stood up.

"Hidden in that cave, we couldn't have seen him from back there," I said pointing a thumb at the canyon's entrance.

I picked up my SR-4, brushed it off, and then reloaded and holstered my H-81.

"Let's go," I ordered.

We resumed our trek towards target Epsilon. Ryan's voice once again came over the intercom, "Our ETA is in twelve minutes. It's me, Max, and most of Second Squad. We lost four guys in the drop and the fight directly after landing, Phil... James... Nevin..." He paused, " I hope to see ya there."

I wanted to respond, but I couldn't. Most COM units were bulky, but Ryan's armor had a smaller prototype COM unit. It was expensive and there were few in existence. Hence they were only issued to the commander's armor.

"I think we could get to the target in eight minutes..." Nevin said. "If I remember right about how this location compares to it."

"Yah..." I agreed.

We ran as fast as we could toward our destination.

Then I saw it. The white orb appeared on my TacMap. It took us nine minutes, but we made it.

"Let's go," I said as the armor's speakers let my words escape.

We approached the door and leaned up against the wall on either side of the door. I pulled out my breaching charge. It was given to us specifically for this mission. All of us had one, but just one. This excluded Ryan, who being our explosives expert, had four. I put it on the door and set the timer to five seconds. I instantly was back up against the wall. It exploded, expelling a column of flame. Immediately three crimson dots lit on my motion tracker. Nevin and I slipped through the door and let our SMG's send bullets across the room. Two dots went black and faded. The other one jerked and the stopped, simply fading off my tracker. We advanced cautiously and I signaled for Nevin to cover one side of a piece of equipment. I moved around the other and fired. A Vorgian grew still as the bullets impacted. I gave Nevin the thumbs-up for all clear.

"Now what?" he asked.

"We wait for Phil..." I answered.

No sooner had I answered, nearly twenty new contacts appeared as they came into range.

"Uh-oh," I said, reloading my weapons. "They should have to use that door to get in."

"Yup," Nevin agreed. We scooted several desks into a line and overturned them. The metal desks were heavy, sufficiently so I probably couldn't have lifted them without my armor. Once they were positioned, I crouched behind one and aimed my SMG at the door. The red dots came closer and closer.

Then, the door sprang open and Vorgian base personnel and Marines came out. I immediately took aim and fired while Nevin panicked and sprayed the entire area with rounds. They dropped fast but there were still many left. A crewman jumped out with a pistol and fired several rounds. They dented my armor, but didn't pass through it. I returned additional fire, dropping the crewman and a soldier. I pulled my head down behind the cover of the desk. I pulled out a fragmentation grenade, activated it, and tossed it into the doorway. A deafening explosion roared as the grenade detonated. The last four crimson dots faded black and then disappeared all together. I peeked up over the desk.

I gave Nevin a thumbs-up and said, "Clear."

"Intense," he responded.

"Let's go were they came from," I suggested.

"But what if the rest of the team gets back?" he asked.

"You're right," I agreed. "Uh… You wait here… I'll see if I can find something."

I took off through the door and barreled down the vacant halls. I finally found a room labeled as *Ops Center*. It was open from its recent abandonment. In their haste they had left the door open. I walked in, glancing at several screens. Suddenly I was interrupted by Ryan's voice over the COM.

"This is Ryan! We have a slight delay!" he yelled over the sounds of explosions and gunfire. "A Vorgian platoon was entrenched on our path. We were almost clear, when a dropship produced another platoon. I dunno how they all squeezed on, but they sure did. We aren't clear yet so I don't have an ETA… Over," Ryan finished, cutting the COM.

I looked around the room and observed each of the consoles. One of them flashed several green dots on a map. I moved close and discovered that is was an old TRIAD display. Each of the four green dots were labeled as Wildcat Support Dropships.

"Prex…" I cursed.

I comprehended what this meant. They had major reinforcements inbound, and we had two soldiers. Our Corsair Heavy Assault Dropships could carry one platoon, or eighteen people. The older Wildcat Dropships normally sustained twelve people, or two squads. But Ryan's COM had told me that they were flying eighteen around on those things.

The first two were labeled with two minute ETA's while the other two were eight minutes. I quickly looked around the room. I saw a map of the building posted on the wall. I searched for an armory. Then I saw it. It was only a few halls away. I darted for the armory as fast as I could, hoping for something strong enough to give us an upper hand. I arrived in less than a minute. The door was open, like the Ops Center. The base personnel must have stopped by for those weapons. I saw two machinegun turrets and a fusion cannon.

The fusion cannon was capable of several levels of spread and ammo consumption. It could be fired with a shotgun-like spread or as small as an AR's spread. In addition it could fire one, five, ten, or twenty-five rounds at a time. To use it effectively the burst size needs to be considered in comparison to spread. With an AR spread, anything more than five was a waste and with a shotgun spread, anything less than ten was too little to matter. It fires small pellets that run through catalyst material when fired. It causes a chemical reaction, igniting it to a superheated state. It does wonders for melting things. It had a magazine box on the bottom that contained a thousand tiny pellets. The pellets are actually smaller than most bullets, allowing more shots to be carried. Our machinegun belts only held three hundred rounds and were slightly larger.

I didn't know how the Vorgians had managed to get a fusion cannon, but I grabbed it and a machinegun and carried the heavy load back to Nevin. I reached Nevin within forty-five seconds, despite the weight of the weapons.

"Dude," I panted.

"What?" he asked.

"Vorgians will show up any second now, a whole lot of 'em!"

"Whoa!" he exclaimed, as if he had thought we'd stay clear.

We quickly set up both turrets and pointed at the door. Luckily it was as simple as spreading the tripod and swiveling the gun. Just after we finished setting up the turrets, I heard the roar of a dropship. Then I heard voices as the dropship's engines faded. They grew louder as they approached. I tightened my grip on the fusion cannon. I didn't know how to adjust its blast radius. I simply hoped it wasn't too big.

The first pair of Vorgians appeared at the door, Nevin let loose heavy fire with his machinegun. Then more soldiers arrived at the door. I pulled the dual trigger, releasing superheated waves of pellets. The Vorgians instantly vanished, taking the rim of the doorway with them. The stream of Vorgians had stopped momentarily. They probably had just realized that the base they were reinforcing was held by hostiles. Which of course was our doing. I had a short sense of pride for the effectiveness of our position, but then I remembered how much could still go wrong.

Outside I could hear yelling, so I listened intently to catch what they were saying.

"There has to be at least a squad!"

"How have they captured the base so fast?"

"Let's try a grenade."

Then one appeared at the door grenade in hand. I fired the cannon and heard the grenade pop as it and the Vorgian were melted by the wave of superheated fusion pellets. Then, an assault rifle poked around the melted opening of the doorway. Nevin opened fire but the gun retracted to the other side of the wall. I turned the cannon and fired at the wall. It, and any Vorgians leaning against it, were gone. Another few came out and met the same fate. Nevin's machinegun had proven effective, but not nearly effective as the fusion cannon.

"We've probably beaten at least half the platoon," I said quietly.

"Yeah," Nevin sighed. "You have."

"Right," I chuckled. "I just have a better gun. Now focus."

I then glanced at my motion tracker, "Prex!" I yelled as I whirled around to see two Vorgians with combat knifes charging at me.

I couldn't turn the turret backwards fast enough so I pulled my H-81 and pulled the trigger as fast as I could. I emptied the whole fifteen round magazine, though both Vorgians collapsed on the ground. Only then did I fully realize that their combat knives wouldn't have had much effect on my battle armor, unless they targeted a soft spot.

"Wow James..." Nevin stated, "Fast reflexes!"

I merely smiled in response, slightly relieved by his uplifting comment. I reloaded my H-81 and looked around the room.

"Apparently there's another entrance," I

murmured.

I returned my H-81 to its holster and picked up the turret. It was unwieldy since its tripod was still extended. I didn't worry about it firing accidentally; it had two triggers, one aft-port and one aft-starboard. Both had to be squeezed to fire.

I set the turret back down and scanned the room. It had a field of fire that covered both doors.

"Nevin, keep your eye on that door," I said, "and I'll keep mine on their back door."

"Okay!" Nevin responded plainly.

We waited there for at least three minutes, ominously uncontested.

"Where is that other dropship?" I asked.

"I dunno, go check," Nevin said.

"Will you be okay?" I asked.

"I'll be fine, just go!" Nevin shouted.

"Okay, Okay," I said as I darted back through the door. I tried to remember where the Ops Center was and after what seemed like a three-minute search, I barreled into the Ops Center. I moved over to the TRIAD console, finding that the other two Wildcat dropships had broke off and were not heading for this base.

"We must've scared 'em off," I chuckled to myself.

I turned around and started my run back to Nevin's position.

"Nevin!" I said as I went through the door.

"Yes?" Ryan answered.

"They're here," Nevin said excitedly.

Ryan, Phil, Max, and Second Squad all stood

in the room with Nevin.

"Do you have the intel?" I asked.

"No, Nev said you would know where to find the console," Phil answered.

"Oh, of course!" I said, "I just came from there."

"I know," Nevin answered.

"All right, let's go," I responded.

We went back down those same halls. Finally, we were back in the Ops Center. Phil observed the room thoughtfully.

"Ah-ha," he said suddenly.

Then he walked over to one of the room's consoles. He began to press buttons and then inserted the data chip.

"Just a few minutes," Phil informed us.

"You better be fast," Ryan said as he began to set up the Eupholium.

We waited several minutes.

"It's almost completed the transfer…" Phil said. "Done!"

"Let's go."

Ryan moved over to the Eupholium and hit a button.

"Timer's on, we have eight minutes."

I was completely exhausted, but I still ran as fast as I could. We ran across Vorga's green fields for at least five minutes without resistance. Then we slid to a stop as we saw another encampment of Vorgian machine gunners.

"Take aim, but hold your fire," Ryan instructed.

The War Across the Stars

I peered through my Oracle Scope. I picked a machine gunner that had a position in a small hole in a cliff. I waited.

"Everyone ready?" Ryan asked in a hushed tone.

We nodded.

"Now."

We all fired. My round missed and hit the rock cliff behind the gunner. Frantically, I fired again. This time I hit. If even one gunner noticed us, he would have had a powerful counterstrike.

"Is it clear?" Sergeant Peterson of Second Squad asked.

"Yeah," Ryan answered as he stood back up.

Then, with the way cleared, we proceeded to the outer perimeter of target Digamma.

"There it is," Sergeant Peterson murmured as it came fully into view.

"Swap for your SMG," Ryan ordered.

We did so and begin closing in on the base. We moved closer to the door. We all leaned up against the wall.

"Corporal Cooper!" Sergeant Peterson said, "Blow the door."

"Yes, sir," A deep voice muttered as a large armored body moved to the front door and set up a charge.

He backed away and five seconds after he placed the charge, flame irrupted into the building. Corporal Cooper was the first to enter the building. Suddenly, several machineguns opened fire, Corporal Cooper stood vibrating from hundreds of rounds impacting his armor. He fell to his knees, and then toppled over onto his face. At least five machinegun turrets were in sight from the doorway.

"Fall back," Peterson ordered.

I stopped where I was. I hadn't made my way inside yet by the time the order was given. But I had seen what happened to Cooper.

"We have a problem!" Ryan said over the COM.

One of the armored Marines backed out of the building firing his SMG-56 through the doorway. Bullets flew out past the soldier. One round hit the soldier's arm and he stumbled. He waved his arm around a second and slipped to safety. Sergeant. Peterson peeked around the doorway and tossed a fragmentation grenade. A loud pop filled the air as it detonated. Peterson peeked back inside and quickly retracted his head.

"Two left," he said.

Then he signaled one of his troops to move in. Peterson and the other soldier entered the room. They each opened fire and took out the remaining gunners.

"Clear!" he called.

"Move in," Ryan ordered.

We all entered the room.

"Phil, get to the data terminal," Ryan said.

"Roberts, Parker, escort him, the rest of my team will make sure to keep the entrance secure," Ryan announced.

"And I'll take the rest of mine to clear the building, Sgt. Peterson said. Peterson and one other Marine left the room. The rest of his squad was either dead or guarding Phil.

We waited and heard several bursts of gunfire over the next five minutes. Then, Phil and his Marine escorts entered the room.

"Done!" Phil said.

"Phil's done and I have the Eupholium set up!" Ryan said over the COM.

"Roger that," Peterson responded, also over the COM. "We're returning to your position now."

Sergeant Peterson was standing in the doorway moments later. Ryan then concluded the Eupholium set up process by configuring its detonation time.

"Lets move!" Ryan said.

We ran from the building on our way to the L.Z. In short time, we arrived at the L.Z. unopposed. We were at the evac site, but no dropships were there to extract us.

"Uh-oh," Nevin said as he noticed the same thing, "I guess we'll wait."

We waited for several minutes before we heard a deep rumble in the distance. It grew louder and louder until Nevin asked, "What is that sound?"

"If I'm not mistaken it sounds like a Preston-class Vorgian Assault tank," Phil answered.

"Get down!" Ryan ordered.

We all hastily dropped to the ground.

The tank rolled up to the clearing, crushing trees as it passed. The gun swiveled around. It was likely using its gun-mounted optics to scan for a target. It slowed as it reached where we were hiding. The tall grass was barely high enough to conceal us.

The gun stopped. Then a man with a tattered desert camo uniform on leaped from a nearby tree. He landed atop the tank. He then pulled out two concussion grenades and activated them, and then placed them on top of the pilot's hatch. Next, he jumped off. The tank and both grenades exploded. The man tumbled into the grass.

Smoke rose from the burnt remains of the tank's cockpit. I was the first to stand back up. I slowly approached the tank. The pilot's hatch had been blown to pieces, though the tank was certainly still functional. Fortunately, it now lacked living Vorgian pilots. I looked down beside me and saw the man who attacked the tank. His shoulder was adorned with the three-stacked chevrons of a sergeant. His desert camo hat was on the ground beside him. He had short, curly, brown hair. I knew I recognized him.

"Sergeant Johnston?" I asked.

The man wiggled.

"Yes?" he replied as he rolled over.

He looked up at me as he lay there on his back. Then Ryan jogged over.

"Dylan! Great timing. Couldn't tell if the tank saw us or not, but it sure looked like it did," Ryan said.

"Dunkelman?" Dylan questioned.

"Yeah, but how did you get here!"

"Long story," Johnston said as he sat up.

The rest of the team wandered over to listen.

"As we ran off back on Sontonos, I took a shot to the leg and fell over. When I managed to stand back up, everyone was gone, other than a few SAS. I took out all three with my AR. All the other SAS had already passed me and continued their pursuit of you. My arm still hurt from Robert shooting us there. I escaped and went further inland. I bandaged up my arm and leg and proceeded to keep fighting. I went around and neutralized several Vorgian patrols in the area. I used my last rounds on a Vorgian sniper. I grabbed the sniper's gun and used it in place of my empty AR-27. I managed to snipe a truck driver through the windshield. The four troopers sitting in the back jumped out and looked around. They all met the same fate as the driver. I captured the vehicle and drove to the nearest town. From there I boarded a civilian transport craft. They simply let me on, way less secure than Elonian spaceports. I had enough money to go since I sold my H-81 to a civilian. It was a decent sized transport craft. It took off from the spaceport and went into orbit. They kicked in Ultradrive and were here within hours. Immediately, I ran out of there into the woods. There had been a lot of commotion in the Capital's spaceport. Word of your arrival in orbit was all over, but they didn't know about the insertion. I assumed that there would be one, so I went to see what I could find. And it looks like I found you," Dylan Johnston explained.

"Wow," Ryan sighed. "Sounds a lot like what happened to me before I was placed on the Rangers."

His eyebrows furrowed slightly, as if he was having memories of his experience alone and on the run. He lowered his head slowly, then jerked it back up when we finally heard the engines of a Corsair Heavy Assault Dropship approaching. It lowered itself into the clearing and opened the rear-boarding hatch. It was primarily atmospheric, but it was airtight and was capable of about an hour of space flight. We walked up the hatch and into the troop bay. We each sat down in one if the eighteen seats.

The hatch closed again and sealed once we were all seated. The Corsair began to rise. The doorway that led to the cockpit was closed, unlike the newer transports that had no door separating the cockpit and transport areas. The Corsair sped up as it soared above the trees. My guess was since we were on the dropship Major Kohl must have secured a foothold.

After a six-minute ride, we arrived at the foothold, just as I had predicted. Several Corsairs were landed at the encampment, and two Paladin Tanks were positioned near the center of the base. Our Corsair lowered itself to the ground and stopped.

"We've arrived," the pilot said.

We exited the Corsair and stepped onto the ground.

Phil was first out and rushed the data to the major's tent. It would be transferred from there, through the COM to Concordia in orbit. We waited there for about an hour as the rest of the bases were neutralized and the intel had been recovered. One by one, other Corsairs flew in and landed, deploying parts of Alpha and Sigma Companies.

Then the COM's in our suits activated, the voice of Major Kohl filling our ears.

"Alpha and Sigma Companies, Rangers, listen up! Our reinforcements are in orbit and coming down on shuttles. You will be joining the attack force when we attack the capital city. Load up and board the Corsairs."

"Well… time to go," Ryan said.

"Part two?" Nevin asked.

"Apparently…" Ryan sighed.

We stood up and walked over to the line of dropships waiting to bring us into the city. We hopped on and strapped into the seats. The hatch sealed and we were on our way back to the action.

We flew for quite a while, since the Vorgian capital city was rather far away from our foothold.

"Alpha Thirty-Five to Command. We are about to land in the capital. Any more need picked up?" our pilot asked over the COM.

"Negative, Alpha Thirty-Five. You wait nearby the city for when we are done. Over."

"Understood, Command. Out," our pilot finished.

Shortly afterward our Corsair touched down on a rooftop of a multistory Vorgian tower.

"Clear the building and move on. The Vorgian troops have taken up positions throughout several of the city's buildings. Just keep moving, and clear as much as you can," Alpha Thirty-Five told us, having relayed the information from Command.

The ramp opened, and we stormed out. I held my SMG-56 tightly in my hands. We arrived at the door, and Ryan opened it swiftly. We moved in and down the staircase. When we arrived at the bottom,

Ryan kicked open the door and searched the room. Several Vorgians were standing around the room with their assault rifles hanging loosely at their sides. We opened fire and mowed the entire room full of soldiers down in seconds.

"Clear!" Ryan said. "These guys obviously didn't expect a rooftop entry."

We charged forward and opened the door to the staircase. We landed on the next level and burst through the door. Tons of red dots lit up on my motion tracker. But when I looked around the room, it appeared empty. But there were lines of desks that enemies could hide behind. We opened fire at the thick metal desks, hoping for a bit of penetration. Suddenly, several squads of Vorgians popped up and tossed grenades. I panicked and darted for the door to the staircase.

"Fall back!" Ryan yelled.

As we hurried back into the stairwell, I saw it. A grenade on the staircase. It was right in front of Phil.

"Gren—" I started as it detonated.

Phil spun into the air and smashed into the railing on the other side of the staircase. Then he slipped and fell down the shaft. He fell two stories and slammed onto another level.

"Phil!" I called.

He didn't respond.

"Max! Nevin! Go get him. James! You are with me," Ryan said.

Ryan and I went back in and shot as many of the troops that were still above the desks as we could.

They too opened fire and bullets pinged off of my armor. Without my armor, I would for sure have been killed. We approached the line of desks as unstoppable juggernauts. We each climbed over a desk and finished off anyone who was left. Another step closer to ending this war. I looked back at the doorway and saw Nevin and Max carrying Phil.

"Is he okay?" Ryan asked.

"I dunno. He hasn't moved…" Nevin said.

The COM activated abruptly.

"All forces, evac immediately. After inspection of information from the labs, we have found multiple nukes stationed throughout the city. We have a list of their locations and are sending EOD teams in to try to defuse them. We have confirmation that they have been activated on a timer. They are repeating what they did on Enphuerzo. Once again, evac immediately," the Major ordered over the COM.

"Oh prex!" Ryan exclaimed. He activated the COM. "Alpha Thirty-Five! Are you available for evacking us?"

"Yessir. I'll meet you on the rooftop. ETA is three minutes," Alpha Thirty-Five responded.

"Roger," Ryan said. "Let's get up there," Ryan told us, after cutting the COM. "We don't know how long we have before those things go off. Our best hope is that EOD gets them disarmed. But if they don't… I would prefer we be a long ways from here."

We pulled back and moved back up the stairs. We arrived on the roof just in time to see Alpha Thirty-Five flying in. Our team hurried on to the

Corsair, with Max and Nevin carrying Phil.

"We have wounded!" Ryan told Alpha Thirty-Five. "Can you take us back to our Base of Operations?"

"We are on our way there now. That is the rally point for everyone we evac," our pilot answered.

We rode quietly in the back of the Corsair as it sped closer to the base. Several frantic calls for help had come over the COM as we came closer to the base. Apparently, a lot of our forces had yet to be picked up. Then, we began to slow down as we neared the base. The rear hatch popped open and we exited rapidly. There were even more tents set up than the last time we were here. We found one with the red plus over the white banner that represented a medical station. Phil's armor had been damaged pretty badly, and overall, he just was not looking too good.

"He's been wounded by a grenade explosion, followed by a several story fall," Ryan explained. "Do you guys know how to handle the armor?"

"Uh… Yes. Yes we do. We will see what we can do," a medic said.

As I looked around the room, I noticed that some of the equipment wasn't set up yet, but there weren't many men in the beds that were in the tent. Most of the wounded were probably still on their way here.

We exited the tent. Several more Corsairs came in from the city and landed in various locations. Then, the ground shook, and a huge plume appeared on the horizon. Then another, followed by yet another. Finally the sounds blasted across us. The thunderous roar of the nuclear warheads detonating shook the entire base.

"What was that!?" a marine said as he jumped off a Corsair.

"Curse it! Curse it all!" I heard the Major yell from his Command tent. "I need casualty reports… how many were still back there?" he started asking.

"The EOD teams must have failed…" Ryan sighed. "Now they are all dead."

We walked over to the Command tent, hoping to get additional information.

"We have more ships in orbit! Nelson's fleet is here. Reinforcements are already en route," someone said from within the tent.

"Well… Bring 'em down," the Major said, frustration evident in his voice.

"Sir! One of the EOD teams survived, they have disarmed the bomb. It was in the northern part of the city… District Four," another officer said.

"Acknowledged," Major Kohl sighed.

"We've lost communication with at least a quarter of our force. And we're still looking for an estimation of casualties. But I'm afraid our loss of communication is just a preview of how many we've lost," one officer pointed out.

A soldier walked out of the command tent and approached us.

"Rangers," he began. "Your services are no longer necessary. You may remain here as an auxiliary force, should the need arise somewhere."

"10-4," Ryan said.

Alex Pennington

The officer walked back into the tent from which he had emerged.

The War Across the Stars

Chapter 9
Pursuit

"Rangers!" Major Kohl said as he stepped from his command tent for the first time in hours. "We have a lock on Vorgian Commander-in-Chief, General Walt Lee. According to our sources, he left the capital shortly after our invasion. He is currently in an APC en route to the city of Ridgefield. We should be able to catch them by dropship, but it is important that you take him alive," he explained. "Understood?"

"Yes sir!" Ryan exclaimed.

"But be careful, we don't have much intel on enemy forces located in Ridgefield, so if he makes it you may be in a lot of trouble."

"Roger that, sir," Ryan acknowledged.

"Remember soldiers, taking him alive gives us exactly what we need to end this war. The highest Vorgian authority held in our custody will cause the rest to crumble. If we kill him, they'll just heap command on someone else and view Lee as a martyr," Kohl warned.

It was time for more action, this time without Phil.

"Let's go guys," Ryan ordered, running over to a nearby Corsair, whose engines moaned to life. We boarded it, and soon were soaring at maximum speed toward the Vorgian city of Ridgefield.

"This is it guys… the end of the war," Nevin said excitedly.

"It'll finally be over? We can stop risking our

lives every other day?" Max asked, smiling.

"No Max, not really. While the war may be over, we're the Rangers. It's up to us to take down pirate groups and anything else that Command feels is worth sending us too. Particularly with our new training... becoming all purpose soldiers is going to make us the single most important squad in the Elonian Empire," Ryan murmured thoughtfully.

After that, the only noises heard were the roar of the engines, and the occasional gunfire from somewhere below. Then, the dropship pilot spoke.

"We're closing in. Lee is on the road just ahead of us. We can't risk firing on him, so it'll be up to you to slow him down."

"Roger that," Ryan stated.

We soared over the APC carrying the general. The road was a thin concrete strip surrounded by trees. The dropship started to lower itself, and turn broadside toward the speeding APC.

"Go! Go! Go!" the pilot ordered.

Our team jumped free from the Corsair and into the grass. The APC had begun to slow down. There wasn't enough room, even through the grass, to get past our dropship. Finally, it skidded to a stop. A lone Vorgian popped up and manned a machine gun on top of the APC. He opened fire on the Corsair. A single shot from Ryan's rifle dropped him limply on the gun.

Suddenly, the armored personnel carrier turned a sharp left, and plunged into the trees. It took down several before crushing its tip into a thicker tree.

"Hurry guys!" Ryan called as we charged toward the woods.

The door opened up and several people darted out. The second was an older man, likely Lee. I took a shot at his leg, but narrowly missed. As we entered the opening carved by the APC, Lee and his officers disappeared deeper into he woods.

"Don't let him get away!" Ryan yelled.

Nevin sped up, leaving us behind him. He entered the deeper region of the woods. I heard various voices. One was yelling out orders, while the others were harder to understand. I tore through the branches and twigs that were in my way.

Then there were several gunshots, followed by the distinctive crack of an SR-4. I flew over a dip and landed beside Nevin with his rifle raised. Bullets whizzed by us. Nevin fired again into the woods. I only saw rustling, and knew that hitting anything would be beyond my ability.

Ryan caught up to us and slowed down.

"Guys, the woods aren't too long. They should be out in the open soon," Ryan informed us.

"Okay, let's do this," Nevin agreed.

We darted further into the trees as fast as we could. Within minutes be burst out the other end to see a road. Parked on the road was another APC.

"Shoot! He's gonna get away!" Ryan yelled sprinting toward it.

Nevin and I followed. Then I heard its engine rumble to life. Nevin leaped onto the back of the vehicle. It started to move. I followed Nevin's act of bravery, barely catching on to the back of the vehicle as it drove off, leaving Ryan and Max behind. Nevin heaved himself on top of the fast-moving vehicle. I looked back, seeing Ryan running after us, however he just wasn't fast enough. Then, I climbed up with Nevin.

"What now? We can't break through the windows," I said.

"Well, you're right. I dunno what we should do. I guess just wait here until the vehicle stops," Nevin called over the wind.

We waited on top of the APC silently for several minutes. As it would seem, the general had no idea that we were on board. But we had no contact with Ryan, so it was up to us. As I looked ahead I saw several large, cecrete walls. Several manned gun turrets were on top of them, as well as a man holding some sort of detonator.

Suddenly, the vehicle began to shake violently. Looking off the side, I saw explosives scattered across the road and even in the grass beside it. Should they be detonated, we would both be dead, but so would the general. The turrets aimed at us, but refrained from firing. Then, to my surprise, the men pulled out rifles and opened fire.

"Nevin! What should we do?" I asked as the bullets pinged around me.

Our armor was taking the blows, but it could only take so many before something came through. I lifted my SMG-56 with one hand, the other still holding on to the vehicle. I sprayed some bursts at the gunmen as we passed the gates. I actually managed to hit one, and he toppled to the ground.

The War Across the Stars

The APC kept driving, and soon the gunmen were out of range. We had to be nearing the city. The checkpoint was likely nothing compared to the forces that will be there.

"There. I can see the buildings. Be ready to take him down as soon as he exits the vehicle," Nevin said.

I steadied my gun. Several Vorgian aircraft soared above us. The general had to know we were here by now. Ahead was a tall building with Vorgian flags waving before it. The APC turned hard, sliding sideways toward the building. I heard its horn honk loudly, likely some sort of signal. A shocking force of soldiers exited the building and opened fire on us.

Nevin hopped off the back and returned fire on the hostile platoon. I remained on top of the vehicle and aimed carefully down my gun's sights. Vorgians continued to pour out of the building.

"Nevin!" I yelled. "He's entering the building, we need to press forward."

I watched as once again Lee slipped away. I jumped down into a mass of Vorgians and entered hand-to-hand combat. I bashed one in the face with my left hand, then sprayed SMG rounds into another. I slipped out my knife and stabbed it into the neck of one right as he shot me at point blank range.

I felt a stinging pain. I realized that a bullet must have penetrated the soft part of my armor. I held my submachine gun at my hip and blasted into the crowd.

Then, I charged. Nevin was right behind me as we slammed through the wall of soldiers. We entered the building and dashed down the long hallway. At the end, I saw Lee turning a corner. A soldier stepped out and tossed a flash-bang down the hall. It blasted open, but it failed to affect us due to our tinted visors.

Bullets flew by us from behind, some denting our armor. I feared taking another… the pain from one was enough. I slipped around the turn and shot the soldier who threw the flash-bang. No sign of Lee. I looked around, and spotted an elevator. The floor number was negative three and decreasing.

"Prex," I mumbled. "He took the elevator." I tried to pull open the elevator doors, but my gloved hands could not get a grip through the seal. "Nevin, use your breaching charge."

"On it," he responded.

I moved back to the main hall and fired some shots at the oncoming mass. Then, a door opened behind me, and more soldiers entered. We were surrounded on three sides. I heard an explosion from Nevin's breach, then turned around and darted for him.

"Go!" I yelled.

He leaped in, grabbing the elevator's cord. I followed suit, and we slid down. We slid for what felt like an eternity, but eventually reached the roof of the elevator, now at rest on the bottom floor. Nevin peeled open the service hatch, and we both slipped into the elevator. It was empty. I slammed a button and the elevator's door opened. We carefully entered the room. It was dark, and unlike the decorative walls and furniture of the upper stories, this room had plain

Cecrete walls and lacked any furnishings.

I could not even see any doorways to other rooms.

"Where could he be?" I asked.

"No idea," Nevin replied plainly.

Then I saw it. There was a manhole on the floor, and its lid was slightly out of place. It had not been placed back on correctly.

"He's in the sewers," I murmured as I moved the lid aside.

I leaped down and landed on a hard surface. There was a river of sewer water running down the center. It was a slimy green color.

Nevin plopped down beside me.

"Which way?" Nevin asked.

I thought hard, but briefly, knowing the consequences of failure.

"Left."

We ran down the hall to our left. My heart beat faster. The running was causing additional pain to my wound, which throbbed continuously like an intensifying fire. The tunnels seemed to stretch forever, with the pain only adding to the feeling.

Out of nowhere, a Vorgian SAS leaped out from behind the curved wall. We fell into the river of muck and began sliding with the current. My gun clattered on the cold Cecrete walkway we had been traversing. I wrestled free of the crazed soldier and kicked him away. Then I planted my feet on the ground and grabbed onto the edge. I pulled myself out and saw Nevin running toward me holding both of our SMG's.

"You okay?" he asked

"Yeah, I'm good," I answered as he passed my gun back.

My armor dripped with the slime. Nevin and I proceeded down the hall. Then we saw him.

"We've got this!" I said as I sped up.

Nevin zoomed ahead and closed in. He began firing his SMG at Lee's guards and officers. The last two of his guards collapsed, one of which fell into the river. Nevin catapulted himself forward, crashing into Lee. The two rolled then slid to a stop. His uniform had *Lee* stenciled on it.

I caught up and reloaded my gun.

"Now what?" Nevin asked, holding down the thrashing general.

"My guess… would be to knock him out somehow," I answered.

"Ok," Nevin said, squeezing the general's shoulder.

Lee suddenly fell limp.

"Nice… Let's go," I said.

Nevin hoisted the frail old man onto his shoulder, and we began to walk down the tunnel. We couldn't go back the way we came, considering the amount of opposition there would be. We had to find another alternative.

As we meandered down the tunnel we heard voices. They were alert, and obviously in search of us.

"Do we fight, or hide?" Nevin questioned.

"Hide," I said, leading the way toward the river.

We both eased ourselves into the water. I heard the footsteps and voices get closer. I held my hand over Lee's mouth and nose and dunked his head underwater. I looked up, but could barely see anything through the slime. Flashlights flashed around above the surface.

At last, they passed. Nevin and I emerged from the water. We pushed Lee back onto the ground. We then pulled ourselves out and picked Lee up again. We quickly moved the way that the soldiers had come from.

"There! A ladder!" I said looking at a rusted ladder.

"'Bout time we found one," Nevin mumbled.

Together, we climbed the ladder pushing Lee up. It seemed to be a long ladder, perhaps stretching clear back up to the surface. We reached the top and rose from the floor. The lid to the hole was off to the side.

"Careful Nevin, I wouldn't be surprised if they have more troops in the building."

"Ya think?" Nevin said sarcastically.

We emerged from the service hole and began to climb the nearby stairway, due to the lack of an elevator. This building was far less elegant than the one we had come down in. As we approached the top of the stairs we heard more voices.

"Hold on," I whispered, letting go of Lee. Nevin still kept a tight grip on the general.

I slowly opened the door with my gun in my other hand. I saw a guard and in response, slammed the door open into another guard. I sprayed a burst into the Vorgian who was standing before me. Quickly I entered the room and went around the door. Three shots entered the Vorgian who was trying to get back up.

"Clear," I called back to Nevin.

He came into the room with me, Lee still hanging limply over his shoulder. We exited the room and entered a dimly lit area. Several mobile stations were set up with large COM and TRIAD modules. Many Vorgians were busy watching the TRIAD.

Nevin and I slowly backed into the other room.

"Ok, so there's a lot of bad guys," Nevin commented.

"Uh… Yeah," I agreed. "Put Lee down, I'm gonna need your help."

Nevin set Lee gently on the floor and pulled his SMG back out.

"Now!" I ordered as we both entered the room.

My first move was to toss a grenade into the center of the equipment. It exploded, shattering several screens and causing ripples in the holo-display. Then I opened fire taking down the survivors as fast as I could. One began to swivel rapidly, clearly attempting to bring me down. I fired another short burst and he fell backward onto the TRIAD.

"Clear," I stated, sweeping my gun around the room. "I'm on my last clip though."

"Great," Nevin said. He pulled out two extra ammo magazines and passed them to me.

"Thanks."

We went back and scooped up the still unconscious Lee. Then we proceeded hastily out of the building. Outside there was a line of APC's and other light vehicles.

"C'mon, hurry," I said as we rushed Lee toward an APC.

I slid open the door and pushed Lee into a seat. I took the wheel and Nevin sat by Lee. I started the engine by turning the switch, then pulled out of the parking lot. I moved the vehicle out to a highway and cruised down the road, attempting to move quickly, though not suspiciously so.

"Ha, I think we did it, James," Nevin laughed. "We're in one of their APC's and they have no way to ID us as Elonian."

"Yeah, you're right. We did good."

We each waited silently for several minutes.

"Where do you think Ryan is? Did he try to continue the mission? Did he wait where we left him?"

"That is a good question. He may even have tried to return to the foothold."

We drove on for a while without incident. Suddenly, Lee woke up. He looked around frantically and grunted. I looked back to see Nevin restraining him. He was pressed hard against the seat.

"Keep him under control! We still have a ways to go!" I yelled to Nevin.

"Working on it," Nevin said trying to stop the old man's resistance. "Ya know, this would be a lot easier if we had some sort of tranq shots."

"I'll bet, but we can thank our superiors for lack of forethought on that one," I said.

Finally Lee stopped fighting as Nevin squeezed his pressure point.

"That wasn't as easy as the first time," Nevin sighed.

Time dragged by but eventually we reached the outer perimeter of the foothold. Nevin stepped out of the APC to go clear us. He approached the entrance with his hands in the air and guns on his pack.

"It's us! The Rangers! We have Lee secured in the vehicle," he called to the sentry.

The soldier on the tower looked around, then looked down.

"You're clear to enter."

Nevin ran back to the APC and hopped in. We drove in and parked near the Command Tent. I exited the APC and walked into the tent.

"Sir?" I said nervously. I was uncertain if I was supposed to go directly to the major, but I figured I would try.

"Wha—" he started. "Oh, it's you," he said, having recognized my armor.

"We... We have Lee. I don't know where the rest of my team is," I admitted.

"You have Lee? Magnificent," Kohl said in awe. He instructed a nearby officer to move Lee to his next location. "Alright, I'll recall the rest of your team. They reported you missing a few hours ago. After that they continued to pursue the objective."

Kohl walked over to a COM unit and

activated it. "Dunkelman, your two missing soldiers just arrived at base with Lee. Sending evac to your location."

"Roger that! Get it here ASAP! We're under heavy fire," Ryan said with sounds of guns in the background.

"On it," Kohl replied.

He then called in a Corsair to pick them up.

Nevin and I paced around the camp, right outside of the command tent. Soon a medic would come patch me up. Yet time dragged on, though the end of the war was coming. It drew ever closer. But I knew that even when the war ended, our training would continue. It would continue until we were the best soldiers the Elonian Empire had ever known.

Alex Pennington

Chapter 10
Treaty of Paix

"Today it was made official that the war is over. The war lasted barely over a month and proved how powerful the Elonian Empire has become. Earlier today, General Walt Lee abdicated command of the Vorgians in what is now known as the Treaty of Paix. Special Forces captured the military dictator earlier this week. His capture disheartened many Vorgians, and with his official abdication, Hothonos, Sontonos, and Vorga have surrendered control to our forces. We'll have more on this astonishing news later, including live at Paix, Euphola for interviews," a news anchor announced cheerfully.

It was done. Phil would recover and the war was over. I would soon be at home with my family. Spend some much needed time with Mom and Dad. I missed my sister Amanda as well. It was incredibly exciting to be going to visit them.

I arrived at the spaceport in Ebony a few days after the official end of the war. Nevin was with me, but we would soon go our separate ways after we left the spaceport.

"Well, that was quite the experience, eh?" Nevin said.

"That is for sure," I replied, walking through the crowds of people.

"It's been a lot better than it could have been, considering we could have not been accepted together," Nevin pointed out, smiling.

"Yeah, having a close friend helps. But man, I

miss my family. I can't wait to see Mom, and Dad, and Amanda again," I said.

We were finally at the door to the spaceport. It was time to split up.

"Well, I'll see you later," Nevin said.

"Yup, you too," I chuckled.

I managed to catch a taxi and was home within twenty minutes. I stepped out, still in my soldier uniform, and approached our house. It looked just like I had remembered it. I rang the door and waited for a response. I could here rustling from within, then the door swung open.

Standing in front of me was Amanda. Her dark hair, barely dangling past her shoulders, was just as I remembered it. She opened her arms and pulled me in for a hug. It was wonderful to see her again. As she let go I saw Mom walk into the room.

"James!" she said in an alerted tone. "Earl! He's here," she yelled to my Dad.

I proceeded into the house and looked around. Once again it had been redecorated and the walls had changed color.

Mom scurried closer and embraced me.

"I'm home, Mom," I whispered.

She started to cry and continued to hang onto me. My dad finally showed up. He had silver hair about the same length as mine, and a furry mustache.

"It's good to see you again, James," he stated.

"You too, Dad," I responded.

At last Mom let go and I approached my father. He reached out his hand, and I returned the shake firmly.

Alex Pennington

"You're stronger," he murmured, his face glowing with pride. "You helped us win out there. I'm proud of you, son. I'm proud of you."

"Thanks, Dad," I accepted, smiling with excitement. It was so nice to be home.

"So... Uh... How long will you be around?" Amanda asked cautiously.

"Well... I only have a week. Then we are back to training. There is only so much that I am cleared to tell you, but we have to become the nation's best soldiers."

"Oh... wow," she said, somewhat sadly, realizing my time was limited.

"I'm sure you can handle it, James," Dad said. "I know you can be the best."

"Thanks Dad."

After our talk, we decided to go eat. We went out to a local restaurant for some food. It was called *Frank's*, which was essentially a burger joint. But despite the low cost and basic menu, the food was delicious.

"Mmmm, this stuff is great!" I said after downing another bite. "It's way better than what we get from the military."

Amanda gave me a look as if she thought I was crazy, but Mom just kept smiling.

"So..." Amanda said slowly. "What's it like out there?"

"Not as fun as it sounded," I stated calmly.

"It didn't sound fun," she laughed.

"Well, I personally had expected to serve Eli as well as enjoy it... But it's brutal. Whenever someone dies…" I trailed off, my smile fading. There was a long pause.

"Well, the business is doing fine," Dad interjected, noticing the awkwardness.

"That's good," I mumbled, still having flashbacks of Steven Roland and Ben Butler, both having been shot right beside me.

"While you were away we made quite a profit. Roger asked where you were last week. He apparently missed your wonderful service," Dad continued.

"Oh… yeah," I said.

I thought about how I would react if Nevin was killed… particularly right beside me. I started to feel light headed. I rubbed the area near my stomach where I had been shot. It was healed up nicely, but it still hurt sometimes. It started up its pain again.

"In fact, we are making so much money that Ross's Rugs might be able to upgrade its store. Wouldn't that be great?"

"Yeah Dad," I said, trying to concentrate on him.

I shook my head to clear my thoughts. Then, I set the few bites of burger that were left back on my tray. "I think I'm done. I need to get some rest," I said.

Shortly after we set back off for home. When we arrived I went up to my old room. My bed was still there, even after several years of vacancy. In the closet hung a few of my clothes, but most of them were stored in a box downstairs along with my other possessions. I changed into a plain white t-shirt and shorts and I sprawled out on my bed.

I quickly fell asleep, with the hope that sleep would clear my head. As I fell into darkness a strange world seemed to form around me. I felt warm... quite warm.

I look around and behind me our house is aflame. I try to move but I seem locked in place. I then look forward again to see my family standing in a line. A man armed with a pistol stood in front of them. He looked familiar. My mind ran through dozens of possibilities before it sank in... He was the first man I killed. The man my scope had picked on Sontonos. I felt a rifle in my hands. I attempt to raise the gun, but still I am unable to move. The man fires a shot into Mom's head. He moves on and fires into Dad's head. I want to call for help, but can't, nothing is responding.

A raspy voice keeps repeating, "Save them! Protect them!" Finally the man shoots Amanda.

Suddenly, Nevin arrives, and kills the murderer. Slowly Rigel Korth approaches from behind, and jabs a knife into Nevin's back. Nevin screams and collapses to the floor. Abruptly, I loosen up, raise my gun, and shoot Rigel.

Then darkness resumed. I woke up and looked around. It had become nighttime while I had been asleep. Everything seemed to be fine.

"Ugh," I muttered. "It was just a dream... just a dream."

I still felt tired, so I rested my head back on the pillow. As I returned to sleep, I hoped that it would not be as disturbing as the last time.

But this time it was not what would occur in my mind, but what would really happen that would be the most painful. I jerked up from my bed and looked out my window. It was early morning.

Car alarms were sounding and gunfire crackled around us. I heard the engine of some sort of aircraft nearby. I quickly threw my combat uniform back on and left my room. After I barreled down the stairs I found my parents in the kitchen gathering supplies.

"James! Help us, we're getting the cans and taking them to the basement. Something is wrong!" Mom shouted.

Suddenly, there was a tremendous explosion. I glanced out the window to see that our neighbor's house was burning and had a massive hole in the upper story.

"Where's Manda?" I asked, worried for my sister.

"She's already downstairs," Dad replied as he shoved more cans in a bag.

I grabbed a package of bottled water and ran downstairs hastily. I saw Amanda folded up at the far end of the room. Choosing to join her, I made my way to her and sat.

Another explosion shook the ground.

"Mom? Dad? You guys okay?" I called.

When there was no response I stood up and went upstairs. There were bullet holes throughout our walls. I looked out the window and saw a Corsair clad in black paint hovering around. My parents were okay and ran to me with the bags.

Alex Pennington

"Let's go, come on!" Dad rushed.

Listening, I followed him straight back downstairs and closed the door behind me. I paused for a moment, and then locked it. The basement was rather bare. One couch, the supplies we had brought, and the box containing my possessions were the only objects occupying it.

"Oh curses," Dad mumbled pacing around. "What is going on!?"

I heard knocking and then more shooting. I wished that I had had a weapon to defend myself, but we didn't own any guns. Plus, all of my military issued guns were at base.

We waited for maybe twenty minutes before it happened. I heard heavy knocks on the door. Then a foot broke through. Men broke through and charged. They held civilian rifles and pointed them around. Dad charged at them but was shot in the shoulder. He continued and bashed one in the face. Amanda screamed and started running. I willed myself forward. I seized one's arm and pulled him over. Then I knocked him on the floor and started kicking him.

I looked over and saw Dad on the floor and one of the pirates approaching me.

"This war ain't over yet," the man muttered.

I reached for the downed man's gun but was then slammed in the face by the stock of the other's rifle. I felt pain for a short time longer before everything went away.

My eyes fluttered open. It was all still dark.

The War Across the Stars

Fires littered the area, and part of the basement's ceiling had collapsed. Dad remained where I had last saw him, but now surrounded by blood. My eyes began to water at the sight.

"No... No... No!" I said breaking into tears. On the staircase was Mom, having not succeeded in her escape. I tried to crawl closer but it was hard. I had blood on my face from a gash in my forehead. My view was still fuzzy from my wounds. I finally managed to reach my Mom. I lay with my arm around her and remained there for what could have been hours. I felt that although I had survived, that they had killed me inside.

I did not know what happened to my sister. I had not seen her in the basement, so I assumed she had escaped. I wished her the best of luck and hoped to find her someday.

Elonian soldiers eventually found me. They took me to a refugee hospital that had been established. I would never forget that day... the pain I felt. It changed me. I knew I had to stop this from happening to others. I had to be the best I could be and put the Elonian people before myself.

Alex Pennington

Part II
The War Across the Stars

Chapter 11
Special Operations

"Move in," Ryan whispered.

Nevin, Cassidy, and I entered a service tunnel, while Ryan, Philip, and Max went down a hall. We moved quickly and quietly down the tunnel. We arrived at a door and stacked up. I signaled for Nevin to move in. He acted on the signal and I heard a suppressed burst of gunfire. I followed him in and noticed the dead pirate on the floor.

We were moving in to the pirate base's command center. Located there should be the pirate leader as well as an Elonian Intelligence officer. The officer had been siphoning sensitive information to the pirate group. His motives were unknown, as well as his identity.

Ryan's team was moving in to disable the power. With the power off, the command center's electronic doors would release.

We darted down the next hallway. Several more pirates were neutralized with ease. These pirates were no match for revolutions of high-level training. We had come far from our days back in the Vorgian War.

We arrived at the Command Center entrance. The door was still locked.

"Ryan, James here... We're at the door."

"10-4, we are closing in on the generator. ETA well under a minute," Ryan said over the inter-suit COM.

"Roger that, sir."

We waited patiently in the barely lit room. Then the lights cut and I heard several machines groan to a stop. I grabbed one side of the split door and Nevin grabbed the other. We pulled it open and Cassidy moved in. Nevin and I followed suit. Quickly we advanced and seized the frantic Intelligence officer. Nevin shouldered his SMG and fired a single round into the pirate commander's head. He was expendable… and better off dead. As for the officer, we needed him alive. I slipped out a tranq needle and jammed it into the man. Nevin and Cassidy cleaned up the rest of the guards and we were clear to go.

"Objective secured. Prepped for evac."

"Alright, we're already closing in on the hangar," he responded.

"We'll be there shortly," I informed him, shouldering the officer.

We needed to get to the hangar quickly. The destroyer *Iron Fist* was waiting outside to obliterate the base after we were off.

We hurried down the pitch-black halls. We had only our gun-mounted flashlights to guide us with the power off. On the way down the hall we encountered another pirate stumbling in the dark. A simple burst and he was down. Before long the whole base would be put out of their confusion. Within minutes we were boarding a solid black pirate Corsair.

"Good work team," Ryan murmured as he started the engines.

We rose out of the hangar that had been

carved into an asteroid. We could see the *Iron Fist* just outside the asteroid field.

"Rangers to *Iron Fist*... come in," Ryan said over the COM.

"*Iron Fist* here, we read."

"Objective secured. You are clear to open fire."

"Copy that Rangers. Clear to open fire."

Our stolen Corsair exited the asteroid field. The destroyer unleashed a massive barrage of missiles into the base. Asteroids exploded behind us. We soared into the open hangar bay of the destroyer.

We exited the Corsair, once again successful. We had made habit of success. We truly were the best soldiers the Empire has ever known, surpassing even the original Rangers.

We were far more organized than before, having more varied roles assigned between us.

Ryan, along with being team leader, was our explosives expert and pilot. He was probably still the most talented person among us.

Phil continued to manage electronics and data, and he tended to carry the SG-13 pump-action shotgun. This allowed him to use his strength in close quarters combat to his advantage.

Max had improved a lot from his days as our local idiot. He still had a tendency to crack jokes at the strangest of times.

Cassidy, ranked sixth in the original contest, had been added to our team to replace Robert. She did nothing but impress after that, having easily matched up with the rest of our team, and was certainly more useful than Max, even after his improvements. She had bright blue eyes and brown hair, about shoulder-length, bound to military specifications.

Nevin used the SMG-56 for mobility over power. He had only grown faster, and now our team made use of it, giving him tasks where his speed could be of aid.

I was proudly our designated marksman. My skills had improved immensely, to the point that I surpassed the rest of my team.

Before this most recent op, Colonel Miller, still the commander of the Rangers, informed us that we had an unusual mission next. He had told us it seemed unfit for a team like the Rangers.

Chapter 12
Operation UNKNOWN

The Rangers sat silently in a dark room. A bright holo-display sat in the center as the only light source. It resembled a TRIAD system, but was obviously modified for other purposes. Colonel Miller sat at the far end of the table. Several mysterious Intelligence officers observed the display.

"This mission is a gamble," one of the officers stated.

"I understand that, but they are the only team that could handle the adverse conditions. If they find what we think they will, we'll need them," another responded.

"I don't like it. What if the Vorgians knew we would collect the data? It may be sabotaged, faulty, a sort of ruse."

"I agree," another chimed in. "Besides, we are sending them through the Black Hole Belt. It's ridiculous."

"Yes, yes, I know. But the Vorgians likely succeeded. I trust this intel," the second officer said thoughtfully.

A man with the lone star of a Brigadier rose from his seat and put his hands down on the table.

"This mission has already been decided. We are contradicting ourselves in a time of great importance. We need to hunt down Rigel Korth before he establishes some sort of new government."

"Sir, with all due respect, it has been over a

revolution since the *Hornet* departed from Vorga. I'm sure Korth has already begun on his new regime," the first officer retorted.

The officer with the strongest support of the mission raised his hand for attention.

"Gentlemen. Yes we need to go. Yes we send the Rangers. But think. He will have a military stronghold at best, not a new civilization. The chances of finding other sentient life forms beyond the Black Hole Belt are astronomically low. We need to exterminate him, but we should not be concerned about his politics."

"He's right. Just be aware that every minute we waste listenin' to this babble is a minute that my boys are not out preserving the safety of our citizens. This whole mission may be the wrong place for 'em, but even so, let's at least get it outta the way," Colonel Miller argued.

Silence filled the room after Miller's statement. I glanced over at Nevin.

"Okay. This is over. The mission is on. Rangers, you will arm up and ship up to the *Procyon*. *Procyon* has a new engine device to allow for you to arrive much faster through Ultradrive. You'll keep a warp beacon on the ship, meant for release once you find this *planet*. Dismissed," the Brigadier concluded.

We rose from our seats and exited the dark room. The hallway was noticeably brighter, and it took some time to adjust. This mission was unusual. Apparently Intelligence thinks that Rigel and Robert are not only alive, but also rebuilding. We boarded the Carrier-class shuttle and prepared to be taken up to Procyon.

"This new ship is pretty exciting," Phil commented.

"Why?" Max asked plainly.

"This is top-of-the-line stuff. It is a new class of heavy assault cruisers. The new Procyon-class will take the place of the current Invader-class."

We continued minor conversations as we waited for arrival at *Procyon*. Once on board the ship we departed for our bunks. This mission would require a lot of waiting before we initiated the action.

The next day *Procyon* launched from Euphola toward the Ontario Black Hole Belt, a region where stars had collapsed onto themselves, then pulled others in to do the same. The strange anomaly had always been enough to dissuade many attempts at passing through it. Fortunately, this ship's Ultradrive should be able to shrink the singularities small enough for us to slip by.

We had a nice arsenal of weapons for the mission. We had all of the usual guns to expect, as well as a few specialties such as rocket launchers and the new SF-42 SOPMOD. The SF-42 was an all-purpose weapon in the literal sense. It was fairly light for maneuvering around, yet has brilliant accuracy. It had a mid-length barrel, which could be shortened with ease for close quarters and heightened mobility. With a scope and semi-auto setting, it made an excellent sniper rifle. While it was inferior in stopping power to the SR-4, with a clean headshot, it worked with the same efficiency. A thirty round clip allowed sustained fire or for a seemingly unending sniper magazine. On full auto it had a reasonable rate of fire as to not waste ammo, but still get the stopping power dished out fast enough. It looked to be an amazing gun, and I was anxious to try it out alongside my SR-4.

Another day dragged on as the *Procyon* flew through a miniscule version of space.

"Attention all personnel. This is Captain Baker. We are entering the Black Hole Belt. Be on station and prepared for emergency. Let us hope we make it through safely," a voice announced over the intercom.

"Phil? Risk assessment?" Ryan asked.

"Well, this has never been tried by us before, so I don't know what to expect. The singularities may disrupt our Ultradrive, dropping us into normal space… in which case our ship would be swallowed by a black hole in seconds. We could also we pulled toward one of the miniature black holes, but that seems unlikely considering their gravitational pull will be greatly diminished," Phil explained.

"Yeah, uh, that is unlikely right?" Max questioned.

"I honestly don't know. This has NOT been attempted," Phil replied.

I pondered what was going on in the bridge. There was a distinct possibility that disaster was coming down on us, and that the bridge was trying to sort it out. The thought of the ship being consumed by a black hole, and us, the Rangers, dying quietly on a ship in the Ontario Belt… it simply didn't seem right.

We waited, soaring through Ultraspace for days. The sheer distance we had to have covered was mind-boggling.

At last, a week into our journey, our captain's voice came onto the intercom.

"Attention personnel and strike teams. We will be dropping out of Ultraspace within the hour. We do NOT know what to expect, and the possibility of Korth having established a considerable force here is not out of the question. With that in mind, we need pilots in their ships, and soldiers locked and loaded."

With that, our team immediately headed to get into our power armor. It had been improved in several ways, yet attempts at neural interface had still failed consistently. We entered the armor fitting bay and to my surprise, found Spc. Wheaton standing by the armor with a grin.

"Hello Rangers, nice to see ya again," he said in delight.

"Likewise," Ryan responded.

We quickly equipped our armor with Wheaton and Phil's assistance.

With armor out of the way we headed for the armory. The SF-42 was only stored in two of the ship's many armories. One was a deployable armory, much like a drop pod, while the other was the heaviest armory in the core of the ship. Chances of immediate deployment seemed low, so we went to the nearest armory, with only the basic weaponry.

"Everyone on station, we are dropping out in ten!" Captain Baker stated again.

I was actually slightly nervous. This strange task had so many unknowns… it didn't feel consistent. I felt a slight whoosh as we reentered normal space for the first time in over a week.

"Multiple contacts," a cautious voice said over the intercom.

"Hail them, keep the intercom going for the crew," Captain Baker ordered.

"Roger that," the COM officer said.

"This is Captain Lawrence Baker of the Elonian ship *Procyon*."

There was an ominous pause with no reply.

"This is Admiral Ronald Cope of the United Earth Defense. We have laid claim to this planet, Marzoc," the COM responded.

"We are seeking fugitives from our nation. One of their starships has entered this system. A man known as Rigel Korth was in command… on a ship called the *Hornet*."

"Fugitives? I am uncertain of what you are referring to. The indigenous people of this planet have a single ship of the same name. So too is their leader named… Rigel Korth. But they welcomed us here with open arms," Admiral Cope announced.

Again there was a pause. I looked over at Ryan and Phil.

"So Korth's here… but he has some cover going and now he has these… these aliens guarding him?" I asked.

"Honestly, it's beginning to look that way James," Phil said with a look of awe still in his face.

Then Baker began to speak again.

"I see. Well they are not native to this planet. They retreated from a disastrous war several revolutions ago. We are here to take them back, and find out what they were doing out here."

"Well you see, um, Lawrence... That's not how this will be going down. We would prefer you stop lying to us, and return to wherever you come from."

Phil had a worried look on his face. "Guys this first encounter is not lookin' good," he murmured.

"Admiral. Perhaps you don't understand. We have traveled for weeks to get here, and our course took us through a black hole belt. A journey like this cannot be disregarded, or failure easily admitted," Baker pleaded.

"Lawrence. It is you who do not understand. We have a clearly superior force and have asked you kindly to depart our lovely ice-covered planet."

"We are getting what we came for. All units! Prepare for deployment planetside," Baker ordered.

"Very well. The choice is made. Not the preferred meeting of gentlemen I had expected Lawrence," Cope said in a disappointed voice. "Open fire."

"Not what I was expecting," Max said.

"Yeah, we need to get to the hangar bay. If anyone is going to make it planetside, it needs to be us," Cassidy commented.

Looking toward her, I nodded. Then I hastily grabbed some grenades, ammo, and my SR-4. We ran down the narrow halls of the Procyon, heading toward the hangar. Suddenly, there was a tremendous rumble, and the ship shook. Max lost his balance a moment, stabilized, and continued.

"How are our shields already down?" Phil exclaimed in shock.

"We don't know what we're up against. I'm not so sure we really know what we are getting into," Ryan stated.

As we reached the hangar door and swung into the large open room, the intercom spoke again.

"Attention ship personnel. I have grim news. We need to abandon ship immediately. We attempted deployment of the warp beacon as to summon reinforcements, however it was destroyed immediately after release. The enemy's missile systems have devastated our shields, and our hull integrity is diving. The bridge crew is already en route to the life pods," Baker spoke solemnly.

Another rumble battered the ship, and static came through the intercom. Then his voice came back, somewhat difficult to hear. "Deployable Armory Alpha is locked in place… We need someone to unlock it so that we may—"

Again static came through. Max skidded to a stop.

"Guys, we need those weapons. I'll go unlock it. Then find a lifepod, or ride it down."

"Max… er… Alright. Go. Good luck," Ryan told him.

He swiftly took off down the hall to try to perform something heroic. Something he never would have done during the Vorgian War.

Alex Pennington

The rest of the Rangers proceeded to one of the Corsairs parked in the large hangar. Ryan entered the pilot's seat in front and we prepared for a rough journey to the surface of the planet.

The main gates to the hangar were halfway open but seemed to have stopped opening, presumably due to damage to the ship. Our Corsair slowly approached the gates, Ryan being cautious to fly straight through. We flew out and immediately headed toward the white-coated planet below.

A mere thirteen seconds after our escape from the hangar, a tremendous explosion propelled our Corsair. Checking the rear video feed, the *Procyon* had been reduced to rubble... Likely with Max still on board.

"Dang," Ryan said plainly. "This is not how this was going to go down."

"I would consider this a serious snag," Nevin said with a solemn face.

Our Corsair, lightly armed, alone, and with limited air descended quietly to the surface. Inside, we had a small survival pack, our personal preference in weapons, and our power armor.

"How many do you think got off?" I asked.

"Not as many as we brought, I can tell you that much," Ryan commented. "What the..."

I walked into the small cabin to see what he was looking at. An immense metal structure shimmered with a spectacular light down on the planet. Looking up, I saw another of the structures above the planet.

"What are those?" I asked curiously.

"You expect me to know?" Ryan asked.

Phil pushed his way in and took a look of his own.

"Uh… Yeah, that is different. My best guess is some sort of heat provider or something to further warm the planet. But the planet is covered in ice, so if that is its purpose, it doesn't seem to work," he said intelligently.

"Do you… Do you think Korth built that? Or these UED guys?"

"I couldn't see Korth having them built, and we don't know enough about the UED. It will take some observing planetside to make a solid hypothesis," Phil told us.

Our lone ship entered the planet's thin atmosphere and came out into a snowy wasteland. Then a startling alarm sounded from the Corsair.

"Missile lock, we have multiple bogies on our tail!" Ryan called out as he swerved the Corsair hard. One of the missiles still nailed our rear engines, spinning us out of control.

"Hang on guys!" Ryan yelled as he managed to regain control and lift back up. He slid in behind one of the fast planes and unleashed a salvo of missiles. The missiles flew quickly after the fighter, barely gaining on it. Our Corsair quickly fell behind, due to the incredible speed of the fighters. Abruptly, the fighter rolled, then pulled up and over. It barreled straight at us and began shooting a machinegun and more missiles. The Corsair's windshield cracked and shattered in some areas as the bullets pounded into it. I ducked down as a blast shook the starboard side of the dropship. The whole ship felt as if it tipped heavily, toppling us to the floor. Then it began to balance out in a rapid descent.

The event made me think back to my first mission, when we were shot down onto the planet's surface, trapped in enemy territory. At last we slid into the snowy ground, sliding quickly, while sinking deeply. The dropship came to a hard stop when it met with a rock.

I heard the fighters fly overhead, but their sound began to grow distant shortly afterword. We were alone.

"I think they're gone. We should move… somewhere," I announced.

"I agree. I don't know what they have out there, but we should go find out, and see what we can do to them."

"They have a clear advantage with numbers and firepower. We're going to have to use guerrilla tactics," Cassidy pointed out.

"Yup. James, you get a recon position on top of that cliff. We're going to go over to the other side and take a look," Ryan ordered.

"10-4," I responded, taking off up the hill with my SR-4 gripped tightly in my hands.

We had landed in a deep snowdrift, with the front of the Corsair submerged purely in snow. Fortunately, its crash cleaned up a path leading up to the cliff side. I ran through the path and then began treading through the deep snow on the cliff. It did not take long before I was atop the cliff, peering out at a massive landscape of snow-covered valleys and several small structures made of stone. Though the view was vast, I saw no sign of life amongst the snow. I clicked the COM link on my helmet.

"Ryan, this James. I have eyes on an expansive, snowy, wasteland with a few structures as points of interest. Over."

"Solid copy, James. You wanna check out the structures?"

"Yessir, they may be some sort of shelter."

"Alright, we have nothin' of interest on this side, but we aren't as elevated as you, there may be more over the next hill, but we'll regroup on you anyway."

"Roger," I said, glancing out at the team powering through the deep snow on the other side.

This place was cold, even with our power armor on. I hated to think about how the Marines from *Procyon* felt in this, granted any survived.

Ryan was the first to arrive at the top of the steep hill. Peering down he saw the same structures as I had.

"Now that is interesting. You ready?" he said.

"'Course sir," I replied.

I was the first to begin carefully sliding down the hillside down into the valley. Behind me was Ryan, who had his pistol in one hand as he proceeded.

The trip down seemed long, but likely was fairly short. From here, the distance to the first structure looked much larger than from atop the cliff.

Realizing the distance we had to cover, we moved as quick as we could, but the snow hindered our movements.

Alex Pennington

"What do ya think those structures are?" Cassidy asked.

Of course, Phil was the first to respond.

"I suspect they are some sort of survival shelter for the inhabitants of this planet, be that Korth's men, the UED, or some other form of native."

"Are you saying that there may be some other species here as well? Even another faction besides us and the UED?" Nevin questioned.

"It seems logical. If there are others, I hope they're on our side. We have enough enemies as is," Phil said wisely.

We continued the trek through the snowy wastes, and grew ever nearer to the ominous structures that loomed over us. The structure was round in shape, like a sort of tower, rising out of the ground. As we came within several meters of it, the snow began to pick up off the ground, and a sort of snowstorm began. We instinctively picked up the pace and slid into the dark interior of the structure. There was a spiraling staircase that passed all around the walls, and there was a metal hatch at the far end. Besides that, the entire room was bare.

"Well then. This is basic," Nevin commented.

"It seems to be little more than a shelter. Perhaps we should check out our paths. You know, the stairs and the hatch?" Phil suggested.

"Right. James, you take your team down the hatch, I'll head up the stairs with Phil," Ryan ordered.

We split into our familiar teams, but without Max. I moved closer to the hatch and grabbed its handle. I pulled it up revealing a wooden ladder that seemed to descend for a great distance.

"Well, I'll go first," I said uneasily as I stepped down onto the first rung.

Slowly I descended down the rickety ladder, hoping that it would hold us in full power armor. The ladder seemed to keep going for much longer than I had initially expected it to.

When I finally reached the bottom the room was lit with strange glowing orbs on the walls. There was a long hallway in one direction, while the side behind the ladder had a stone wall. I pulled out my H-81 and clicked on its under-barrel flashlight. I advanced quickly down the hall. At the end was a door of solid steel. I grabbed its handle carefully, and as I entered the room I kept my pistol pointed forward. There was a series of symbols carved into the wall, several desks and electronic equipment, and three men standing there. I hesitated, completely clueless what to do.

"You! Who are you?" one asked, grabbing a pistol off one of the desks.

"Uh… I'm James. Staff Sergeant James Ross. Who are you?"

The man glanced behind him then looked at me nervously.

"I'm Dr. Jake Thomson of the UED Research and Discovery Corps. To whom do you affiliate yourself?" he responded.

I steadied my gun, unsure if he knew about the recently initiated war across the stars.

"Elonian Rangers. Special Forces. I've been tasked with retrieving Rigel Korth and Robert

Washington from this planet."

He started backing up again toward the desk. I caught eye of a handheld COM laying on it. His hand quickly darted for it. In response, I let off a shot, shattering part of the device. The man then shot me, hitting a hardened part of my armor. I unleashed a flurry of carefully aimed shots at all of the men, just as Nevin and Cassidy bounded into the room with their guns raised.

"Um... What did you just do?" Nevin asked.

"Well, these guys just tried to kill me. But they're... they're human. At least they look human. They said they were UED. How could the UED be human like us?" I asked.

"We need Phil," Cassidy said blankly.

I activated my COM system.

"Hey Ryan? James here," I said.

"Yeah, what's up? Find anything?" he asked back.

"Yeah, did you?" I asked.

"That's a negative. We've climbed a ways and found some windows with nice views. That's about it though. We're nearin' the top. I think."

"Alright, well when you guys get a chance, we have some interesting markings down here, and... well the UED appears to be a human race just like our own. They had scientists down here."

"Okay. That is a bit unexpected. We'll report back to you when we reach the top. See what you can do until then," Ryan ordered.

"Copy that sir, we'll see what we can do." I clicked off the COM and approached the computers.

The War Across the Stars

I observed the markings on the wall, and then looked at the computer screen. To my surprise, I was able to read everything onscreen. It had some sort of matrix running on one, rapidly flashing thousands of words and letters constantly, while on another there seemed to be a sort of science log.

1 December 2197
We've been studying this rock structure for while, thus far, with little luck. O'Brien had a minor success when he translated a few of the cultural notes. Apparently, this planet was known as Marzoc by some race known as the Tredecim. They were the indigenous people here, and had some sort of empire going for an extended period of time. The story details the construction of some super-computer, perhaps an AI, known as the Beholder. After its creation it essentially became their god.
-Dr. Jake Thomson
UED RADC

7 December 2197
Jackpot! We ran across a sort of Rosetta Stone for this language. It has allowed us to dig deeper into their culture and beliefs. They seem to have only been quasi-advanced, yet the Beholder appears well beyond them. We believe the Beholder is located in a massive complex underground where their capital was located. It honestly seems as if they had a golden age, then fell into a dark age from the sudden drop in advancement and technological use.

Alex Pennington

Some time before the Beholder's construction they created Facticius Phoebus Platforms. They were an array of machines meant to act as the planet's suns, considering the planet was out of range of any star, which in itself seems an impossible anomaly. The planet does appear to have a higher than average temperature near the core, which may be part of how these species survived. The deeper they go the more heat it provides. These platforms were intended to provide a light and heat source to the planet with their tremendous energy emission. I'm astonished that they worked, and that these Tredecim even had starships to get them into space. So far we haven't found much out as to why they are no longer present on the planet. In truth, they may still be here, just hidden in some underground network that we have yet to find.

-Dr. Jake Thomson
UED RADC

13 December 2197
Intel came in from Cope that there might be hostile personnel in the area. He mentioned it was unlikely that they'd show up here, and that most are likely dead, but apparently we've made a new enemy. Perhaps the Tredecim have emerged and are attempting to combat us. He said they were going by "Elonian" though, so it may be some other alien race. Exciting!

-Dr. Jake Thomson
UED RADC

I looked back at the bodies lying on the ground. It seemed odd reading what they had written mere days and hours before we killed them.

"Well, this place is fairly strange. Interesting information on that terminal," I said.

Nevin, looking up from having read it himself, nodded in agreement.

"Tredecim," he murmured.

"Yeah, I think this would fascinate Phil to no end," Cassidy pointed out.

Once again clicking the COM, I planned to inform Ryan of our new intel.

"Sir? We've come across UED terminals loaded with valuable information about the planet, its prior occupants, and those light stations we saw on our way down."

"Yeah, alright, we'll head down. This top room seems to be little more than an observatory," he returned.

We searched around the mid-sized room looking for any other high-value discoveries. We managed to locate a tunnel leading deeper into a pitch-black region of the cave and more of the strange symbols on the walls.

"You two wait here for Ryan. I'm gonna check this out," I told the others.

I stepped into the dark area, pointing my pistol around, its light illuminating the darkness. As I proceeded deeper into the tunnel I thought I heard some sort of scampering noise. I searched the area, but saw nothing that could have been the source of the noise.

I turned back around, ready to head back down the path, but to my surprise I saw Rigel Korth before me. I swung for his face but he narrowly ducked, then took off down the hall. I pursued him, aiming my gun. He slid, and then turned left. As I arrived where he had turned, I too swung around to follow him, only to find a stone wall. There was no door, or even a sign of movement. I looked behind me, but nothing there either.

"Surely I didn't imagine that," I mumbled to myself. Though as I looked around, I began to question if maybe I had.

I shook my head and returned to my team, unsure whether to tell them what I saw. I was second in command, the executive officer... I could not let them believe me to be insane.

When I arrived, Ryan's team had returned. Ryan looked up from the computer.

"Hey James, you see anything?" Ryan asked.

"Uh, no, not really. It was just a long tunnel," I told him, fairly honestly.

"Think it's worth exploring?" Ryan inquired.

"Well, it's probably better than the arctic wasteland up there."

Phil finally looked away from the computer.

"This is amazing. Simply amazing. I can't believe we stumbled on something like this. And for these aliens to speak our language! But they're human... How?" he said in disbelief.

"I dunno, but when those Intelligence guys

said that this would be an unusual mission, they weren't kidding, that's for sure," Nevin said.

"So Phil, any clue about that matrix, or these symbols on the walls?" I questioned.

"Well, the matrix is some sort of translator, rapidly processing a bunch of these symbols into words. I assume this is how the UED came up with the information in those logs."

"You want us to stay here for a bit Phil?" Ryan asked.

"Actually, as much as I'd love to keep reading the new translations, I suspect the UED might be looking for their scientists soon. We should keep moving."

"Alright, its your call. We'll go downs James' tunnel," Ryan decided.

I was a little concerned, as the tunnel just didn't feel right. It was a fatal funnel if something were to try to kill us. We had no escape routes, or any cover. We'd just have to trust in our armor.

"Phil, you're on point," Ryan said.

Phil entered the dark hall and turned on his flashlight. He had his SG-13 ready in case of trouble. As a team we moved down the narrow hall, with no end in sight. The path would occasionally turn slightly, making some sort of trail to somewhere.

Then we finally saw light. It was more of the bluish orbs.

"Take it nice and slow. We don't know what's over there," Ryan said calmly as we lessened our pace. We all turned off our flashlights as we drew nearer. As we came within a few meters of the lighted room, I saw an armed soldier walk by. He did not look down the hall at us, but it meant the room was under watch. I looked back at Ryan. He pulled out his combat knife, and motioned me to do the same. I did so, and held the knife firmly in my hand. He signaled to move in.

As I entered the room there was a guard to my immediate left and right, plus the guard who had been walking around. I plunged the knife into the man on the left's throat, one of his only unarmored areas. Kicking him over I saw Ryan taking out the door guard and Cassidy knifing the patrol.

They had hardly had time to scream before our team had neutralized all three. Their weapons lay unused on the ground. Their assault rifles were quite short in comparison to the longer barrel of the AR-27 and other rifles in service. They also used a bull-pup design for the magazines.

"I take it this facility has some significance to the UED if they have guards here," Ryan pointed out.

"I agree, we should stay sharp," Nevin said.

We concluded that the only place to go from the room was up a ladder. Like the ladder before, it was rickety, and we had to advance one at a time, Phil going first. I went last, but as I neared the top, the ladder shook. Then the rung snapped, and my foot fell fast into the next one, breaking it as well. I held on tight to the ladder, as to not slip and fall clear down to the floor.

"James?" Cassidy asked, concern lining her tone.

"I'm good," I said, my arm reaching the top. I

lifted myself out and pulled my pistol out.

The room we were in was round, and oddly unguarded. It seemed to be exactly like the structure we had found originally. I saw the same stairway curving upwards, and the same doorway into the wastes. Beside the hole was another metal hatch. Through the doorway I could see a horrible snowstorm blowing snow powerfully.

"Well, let's check upstairs. The UED has to have something here, right?" I said fairly quietly, concerned the UED could be near.

We moved up the stairway, taking small, quiet steps. It seemed that the stairway was incredibly long, but as we neared the top, I heard voices. Phil's hand came up in a fist, inferring we stop.

"Oscar Papa Nine, you may have company soon. We've lost contact with the RADC team under Oscar Papa Eight," a voice said through a COM device.

"Copy that HQ. We already have a team downstairs on watch. Over," a nearby voice replied.

"Affirmative Oscar Papa Nine. Just keep hold of that observation post, we need to hold as many of 'em as we can."

"10-4," one responded.

"That's all, over," the radio replied.

"Ramirez, how are things goin' down there?" the voiced asked into the radio. "Ramirez? Come in. Something must be messin' with our signal. Holton, go check it out."

"Yes sir."

A soldier approached the stairs and turned the

corner. As he took his first step down, Phil fired a shotgun blast into the man. He flew backwards, and our team moved in.

"Keep one alive," Ryan ordered.

As I popped up to the top level I saw four men. One of them wore a hat in place of the helmet worn by the other three. I assumed him in charge and shot his leg. He went down, but drew his pistol and took several shots at me. I stepped closer, knocking it out of his hand with my gun. The pistol slid across the floor and over the ledge to the stairway.

"Very nice," Ryan commented, looking at the three dead soldiers and our new prisoner.

"Who are you?" the soldier said through clenched teeth.

"Lieutenant Ryan Dunkelman, Elonian Rangers. So who are you?" Ryan said.

"Master Sergeant Christopher White. UED Marine Corps."

"What are you doing here?" Ryan asked.

"Look, I'm not telling you anything. Just kill me."

"We're not going to kill you. In fact, I could be convinced to let you live after you've told us what you know."

"Why should I believe that?" he asked angrily.

"I don't see a lot of choice right now," Ryan pointed out.

"I'd rather die than betray the UED!" he screamed.

Ryan slammed his armored boot into the sergeant's stomach. He screamed in agony as Ryan repeated it.

"Now?" Ryan questioned.

"NO!" White replied, his eyes filled with determination.

"Ya'know… you are actually a pretty good soldier. It'd be nice to have more men like you on our side."

"You're not going to convince me to be one of you! Don't even try!" White protested.

"Oh, I'm not. I was just letting you know before I started the real interrogation," Ryan said, with feigned excitement.

"What do you… Oh…" White said as Ryan pulled out his combat knife.

He then seized the man's hand and pressed the knife close to his fingers.

"Round one," Ryan said as he began to press in on the knife.

Sergeant White's face contorted with pain as his fingers began to drip blood.

"STOP! I'll talk… I'll talk. Just… stop. Please," he begged.

"Oh, unexpected. I was getting excited for round two," Ryan replied. He had used this tactic before, creating a sense that he enjoyed their suffering, and that he had no limits.

"Okay…" the man's face winced. "What do you want?"

"What is the UED doing here? Exploring, Colonizing, Protecting?"

"Originally, we were exploring for a new colony. We had encountered another alien species on

Corzam, and wanted to be prepared if we ever found another. So we… we sent multiple warships in each scouting party. When Cope found this planet, without… a star, we realized the significance immediately. We deployed forces to the surface, and were contacted by the locals. Korth, I think he said his name was. Look, I'm really just a grunt, I don't know everything," he explained.

"You're doing well so far," Ryan said, spinning his knife. "With that in mind, I'd continue."

"Okay, okay. Uh… We've been ordered to hold these… these… towers. We've dubbed them Observation Posts, it was the best our teams could come up with for their purpose. Command is sure that these are important."

"What do you know about the Tredecim?" Ryan inquired fiercely.

"The who? Oh, yeah… the other natives. We've been instructed to keep an eye out for them. That's all I know."

"Who's in command?"

"Cope. Admiral Cope."

"Where can we find him?"

"Last I knew, he was still in orbit on board the *Odyssey*."

"Anything else you want to say?" Ryan asked, waving the knife slightly.

"No… that's all."

"How strong is your force planet side?"

"We have multiple battalions deployed down here. You know you don't stand a chance," he said boldly.

"What's that device on your ear?"

"My communicator… that's it."

"Give it to me," Ryan ordered.

"Fine, here," White said, removing it and handing it over.

Ryan observed it carefully, and then slipped it into one of his ammo pockets.

"We're done here. Best of luck to you Sergeant. Rangers, let's move," Ryan concluded.

He put away his knife, pulled his gun back out, and started down the stairs. We followed quickly, ready to further explore this planet.

"Good work there sir, as usual," Phil said, laughing.

"It's really not as fun as it looks. But yeah, we're slightly better off."

"So, where too? We have one exit that we haven't used yet, so… back into the snowstorm?" I asked.

"I guess so. Maybe we should look for the Beholder. If it's still intact," Cassidy suggested.

"It's a start. We need a goal. Surely their former capital won't be too hard to find. But we also need to find Korth," Nevin pointed out.

We filed out into the raging snowstorm once again. We had no idea which direction to go, only that this landscape, one filled with towers and mountains, would not be the easiest to explore.

"Let's get up on another one of these hills. Get as high as we can to get a good view," I suggested. "All things considered, there may be other survivors."

"We can only hope," Ryan responded.

The hill was slick and icy. Large rocks protruded from it in various locations. With each step our boots would sink into the deep snow. As we finally reached the peak, we were met with a surprising sight. Rows of tents set up in the center of the valley. They were blowing violently with the wind, rippling, but remaining planted in the ground. A flag was blowing in the middle of the camp with seven stars encircling what appeared to be a planet.

"Sir… I think we found something," Nevin said, staring at the encampment.

"That's got to be UED," Phil commented.

"Let's hit it, see what sort of damage we can do," Ryan said.

"Anyone else getting the feeling there's gonna be a lotta guys here?" Cassidy asked as we began descending the mountain.

"Actually, James, you wait here. Snipe 'em off 'till we give the signal," Ryan said, looking back at me.

I nodded silently and took the few steps back to the top. The rest of the team made their way to the base of the hill as I set up. I lay in a prone position, and had my SR-4 up to my eye, observing the base. It was fairly close, meaning most shots would be easy to hit.

In less than a minute the group had arrived at the edge of the encampment and I saw them all raise their guns into a combat stance. They advanced steadily, searching for targets. I expected one to emerge from one of the many tents at any moment, but still nothing. They turned a corner down one of the alleys of tents. I was unable to see what was in front of them, as it was obscured by the rows of tents. Then Phil, who was in front, stopped, raising his left arm to a ninety-degree angle.

My COM crackled, making me jump with surprise.

"James... Come on down. Be careful. We've got a blood trail and a lot of blood. No bodies," Ryan stated.

"Copy that. On my way down," I said, exhaling.

As I moved down the mountainside I started to wonder what had happened. My first thought was that some of our Marines had survived, but I could not think of a reason that they would move the bodies. The thought bothered me as it left so much unanswered.

"Sir? Could it be a trap?" I finally said.

"We've considered, not seeing any signs of it though. Checked a few tents already and still nothing but blood. These tents 'round here are in pretty bad shape as well," Ryan replied.

My slow jog broke into a sprint as I tried to regroup with them as fast as I could. Something didn't feel right, but I couldn't place what it was. I finally caught up with them and saw the scene they had been describing to me. It definitely didn't look like something Elonian Marines would take the time to do.

"Well, I see only one logical option," Phil said, staring at the bloody trail leading away from the base. "We follow the blood."

Ryan nodded in agreement and we began to trek alongside the trail of blood. The snowstorm remained harsh, and as we moved further along the trail, it became less and less clear. Two hundred meters from the camp, we found that the blood led into a cave in the mountainside.

"Why am I not surprised?" Nevin asked. "A cave."

Cassidy laughed softly, but Ryan gave me an uneasy look.

"Well, this may be our worst decision yet, but let's head inside," he said. "Phil, you're on point."

We moved into the dark tunnel, moving slowly, trying to be prepared in case anything was to attack. I placed my sniper rifle back on my pack, pulling out my pistol and clicking on its under barrel flashlight.

I heard rocks tumbling, somewhere to the left of me, and quickly swung my aim in that direction. I saw nothing unusual, and then realized how complex this cave system must be. The rocks must have been somewhere on the other side of the wall before me. The ambiance of the cave was unsettling, but fortunately it kept me alert.

Phil stopped abruptly and backed up a step. Shining his light ahead, I now saw what he had found.

"Well, I guess we found the bodies," Phil murmured.

Before us was a stack of nearly twenty dead UED Marines resting in a pool of blood.

"What… could have done this?" Nevin asked

thoughtfully, taking several steps closer to the pile.

"Careful," I warned, still keeping my guard up.

Each man seemed to be wearing a white camo outfit with some sort of vest for armor. Many of them had pairs of gashes as if a two-fingered claw had attacked them. As I observed the bodies, something flashed out of the corner of my eye. The next thing I knew Nevin was gone. I quickly looked left to see a large creature rolling across the ground with him, slashing at his face. I lifted my pistol to shoot when I too was knocked over, dropping my pistol. It slid across the cave floor, its light illuminating various markings that adorned walls before coming to a stop facing the body pile.

I looked up to see a wide-faced monster barring its rows of dark teeth at me. Its skin was a dark brown, almost magenta color, and it seemed to have a strong, yet agile build. With one of its mighty hands it held me to the floor while the other one repeatedly began to bash me. I struggled to punch back, but its grip was too strong. My heart began to race as I ran out of options. So far it hadn't gotten through the tough armor, and as I fought to get it off I could only hope it wouldn't. At last, after a seemingly long time, I heard Phil's shotgun fire a blast into the creature on top of me. It rolled off of me from the force of the blow, but appeared to be getting back up.

It then uttered something that almost sounded like a sentence, as opposed to an unintelligible roar, before being battered by another blast from the SG-

13. It collapsed to the ground, its dark blood spraying onto the cavern wall behind it.

I quickly looked over to Nevin to see the creature that had been on him now sprawled motionless beside him. He slowly started to get up, but as he looked at me I noticed his visor had a small crack in it.

"What… was that?" Nevin finally asked.

"I have only one guess," Phil stated. "Tredecim."

Chapter 13
Tredecim

"So… *that* is a Tredecim?" Cassidy asked, leaning her head toward the dead creature.

"Purely hypothetical, but I'd say… yes," Phil declared.

"It's strong. I couldn't get it off me alone," I added.

"Agreed," Nevin nodded. "It cracked my visor."

"Is your HUD okay?" Ryan questioned.

"Yeah, its good. Not sure if I'm airtight anymore though. Can't tell so far."

I moved closer to the dead creature that had assaulted me. It was tall, likely near three meters in height. It had two long, bladed fingers on each hand, as well as rounded thumb. Its face seemed to be terribly misshapen, being quite wide with a large mouth.

"Could these things have been collecting these Marines to use as food?" I asked, looking over to see Phil observing the body with me.

"Entirely possible. Given the fact they took the time to collect the bodies says a lot itself," he replied.

"Stay alert team, there may be more," Ryan warned.

I reached down and scooped up my pistol from the ground. Observing it for a moment, I held it up in a tactical stance and approached the body pile. I heard a slight chatter and a moan nearby. Ryan shot me a quick glance, then nodded. He had heard it too. I slowly stepped around the pile to see that the cave forked off into four directions, giving the enemy multiple points of attack. Phil moved in on the other side of the bodies, and aimed his gun down one of the caves, illuminating it.

"Clear," he said quietly.

I pointed my H-81 down the nearest tunnel and fired when I saw one of the creatures crouched before me. I managed to get off three shots before it tackled me, sending me into the pile of corpses. I held on tightly to my pistol, not letting it slip from my hand. As the Tredecim attempted to begin bashing me, I turned my wrist so I could fire again, putting four shots into its head. It fell limp, its weight still holding me down. I sighed, satisfied with the kill, and slid it off me.

"You good James?" Phil asked as he relaxed his readily aimed shotgun.

"Yeah, that one wasn't so bad."

The others made their way around the bodies and looked at the corpse before me.

"This is why we need to stay in each other's line of sight," Ryan said.

There was a brief moment of silence before Nevin spoke up.

"You guys think these caves lead to their capital?"

"Honestly, no. I suspect that this is nothing more than a village of them," Phil said.

"Agreed," Ryan said flatly. "Though I still

think we should explore. We need to better understand these things… and we still don't know for sure they are Tredecim. We're making assumptions."

"There's four routes. Which should we take?" Nevin asked.

"Well… Gah, I hate to split us up after all this, but we need to cover ground too. We'll do teams of two and three. Phil, you're with me. Cass, Nev, you two go with James," Ryan ordered.

"On it," Nevin said, moving to stand by me.

I reloaded my pistol and moved slowly down the tunnel that the creature had recently emerged from. Nevin moved up beside me, his SMG-56 held at his shoulder as we progressed. Ambient drips and crumbling sounds kept me on edge, ever wary as to what may lurk ahead. We had gone far enough into the cave that our only light was from our flashlights, with all other areas being shrouded in a veil of darkness. I slowly swayed the pistol, trying to get an idea of every corner, crevice, and crack that the cave wall had.

A short distance ahead, the cave suddenly dropped off, the sound of running water filling the air. I held tightly to the edge and lowered myself down, landing softly on the rock below. This area appeared to be a sort of underground river, though the water couldn't have been more than a meter deep. I heard Nevin and Cass splash down behind me as I began walking down the river, following the water. On the edges, the water went no higher than my ankles.

"This appears to be water, but surely not enough for them to survive off of," Nevin said quietly.

"We don't know how much water it takes for them to survive. Perhaps its not nearly as much as humans," I replied.

"We're assuming they even need water at all," Cassidy added softly.

As we proceeded down the river, faint noises could be heard from various directions. I could tell the cave wasn't clear yet, and that somewhere, more Tredecim still lurked.

"I hear something. I think it's a waterfall," Nevin stated.

I listened carefully and before long I too heard the noise. We picked up the pace, moving quickly in the direction of the sound. It was a short amount of time before we reached the edge of the water, where it poured gently into a massive cistern. The three of us scanned the area with our flashlights, unveiling a tremendous clearing in the cave, with the center filled with water. Along the edges appeared to be structures, carved out of the cave's stone walls.

"Shoot!" Cassidy exclaimed, abruptly pointing her light straight up. "Four of 'em, they saw me."

She turned off her flashlight, with Nevin and I following suit. We could only hope they wouldn't find us without any light.

Just then, my COM activated.

"James, this is Ryan. We found some sort of camp of them. Just had a rough fight. Three of them are dead. They appear to be able to see in the dark without trouble… there are no lights around here and they still located us fine. Phil says they may be using some sort of echolocation or sound-based detection method, but I think they just have good eyes."

Before I had a moment to respond I heard a splash followed by a large hand securing itself around my leg and pulling me off the edge. I had originally estimated it was about ten meters from the start of the waterfall to the surface of the water below, and I now found myself falling in complete darkness that entire distance. The fall felt longer than it should have, perhaps a mental illusion from the lack of sight.

I felt the impact as I splashed into the water below, still being grasped by the creature. I frantically moved to turn on my light, now seemingly the best way to even the playing field.

Continuing to sink, I felt the monster begin its attack, taking heavy swipes at my armor. Then, two lights illuminated the water. The renewed ability to see gave me a chance to click my light back on, then take a swing at the Tredecim. I landed two blows to its face, causing it to relent its grip on my ankle. Immediately I began moving back upward, grappling protruding stones along the edge, in an attempt to escape the water. At last I breached the surface, pulling myself onto the hard shore.

The moment I was able to, I turned around, seating myself on the rock and aiming my pistol back into the cistern. As expected the Tredecim burst forth, giving me a clear shot at its face. Four subsequent 9mm rounds to the jaw and brain silenced the substantial creature.

"Nevin! Over here," I called, hoping to

regroup.

"We have a plan, you're our distraction!" Nevin replied, aiming his light straight at me as yet another Tredecim knocked me to the ground.

As I slammed face-first across the cave floor, I realized that these beatings were getting old... fast. Nevin unleashed a long burst from his SMG to free me from the beast. I began crawling forward as quickly as I could, then heard another approaching from behind. Quickly, I did a roll to the side, resulting in the Tredecim missing me and sliding past. I hopped to my feet and put several rounds into the creature as Nevin's SMG added support.

I saw one of the doorways into the structures along the edges and sprinted toward it. As I neared I dove forward, ending in a roll. I landed back on my feet inside the stone cutout and carefully observed my surroundings.

Firstly I noticed more writing on the wall, similar to that found near the entrance to the cave. Secondly I saw a bowl shape carved into the floor, approximately four meters in length. The inside of it was incredibly smooth, leading me to believe it may have been some sort of bed for the creatures. Scanning quickly, I saw two others bowls, as well as a large pile of sticks with three propped against each other. I immediately assumed they were for use in the creation of fire, adding another layer of intelligence to these creatures.

I heard one of them let loose a series of unusual noises outside the doorway. In response, I quickly moved against the wall, completely hidden from sight from outside. I tried to keep calm, calling on all of my training, though the situation I found myself in was one we had never trained for.

I heard footsteps approaching, coming ever closer to my doorway. One of the creatures stepped in looking away from me first. Knowing it was a head's turn away from seeing me, I aimed and pulled the trigger three times. I was treated with a *bang* followed by two *clicks.*

"Prex…" I mumbled to myself, realizing I had to reload.

The bloodied Tredecim lunged toward me, and acting fast I pulled out my combat knife. The monster drove itself into the knife, spurting its dark blood across my visor. Its two great arms swung around me hard, as if in a bear hug. It began to squeeze, creating noticeable pressure on my armor. Breathing quickly became difficult, causing a slight panic to start in my mind. I tried to move the knife for another stab, but did not have enough room to move, so I jerked the knife upward, pulling toward the beast's neck.

At last it released, allowing me a gasp of air and another moment's peace. I slid my knife back in its sheath and reloaded my pistol as fast as I could.

I exited the structure to see Nevin and Cassidy on the other side of the cistern, engaging several of the Tredecim. I took this as an opportunity to update Ryan.

"Sir, we've got a serious problem," I panted. "We ran across some sort of nest of these things. I might even go so far as to call it a village. We can talk specifics later, but I don't think we can kill 'em all."

"A what? An entire village? They're civilized? Uh…" Ryan paused for a moment, trying to decide how to respond. "Push forward. Keep going in until you get out. Phil and I's path appears to be leading us upward, we're thinkin' to one of those Observation Posts the UED guys were talking about."

"Copy that, keep pushing forward," I replied, moving in toward my teammates.

"James!" Nevin called out, noticing my approach. "We can't take all these things. We're takin' a—" Nevin was interrupted by yet another Tredecim knocking him to the floor.

I placed several rounds in its skull before responding to Nevin.

"I know, we need to go. Now!" I ordered.

The three of us took off in a dead sprint toward another tunnel at the far end of the cavernous room. The opening was about the size of the original cave entrance, meaning simply getting there would do little to stop the Tredecim rampaging behind us. I looked back over my shoulder to see a group of three of them gaining on us.

Looking ahead I tried to run even quicker, even to the point of keeping up with Nevin. We entered the smaller tunnel, which immediately took a hard turn to the right. Nevin reached out his hand against the cave wall and twirled around the corner, with me pulling a similar stunt. Upon further thought, the tunnels may not *stop* the Tredecim, but their substantial size would complicate fitting multiple at high speed into the small space.

We barreled down the next direction with Cassidy doing her best to keep up with us. To my surprise, Nevin disappeared from before me, falling down into something. I tried to slow down, but was too late, joining him in the pit. To my pleasure however, I saw snow.

"Hop down!" I called out to Cass, figuring she was holding position after the falls.

I immediately began running down the narrow, declining path toward the snow. As I reached the base I leaped forth, both hands extended in front of me. The fall was just five meters, but was still enough for a deep impact in the snow. I found myself completely submerged by it, though not overly deep. I heard a second impact behind me, followed shortly after by a third.

Despite the urge to get up and run, I just lay there, face down in the snow, making no attempt to escape further. I lay there for as long as a minute not bothered by anything but the silent patter of snow in the hole my armored body now filled.

"You good James?" I heard Nevin ask from behind me.

I stood up slowly, looking back toward the hole I had jumped from to see a single Tredecim doing nothing but watching. Then looking to the right, I saw Nevin, standing directly beside me.

"Yeah, I'm fine."

"It's just watching us. Perhaps it only attacked 'cause we were in its territory," Nevin suggested.

"Maybe…" I murmured.

"I say we rendezvous with Ryan ASAP," Cassidy said plainly, rising from the snow.

I clicked on the COM, hoping Ryan and Phil would be easy to find.

"Ryan, James here. We're out. One of 'em's watching us. You say you were near one of those towers?"

"James, I think we see you. Look up," Ryan replied.

I allowed my eyes to rise, before long they arrived upon a tower, exactly like the others, placed atop the mountain.

"Yeah, I can confirm. I see the tower. Anything good in there?"

"A dead Tredecim."

"Dead when you got there?" I asked.

"No. It was acting awfully odd though. It was hunched over on its knees with its arms pushed out in front of it. I dunno, maybe a stretch or prayer pose?" he replied.

"No clue. Where're we going to regroup?"

"Give us a sec, I'm still checking out the surroundings. There. That might be a good sign. I see some pretty heavy smoke coming from a crater a little ways out. If I were to take a guess…" Ryan paused. "I'd say it's a life pod."

I became excited. A life pod meant that there might be survivors… Fellow Elonians who could join us. Perhaps it would even be Max. I still had difficulty trying to decide if the squad was better off without him or not, but the thought of him being dead bothered me. He was one of us… a Ranger.

"Alright, Phil and I are coming down. The cliff face to our left appears to be traversable. Barely. You three move around and meet us at the base."

"10-4," I said plainly, taking a final look at the Tredecim that still stood watching us.

As we began to move away from the opening in the mountain, I heard a noise behind me, causing me to quickly look back. The Tredecim was gone, the cavernous opening now empty. I brushed it off and continued to trek through the snow. It had to have been several hours since our crash-landing in the Corsair.

As we turned the curve of the mountain we could see Phil and Ryan sliding down the mountainside. They seemed to be carefully moving between various outcroppings that allowed them to keep their speed in check.

At last they arrived on ground level. It was nice to be a full unit again.

"Before we get rolling, let's run a status report. Mine and Phil's armor's fine, essentially undamaged, though we are both running a little low on ammo. Phil has more than I do though," Ryan announced.

"My armor has taken a beating, but nothing worse than you already knew. James took almost all the hits in the tunnels," Nevin said, nudging me slightly.

"I have a few mags for my H-81 still, and haven't fired my SR-4 since we got here," I began.

Alex Pennington

"As for my armor, it feels fine, but I've had at least four of those things roll around with me."

"I think they're afraid to hit a girl, I mean... I haven't been hit yet. Ammo's a bit low though," Cassidy said with a smile.

We laughed a bit before deciding it was time to move. Though it seemed the Tredecim were content with remaining inside their cave, it was clear from the UED camp that they were willing to leave it when they needed to. With haste we made our way toward the billowing smoke cloud that lay before us. It was a fairly long run, through a plain environment seemingly devoid of life.

Chapter 14
This Is Real War

When at last we arrived at the crater, Ryan's suspicions were confirmed. Lodged into the ground was an Elonian life pod, smoke rising from its nose. A small amount of blood seemed to be leading away from the tail door before being covered by the endless snow. Ryan and I hopped down into the crater, no more than two meters at its deepest point, and approached the pod.

I looked inside the damaged craft and images started playing in my mind. Enphuerzo. Our flaming transport descending at incredible speeds toward the ground. Jenkins. Rob.

I came back to reality and saw an empty pod. A blood splatter adorned the floor in front of one of the seats, though no other signs of life were present. It certainly wasn't Max's escape pod.

"They're still alive. Just… where did they go?"

"Uh… I… I don't know. I'd expect them to look for shelter though, considering they don't have power armor to help deal with the cold," I suggested.

"Agreed. Most likely they would find one of those towers and camp out inside it."

We moved on, heading toward the next structure that jutted out of the ground. We had to be close. We couldn't be the only Elonians who lived.

"You know…" I started, thinking back to the caves while we walked. "There were sticks in one of those structures… but where are the trees?"

Nevin turned and stared at me, clearly thinking.

"I… I'm not sure," he said shortly afterword, the others clearly reaching the same conclusion.

"I don't see how trees could survive out here, the snow's substantial and if this planet doesn't have a real sun, I can't imagine plant life ever being supported," Philip pointed out.

"Just another mystery to solve," Ryan said thoughtfully, exhaling as he spoke.

We walked silently for several more minutes before finally reaching the next Observation Post. There was blood splattered across the side of the doorway. To the left of the tower was a small mound, mostly covered in snow. Despite the cover, it appeared that the mound's base was composed of bodies clothed in arctic camo. UED.

"Alright team, we're here. Phil, stack up," Ryan ordered as they each took a side of the open doorway.

He took a deep breath, before making his move.

"Now!" he ordered.

Both soldiers turned into the doorway and moved in.

"Clear."

Nevin, Cassidy, and I entered the doorway behind them. A blood trail led up the stairs. It had to be them. It had to be the survivors.

Phil started up the stairwell, Ryan and I following close behind. Nevin and Cassidy waited near the hatch that led underground. As we neared the top I heard hushed whispering. Phil was the first to the top, his head poking out above the floor. Immediately a loud *crack* sounded, followed by the sound of a shotgun pump. Phil flew back against the tower wall, his visor strewn with cracks. Ryan was next to the top, but held his hands above him, one clutching his AR-27.

"Friendly! Friendly fire!" he beckoned, gazing upon Elonian Marines clad in black.

"Whoa, stop. Put the gun down. Put it down," the soldier with the shotgun ordered.

I also rose into sight, and slowly lowered my H-81 to the floor.

"Lieutenant Ryan Dunkelman, Elonian Rangers," Ryan said calmly.

Phil, having recovered from the shock of the hit, held his own shotgun pointed at the lightly armored Marine.

The shotgun armed Marine remained still for a moment longer, before lowering his gun.

"Sir. First Sergeant Dakota Boone. I'm sorry. We thought you were the enemy," the lead soldier defended.

"Phil, you good?" Ryan asked, looking over his shoulder to see Phil had lowered his gun as well.

"Yeah. Though I'd immensely prefer not to be subject to attempted fratricide again."

"Understood sir," the Marine said obediently.

Phil was only a standard sergeant, so the Marine either hadn't taken note of his rank patch on his armored shoulder, or was simply showing respect for us being Special Forces.

Ryan's COM clicked, likely Nevin checking on the gunshot.

"Hey Rye? You good?" I heard his voice ask.

"Yeah we're good. Just a misunderstanding. Hold position."

"So Boone," Ryan started, looking around at the twelve men standing in the room, and the one sitting on the floor clutching his stomach. "Status report."

"Baker gave the order to get off the *Procyon* and Alpha and Epsilon squads made their way to evac. I've got the whole of both of those squads, and a crewman from *Procyon*. Alpha's my team, Epsilon's under Sergeant House, but he isn't combat ready. On impact with the planet, Private Wells' rifle discharged, shooting the man directly across from him… his own CO," Boone explained.

"I'm sorry! I've already said I'm freakin' sorry! You keep bringin' it back up an'—"

"Private. Shut up. You need to keep it together out here," Boone told him coolly.

The private didn't reply, but closed his mouth, which had been left hanging open, then tried to regain his composure.

"So, we saw this structure and made our way to it as quickly as we could, helping House along. It is frigid out there sir. Absolutely frigid. We arrived here and killed the guards. We then took over the tower and camped here since. Far as supplies, we've got a water apiece, excluding the swabbie, and a small amount of food," Boone concluded.

Boone was wearing a pair of sunglasses,

which seemed out of place, though it added an air of command to him. In addition to aesthetics, at least it provided him something to keep the snow out of his eyes. His face was clean-shaven, and he seemed to have a bandana around his neck for face coverage.

"Well, it's good to see other Elonians," Ryan said. "We don't plan on just waiting around to die, so will your team join us?" Ryan asked, giving the squads a choice. "We'll have platoon numbers then, and can really inflict some damage on the UED."

Boone looked back at Sgt. House, still reeling in agony against the wall. He then looked at all of the soldiers standing behind him, and looked back at Ryan.

"What about House? He can't keep moving around. He needs rest… heck he needs medical attention but we don't have any med supplies."

"I have basic medic training," Phil said, stepping forward. "But I only have a few bandages as far as supplies are concerned."

Boone looked back at House. I could tell they knew each other, likely good friends.

"Anything. Just do what you can. Lieutenant?" he said, turning back toward Ryan. "Alpha's behind you. I'd like to have Epsilon hold here and stay with House. We can run this like an HQ, a base of operations."

"Our numbers don't really constitute an HQ, but given the circumstances… We'll make it work. We will need a way to communicate back. All of us have a COM system, but I don't intend on leaving a Ranger here to run COM duty," Ryan said.

"I understand sir. It appeared the UED may have some form of advanced COM device. Maybe we could use those."

Ryan reached into one of his ammo pockets and extracted the communicator from the sergeant he had interrogated.

"Phil. Figure this out. We're gonna go get some more," he said, flicking it over to Phil.

Ryan began down the stairs, and I recovered my pistol and followed closely behind. I was elated to see friendly faces, even if our initial encounter wasn't so pleasant.

We moved down the stairs hastily, and with a purpose. When we reached the bottom I saw Nevin and Cass, still hanging around the hatch.

"Hey, go check it out down there. Give us a better idea of what we're settlin' into. This is our Base of Ops for a while," Ryan stated.

"On it," Cassidy said, lifting the hatch and descending the ladder into darkness.

Ryan and I exited back into the ferocious snow and moved around to the mound. We then dug away at the snow, finding the heads of the dead soldiers. It somehow seemed wrong, despite all the times I had taken weapons of the men I had killed, something about pulling these earpieces from their skulls didn't seem the same.

After we had collected three of the devices, we returned to the tower. Climbing the steps, I toyed with the two devices in my hands. They seemed to be an incredible piece of technology, much like the COMs we had in our suits, though cheap enough to be deployed to all soldiers.

When we reached the top, most of the men had dispersed. House appeared to have been bandaged up, presumably by Phil, who now was standing near Boone holding the earpiece Ryan had given him.

"Phil, Boone. We're back. Three more. This'll give us a total of four. I'd say two on Alpha squad and two here at HQ with Epsilon."

"Good with me, if they work," Boone replied.

"I think they do. I just required another to receive and send to prove it. Hand me one," Phil asked.

I handed Phil one of the ones I had collected, and he flipped it around in his hand until he found what he was looking for. A small button juxtaposed to an equally small screen displaying a number. He tapped the button several times, before stopping. He motioned for one of the soldiers on the floor to come, and he did. Phil handed it to him, and then gave instructions.

"Put it on your ear. Then hold your hand up to it, and apply a light pressure to the device."

The soldier immediately did as he was told.

"Did it work?" he asked.

Phil glanced back at Boone, whose helmet was in his hands and the device in his ear.

"Yeah. I heard him loud and clear straight in my ear," Boone replied, a smile splashed across his face.

"Knew you could do it Phil. You always can," Ryan said, patting Phil on the back.

"We simply had to adjust the frequencies to be the same, and the pressure activation was fairly obvious," Phil said modestly.

"Obvious may not have been the word I'd have used," I pitched in.

Boone replaced his helmet on his head, fitting it snugly over the device. "Let's hit 'em."

"Well, before we found your pod, our plan was to find the Tredecim capital. We assumed it would be valuable in information and targets," Ryan said.

"Wait... Tredecim?" Boone asked, perplexed.

"Natives... basically huge bipedal creatures with razor claws. Probably about two to three meters tall. We found some UED intel on them in another one of these towers, then we found a cave full of the things about an hour ago."

"Their capital is supposed to hold some sort of supercomputer known as The Beholder," I said. "It was like a god to them."

"So these things... Tredecim... they built a computer then decided it was so great they started worshiping it?" Boone inquired.

"From what I gathered from the UED data logs... yeah."

Boone laughed for a moment, then his face became serious again.

"So, this computer might help us?" he asked.

"We don't know. We're just going to find out," Ryan answered before I had a chance.

"Eh, alright. Let's make it happen," Boone said casually. "Just gimme one sec."

Boone walked over to House, who seemed to have fallen asleep.

"You hang in there soldier. We'll be back for ya," Boone whispered quietly.

Boone then stood up and approached the stairs, the men affiliated with Alpha squad filing in behind him. I tossed the other COM device to one of the soldiers in the room before turning for the stairs myself.

"Nev, what's it like down there?" Ryan asked into the COM.

There was a several second pause, creating a bit of concern in me.

"Writing. More Tredecim writing. UED looks like it was tryin' to set up another decoding station, but the guys manning it are gone. The place is only halfway set up, several crates with more parts in them. Literally no sign of the eggheads though," Nevin replied at last.

"Any escape routes?"

"Yeah, a single tunnel, just like the other one. We haven't gone down it, should we?" Nevin asked.

"Negative. Regroup up here. We're headin' out."

"Copy that, on our way up."

We waited for the two to make their way up the long ladder back to the surface. When they arrived, we were ready to move, and proceeded into the snow. I felt bad for the Marines with us, as their standard issue BDU with an assault vest would do little to keep out the cold.

We tread through the snow for at least half an

hour before spotting anything of significance. We saw it from afar before ever closing in, but it appeared to be mighty tower at least three times the height of the observation posts we had grown accustomed to. As we grew nearer, I looked back at the group. It was then that I realized how severely Phil's visor was messed up. I was surprised he could still see well enough through the cracks and fissures. It looked worse than the damage done to Nevin's, but I knew Nevin's was pierced, whether Nevin felt it was or not, I could tell. Phil's, having only been hit by a shotgun, had held firm.

"You sure you wanna keep that thi—" I started, before being cut off by a scream and a spray of blood from the Marine behind Phil.

"SNIPER!" Boone called, diving into the snow.

I immediately crouched and pulled my SR-4 off my pack. I took aim at the tower through its Oracle scope, but couldn't seem to find the shooter. Every second I wasted could have been the life of another Marine. My heart started beating quicker as I searched for my target.

Another shot was fired, but I didn't hear any soldiers scream in pain. The shot had given away his position however, located on the fourth story. He appeared to be wearing a white ghillie suit, well suited for sniping in snow.

Quickly as I could, I lined up a shot. My crosshairs hovered over his head when I saw it go off again. I took the shot, the bullet soaring through the air before planting itself in the sniper's brain, causing his body to fly backwards. I looked around, trying to see where the last shot went. Then I saw Phil, his visor shattered, and blood running down his cheek.

"Phil?" I asked, looking at him as he raised his hand to feel the wound.

"I'm… I'm good. He only grazed me. My injuries are insubstantial. Let's keep moving."

"You sure Phil?" I asked him, blaming myself for his pain.

"Yeah, I'm fine. Really," he said, rubbing the line of torn skin along the side of his face.

"Boone, how's your guy?" Ryan asked, looking at the soldier on the ground, a circular hole of blood placed precisely on his forehead.

"Dead," Boone replied plainly.

"Alright… Let's keep moving. We'll make 'em pay."

Our unit moved forward rapidly, approaching the doorway to the obelisk. We closed in quick, stacking up at the door. Ryan was on one side of the door, and Boone on the other. Phil hung back, still assessing his own injury. I stood behind Ryan, and another Marine stood behind Boone.

Silently, Ryan raised his hand and put up three fingers. He reduced it to two, then one, then turned in, aiming his rifle through the doorway and pressing in. I heard him open fire… it wasn't clear. Boone was next in, then it was my turn. I moved forward, pistol in hand. Looking in, there were five enemies, two of which were already in the process of dying. I turned to my left and fired two shots into the chest of the soldier waiting there and then looked back to my right.

The last man ducked back behind his cover, concealing himself from our fire. In a single quick move, Boone ran forward then slid, progressing rapidly across the floor, shotgun raised. As he passed the cover he immediately put a burst into the man, and from the doorway I saw him jerk upward into the air.

"Clear," Ryan announced as more Marines continued to enter the doorway.

"You two… hold here. Watch our six while we take the rest of the tower," Boone said, eying the last two soldiers to enter.

"Got it, Top."

We began to move up the stairwell, intent on capturing the tower. Again Ryan was on point, and when he reached the top of the stairs he turned and unleashed a powerful spray onto the foes who waited in ambush. Boone placed his shotgun blasts primarily on a tight group of UED troops that were in cover behind an overturned table. A single burst from Boone nailed multiple targets, dropping them.

I bolted forward, taking a few bullets to my armor, distracting them away from the lightly armored Boone. I felt as if it was somehow my responsibility to take the bullets, being as my armor was so superior. Overtaking the enemy cover I fired several rounds into the white-clad men.

"We're clear," I proclaimed, scanning the room.

I reloaded my pistol slowly and precisely. I began to feel as if something was going to go wrong.

We were doing too well.

"Hood, Rush, watch the stairs up. We need to investigate," Boone called to his men.

I began to wonder what he meant by investigate, when I noticed several carefully stacked laptops near the wall.

"This place had to be important to these guys," Boone pointed out, grabbing a computer and opening it up. "Password. We need to catch 'em before they get packed. Let's move!"

Boone charged forward, pushing between his two men to take point.

"Hold up Sergeant!" Ryan called, chasing behind him. I moved in behind Ryan who was alongside Hood and Rush. I could see Boone reach the top and take a shot. Immediately after, two clouds of rock burst off the wall behind him before I saw a puff of red come from his shoulder.

"Boone!" Ryan yelled, himself reaching the top.

Boone yelled in pain but continued the fight relentlessly. Moments later we had seized the third story. That marked the halfway point on the tower. The moment it was clear Boone proceeded full charge up the next flight of stairs. I heard the click of a grenade's pin being removed as Boone bounced one off the wall and onto the next floor. The following explosion was mixed with the sound of electronics fizzing out and screens shattering.

As we moved up, the room was free of enemies, all of them dead and strewn about the room. The sniper from earlier still remained on his back near the window. Boone ceased his rampage when he saw an intact computer near the edge of the room.

"Hood, secure that computer," he ordered.

He then glanced at his shoulder, and ran his hand over it. Despite the cloud of blood that I had seen burst from it at first, the injury seemed insubstantial. We were getting lucky, but at the same time, it had been ages since I had seen a mission like this.

The Rangers generally operated alone, making use of small team tactics to take out larger forces. Thanks to our power armor, casualties and even injuries were almost completely eliminated. Fighting alongside Marines reopened the opportunity for death. Even those I thought were safe... those of us in power armor... weren't as safe as we thought.

"Boone, what was that?" Ryan asked, walking closer to him.

"We needed to secure a computer sir. The information on them could be vital. We had to move as fast as we could."

"Right, well next time you might check with me before you go on a suicide run. But it worked. Good work," Ryan replied.

Boone was probably used to being the top guy on the field, not having to confirm with superiors for quick battlefield judgments. I looked at Boone and could tell he wasn't trying to be a hero. All he wanted was success, and to defeat the UED. It was nice to have a soldier like that with us.

"Top," Hood said. "I got somethin'."

"What is it Corporal?" Boone asked,

dismissing his injured shoulder and approaching Hood.

"We've got access to all sorts of data. Multiple logs left by one of the scientists… UED fleet data… and presently we have access to some sort of data server," Hood explained.

"Excellent. Reset the password, close'r up and let's get moving," he said, a faintly distressed look on his face.

Ryan and I were the first up the stairs to the fifth story, ready for another fight. As we each popped up over the top, we were treated with a vacant room, computers broken and desks overturned.

"It's empty," I murmured.

"Either a trap… or they're all on top," Ryan returned.

Carefully fanning out and checking behind the desks, we confirmed it to be the latter.

"This'll be it. They've got everything on top. We take them down, then we've secured this post."

Nevin moved up beside me, his visor scarred horribly from that first encounter with the Tredecim.

"These guys aren't so tough," he said plainly. "I expected more of a fight."

"Doesn't it seem… too easy?" I asked him.

"James, you're always thinkin' of some sort of disaster aren't you. We're the best. We're the *Rangers*. These guys haven't fought anything like this," Nevin said confidently.

He was right, we did represent the greatest that the Elonian Empire had to offer. We were picked for this operation for a reason. It was time to fulfill it.

"Go, go, go," Ryan ordered, taking point up the final staircase.

Nevin and I were behind him, with Boone and members of Alpha trailing us. The moment we reached the top there was a hail of gunfire from the entire room. Every soldier there had their rifles trained on us. I felt my suit vibrate intensely as bullets hit me. I desperately hoped that none would find their way to the lighter mesh that was located at all my major joints.

Then everything seemed to slow down. I noticed small, light brown packs stuck to the walls all around. There was a small panel attached to the package, the defining sign that they were what I feared... Explosives.

"FALL BACK!" I yelled at the top of my lungs.

Over the chaos of the battle I heard a voice come from a UED soldier.

"It's been an honor servin' with ya boys."

Those were the last words I heard before a split second *beep* followed by the roar of an explosion. I felt the substantial addition of heat from inside my armor and immediately I grew concerned for the Marines. Before I had another thought I was struck by a collapsing chunk of rock propelled by the explosion. Everything went dark for a split second, but I could see again seconds later as I fell backwards out of the tower. Above me I saw the sky and around me was snow. Then I felt a thud as I hit the ground.

Everything became blurry, fire still rolling lightly out of the top story. The deep snow covered most of my peripheral vision. I tried to take a breath but realized I couldn't. Panic started to set in as I began to contemplate how badly I was hurt. Immediately my memories began to play back Phil's fall on Vorga.

At last I managed a gasp of air, unsure how long I'd been without it. I breathed heavy and fast for several seconds before calming. I tried to get up, but found my body unresponsive. Then I saw Robert. He reached down, as if offering his hand to me. I felt around in the snow for my pistol, but couldn't find it. Instead I grasped his hand, ready to pull him down hard, when suddenly my view4 cleared.

It wasn't Robert I saw holding my gauntlet, but one of the guards that Boone had stationed at the entrance.

"You okay?" he asked, pulling.

To my surprise, I could feel my body again, and stood up as he pulled. His hand likely did little considering the weight of my armor, but something about the contact had restored some of my energy. I felt at my visor, hoping it had withstood the blow… It had. Looking back up the explosion was over and it seemed only the top floor had been affected.

"I… yeah. Yeah, I'm fine," I stuttered to the Marine.

I hated the sound of my words. They didn't come across as confident or noble. I was a Ranger. The best. We had to seem as if we were more than we were to keep the Marine's morale high. I shook the thoughts out of my head and started walking. It was fairly painful… the fall had certainly done some damage. I saw the silhouette of my pistol in the snow and reached in the hole to grab it. Pulling it out, I observed it, noticing a large scratch on the left side of it, likely from the rock that had struck me.

"James… come in. You there?" I heard Ryan's voice say over several rough coughs.

"Yeah. I made it," I answered softly.

"Good to hear you're voice. I thought you were dead," Ryan said solemnly. "Nevin and I got blown down the stairs, Boone and Hood weren't in the blast radius yet…"

There was a brief pause.

"So we're all good?" I asked.

"Not quite," Ryan said. "Rush had just reached the top, he's got some severe burns all over. He's barely breathing… gah, I don't think he's gonna make it."

Another man down. Two KIA, two WIA… this was definitely a throwback to the Vorgian War.

"I'm on my way back up," I said.

My body ached all over and I still didn't feel like I was walking straight. Then I realized I was glad it was me instead of a Marine. Without my armor, that fall would have meant death.

I made my way to the fourth story, where a majority of the men were huddled. Not seeing Ryan or Boone I proceeded up the next staircase. Ryan looked fine, but Boone looked rough, having several cuts and bruises from the pressure knocking him down the stairs. On the floor at the base of the ascending stairs was Rush. His helmet was on the ground beside him, scorched, but not noticeably so due to its black shading. Rush's face was a revolting mix of red and black, to the point he didn't look like he should be alive. He seemed to be mouthing something, but no words came out. Phil was crouched beside him, holding a canteen. Carefully he moved it to Rush's cracked lips and let some water into his mouth. He swallowed, then began to choke. Phil stopped the water flow, and Rush calmed down.

He tried to speak again, seemingly trying to convey something important. His left arm moved over and reached into one of his assault vest's pockets. Then his hand grew still and his craning head fell back onto the rock. Phil reached down and closed the dead man's eyes before moving the hand and reaching into the pocket. He pulled out a piece of paper, likely a letter, with singed and curled edges.

"Trisha?" Phil asked, reading the name written in excellent calligraphy on the front of the folded paper.

"Ah, dang it…" Boone muttered. "His wife. He always talked about her."

Boone reached out his hand, taking the letter from Phil. He carefully slid the letter into his own vest's pocket before turning to head down the stairs.

"You alright Phil?" Ryan asked, looking down at Phil, still crouched beside Rush's body.

"I'm fine. Never like to lose a soldier, but this is war. It happens," Phil said plainly, standing up and following Boone down the stairs.

Only Ryan and I were left in the damaged room. Several pieces of rock had broken from the ceiling above and fallen in. Snow was filtering in through the newly formed holes and what was left of the staircase now led to nothing.

"We did fine James. Look how many of their guys we brought down. We took the ground, we did more damage… we won," he said, trying to move on from the loss of two men.

"And every victory has its price… it's just been a while since we've paid in blood," I said, hobbling toward the stairs.

"James. This is real war. Get used to it," Ryan said in an unexpected reply.

I looked back and nodded grimly, then carried on down the stairs.

The War Across the Stars

Chapter 15
Discovery

We waited around the tower for nearly an hour. Several of the Marines took advantage of the time to sleep, though the Rangers chose to stay awake and discuss what was to come. Ryan felt we should keep our momentum and keep pushing for the Tredecim capital. Cassidy wanted to focus on finding Max. Phil wanted to stay low and conduct research on the area and extract more data from the captured laptop. Nevin and I were open to anything.

"We've already decided our objective. If we see signs of Max and the armory, by all means we'll investigate it. Staying passive has its advantages, but we are already prepared for that. We have an HQ now, and they can handle the research," Ryan explained.

"May I stay with them? Help with the data combing?" Phil asked.

I could tell Phil had other reasons to avoid the frontlines, most likely a result of coming a centimeter from death.

"I'd prefer to keep the team together Phil," Ryan replied.

Phil looked at Ryan thoughtfully.

"Alright. I understand. I was just thinking Hood could use some assistance."

"So how do we find this capital?" Cassidy asked intensely.

"How do we find *Max*?" Ryan countered.

Cassidy opened her mouth, then closed it

again, understanding what Ryan had said.

"Finding the capital has to be easier than finding one life pod," Ryan finished.

With that, Ryan had shot down every opposing idea, which clearly showed why he made a strong leader. He knew where our priorities had to be, and what to reasonably expect.

"When do we roll out?" Nevin asked.

"I say now. We ought'ta contact Epsilon again… Let them know we're leaving," Ryan said.

Ryan moved over and woke Boone. Despite his minor wound having been patched up, he looked a little pale.

"Sergeant, we're moving out. Call up Epsilon, give 'em the heads up," Ryan ordered.

"Yes sir. Right away," Boone said, quickly standing up.

He reached his hand up to the small device in his ear and began to speak.

"Epsilon, this is Boone, come in."

"Private Wells here sir. We're good," the voice replied, though barely audible to me.

"We're packin' up and about to make another move… hopefully toward the Tredecim capital."

"Copy that sir, you're on the move. Over."

Boone pulled up his bandana over his mouth and made his way toward his Marines.

After we woke up the soldiers and checked our gear, it was back into the snow for us. We exited the damaged tower and were hardly thirty meters out from the tower when I heard a loud engine roar. It grew louder quickly, then I saw it. A single UED fighter like the one that had shot us down earlier zoomed across the sky. Its thin and sleek design tore through the air effortlessly. Just before it passed over the tower it deployed a barrage of four missiles, two from each wing. The missiles almost instantly connected with the structure, blowing it to pieces. What was left groaned under the stress and soon collapsed straight down.

"What just… What just happened?" one of the Marines asked.

"No way… No way they were that close," Ryan stated, shaking his head in disbelief. "They couldn't have been that close."

"Wait, are you suggesting they deliberately missed?" Boone asked. "That doesn't make sense, there's no point!"

"But surely they saw us. Why didn't they shoot us? Why still shoot the building?" Ryan questioned.

"We don't know they saw us," Nevin pointed out.

"Yeah, like they won't notice almost a dozen people thirty meters out the front door," Cassidy added. "I don't know which side to choose on this. They should have seen us, and they should have shot us."

"Let's not build ourselves some over-hyped conspiracy here. Let's just get moving and drop the topic," Boone suggested forcefully.

"Yeah, maybe you're right. We can deal with it later—" Ryan admitted.

"*If* it becomes relevant. With all due respect

sir, I believe it was just our luck," Boone interjected.

We tried to push the issue out of our minds. Considering we had been in control of the tower for over an hour without consequence, an attack the moment we leave did seem suspicious.

The wastes of Marzoc were repetitive. Everywhere it seemed to look the same. White snow everywhere, with occasional towers of stone jutting forth. Natural rocks and caves bursting forth from the ground in some areas.

After another half hour or so of searching for signs of their capital, we finally spotted something unusual. One of the observation posts appeared heavily damaged. A large hole was torn in both sides of it, as if something had pierced through. Immediately my mind shot to the possibility of another lifepod.

We quickly made our way to the broken structure, and as we reached the top of the small hill before us, we could see a large, rectangular box planted in the ground beside the tower... the deployable armory.

"Sir, that's—" I began.

"I know. That's Max."

"Who?" Boone asked.

"Our sixth guy. He stayed behind on the *Procyon* to unlock the armory for launch. I honestly thought he was dead but... that's got to be him," Ryan said calmly.

We approached the armory and soon reached the hatch in the back. It was about a meter off the ground, with the front of the armory dug partially into the ground. Ryan and I both pulled ourselves up and stood on the angled pod. Ryan tapped the button to release the door, but the thin screen above it displayed "Armory Locked". I tapped the door several times, hoping to get a response.

"Max? Max, come in," I said into the COM.

"If he'd have lived, he would have responded to our contact attempts earlier," Nevin said, looking disappointed.

Ryan kicked at the doorway while holding on to the edge of the pod.

"Max! It's us! Friendlies!" Cassidy screamed at the armory.

"Well, I guess we blow the door to get the supplies…" Ryan murmured, seemingly giving up on Max's survival.

Suddenly, the doorway slid open, revealing an armored figure, helmetless, standing before us. The man before us had a crooked smile and sandy blonde hair.

"You miss me?" Max asked.

Despite my uncertainty of Max, I couldn't help but smile to know he was alive.

"Yeah. But it's just like you to still be in the safety of the armory," Ryan said, smiling as well.

"Hey, I have an excuse this time. Had to keep the weapons safe for you guys," Max replied slyly.

"Are the 42's in here?" I asked, getting back on task.

"Yes. A few of the weapons broke out of their bindings on impact… my helmet's busted bad… but the 42's are fine."

"That explains the lack of COM," Cassidy added.

"Well, let's arm up," Ryan suggested, slipping by Max into the armory.

"Did you go *through* that tower when you landed?" Nevin inquired.

"I'm pretty sure I did, ya know, judging by the giant hole and the huge crash that came before I hit the ground," Max replied matter-of-factually.

I followed Ryan in, looking at the compact, yet well supplied, armory. Weapons lined the walls, attached using the same magnetic binding that was employed on our packs. A single Sparker Rocket Launcher was placed on the wall. Near it was a collection of AR-27D's and two BR-26's. The single shot battle rifles were quality guns, I had used them extensively during our enhanced training. A twenty round mag coupled with precision accuracy made it an excellent marksman rifle. Then I saw what I was looking for: the perfectly crafted SF-42.

I reached out and removed it from the wall, turning it over in my hands. This one was loaded with attachments, including a silencer and an ACOG scope. I scooped up some ammo for both the 42 and my pistol. I moved back to the raised end of the pod and jumped out into the snow.

"Nice," Nevin said, looking at my new gun.

I nodded as he climbed into the pod to grab one for himself. Several of the Marines followed him in, all hoping to restock their ammunition.

"Alright, so we need to get movin'," Ryan stated. "I take it you've explored that Observation

Post, Max?"

"Now why would I do that?" Max asked, smiling. "Yeah I did. Nothing to report though. Empty second story and a dark basement."

"So still no clues as to where this capital is… This is proving to be difficult," Ryan muttered.

"Capital?" Max inquired.

"Native population. They have a capital and some sort of AI. We're going to find it."

Max did a three-sixty spin and then spun once more, stopping in a random direction. It happened to be the same direction that his crashed drop pod was facing.

"That way," he said with a grin.

Boone looked at Ryan, who actually seemed to be considering the idea.

"Max is alive right now for one reason, and one reason only," Ryan said. "Luck. We're goin' this way."

"Hey, I have a little bit of skeel, don't I?" Max asked, his grin only partially dampened.

Ryan casually ignored the question as he began to walk in the direction Max pointed. We fell in behind him as he proceeded through the snow. As we slowly walked away, many of the Marines rushed in and out of the armory, trying to rearm and get the best weaponry for their own skill sets.

Again I observed my new gun, checking for any sort of settings such as fire mode. In the end I had adjusted my scope, set it to semi-auto, and loaded the gun.

"So how'd it go down Max? How'd you

make it?" Nevin asked.

"I left you guys and bolted in the direction of the armory. I'm glad we looked at it as much as we did over the trip here... I knew right where it was. I got to it and turned off the lock, and then it was all *whoosh* and I was hurtling toward the planet," Max replied. "Then after a rough landing I just stayed inside for a while before checkin' out the tower."

"The chances of us finding you in this wasteland were pretty slim," Phil pointed out. "It's a miracle we found you."

The thought of finding Max had bolstered my hopes, that perhaps we stood a solid chance out here. Already we had a fighting force capable of standing against the UED. It wasn't long before we were met with another shocking surprise.

A large wall made of the same stone material as the observation posts towered before us. A part of it was blown out by missile fire that was coming from two nearby Corsairs. On the surface was a Paladin tank, supported by a sizable team of Elonian Marines. The tank was rolling toward the hole punched in the wall.

"You seein' this?" Ryan asked, looking in awe at what would soon be our reinforcements.

Boone just nodded his head, acknowledging his own satisfaction to see our own guys. In their wake I saw a number of bodies, some half buried by snow.

We moved closer to them, keeping our arms over our heads, Ryan even swinging his and calling out. Several of the soldiers at the rear of the unit turned toward us and began approaching, rifles raised, though not firing.

"We're Elonian! We are friendly forces!" Ryan called out over the brewing blizzard. "We are the Rangers and what remains of Alpha!" Ryan yelled.

The oncoming Marines slowed down and lowered their weapons when they could tell we were telling the truth from our uniforms and armor.

"Sir," one of them said, snapping a quick salute before gripping his rifle again.

"Boone," the other stated, nodding at the First Sergeant.

Silently, Boone returned the nod.

"So what's going on here? Is this…" Ryan paused, thinking for a moment. "The capital?"

"Captain Malum tells us that this is some sort of UED stronghold," the soldier answered. "A lotta scientist types alongside their troops, too."

Ryan looked at Boone, then at me.

"I think this is it. The UED didn't build this, this had to be the Tredecim capital. Have you seen any Tredecim? The big… I dunno, monsters?" Ryan inquired.

"Well, we saw a few before we got to this place, but so far only UED guys fightin' here. Though Malum thinks the UED are fighting two fronts at this place. He says that central structure prob'ly leads underground and that we might have people there… you think its Tredecim?"

"I guarantee it," Philip added.

"C'mon, let's go talk to Malum," the soldier

said after a slight pause.

We followed him through the snow toward the Elonian vehicles. The tank had begun rolling over the rubble left of the wall. The dual Corsairs each hovered menacingly over the tank.

I had heard a bit about Captain Malum before the mission. He was one of the primary infantry commanders assigned to Operation UNKNOWN. He was supposed to be ruthless though efficient. I had yet to meet him.

We moved swiftly through the snow toward the hole in the wall. My guess was that we were heading for the tank. As we climbed over the debris, the Corsairs above us let loose a withering spray of bullets onto a UED entrenchment up ahead. Ryan and I opened fire on the enemy position, providing any assistance we could.

The firefight lasted only a few minutes before it fell quiet, only the roar of engines filling the air. The soldier who had escorted us walked over to the Paladin and hopped onto it. He knocked on the hatch a few times and leaned back. It opened, and he exchanged words with the pilot that were inaudible at this distance.

When he finished, he climbed off and one of the Corsairs moved forward and then lowered itself slowly to the surface. Malum must be inside. When it landed, my suspicions were confirmed as a middle-aged man with the double-bar insignia of a captain emblazoned on his shoulder stood in the hold of the vessel.

I briefly considered saluting, though refrained,

considering this was a battlefield mere minutes ago. Instead I nodded slightly and waited for him to speak.

"Name's Malum. You're the Rangers?" the man said sternly.

"Yes sir, that's us. We're with Alpha too," Ryan replied.

"First Sergeant," Malum said to Boone with a scowl.

Boone showed no sign of acknowledgment, now seemingly unimpressed by the sizable Elonian force present.

"Now what we have here is a substantial UED stronghold. My present theories include that it contains Korth and his Vorgian goonies, or that we have forces stranded inside being pushed deeper by the UED."

"Sir, I believe that this location is the ancient Tredecim capital. Within it should be the knowledge bank we've been looking for, the Beholder," Ryan said.

"Lieutenant, while I appreciate your detective work, we have bigger things to deal with right now," Malum said matter-of-factually.

"Sir, this information could be of significant aid against the—" Ryan said before being cut off.

"Soldier. Listen. We're runnin' this my way, and it'd be a heck of a lot easier if you let me call the shots," Malum said impatiently.

There was a pause as the two stared at each other. The Marines outside the Corsair appeared to be freezing, though those inside had the benefit of some degree of thermal control. For a moment my mind flickered to what the terrible planet's environment would be like without my armor.

Ryan looked over at Boone, breaking the stare-down with Malum. Boone gave a casual shrug, as if he was used to the sort of treatment being given to Ryan.

"Are we clear now Lieutenant?" Malum asked.

"Yes sir," Ryan said obediently, though I could tell he was reluctant to submit.

I shifted my rifle uneasily in the silence to come.

"Now whatever greater purpose you want to search for in there is up to you, but I plan to deploy you immediately. I'll continue my advance as scheduled, but with your power armor, I'll have you and Alpha push down into the tunnels. From what I gather, this stronghold is based primarily underground. A fair amount does rise above, as you can quite clearly see, though I doubt that is little more than a recon post to keep an eye on intruders such as ourselves," Malum explained.

"Sir, we've commandeered some UED communicators, and have been in contact with Epsilon since our landing. Would you like us to try to have them regroup? House was injured, I'm not sure they are prepared for the journey but..." Boone said.

"Just call 'em. Get them here. If necessary leave House. We need the manpower. We can't afford to delay over a single soldier."

Without responding Boone turned away, clearly offended by Malum's disregard of Sergeant

House's life.

"Epsilon, come in? This is Boone. Wait, hostiles? How close? Is everyone alright? How could the COM's be tracked so easily? Okay, hang in there, we've located the capital as well as a contingent of friendly troops. Yeah, its Malum. I'll try to get a team sent to pick you up," Boone said over the COM.

"What's going on?" I asked, having clearly been able to observe something being amiss.

"They believe the communicators we're using can be tracked, and the UED picked up that they were still in use after their guys died. They've sent a force and are closing in fast. We need to get some help over there if we want them alive," Boone said, loudly enough for Malum to hear.

"Denied soldier. We need the Corsairs here. If we get hit by another air raid, we'll be defenseless without both of them. They'd take out the Paladin and then we'd be back to square one. As much as I'd like to add six men to our unit, the Paladin is more valuable," Malum reasoned.

"With all due respect sir, there is no guarantee that the UED will launch an air strike here. If we do not go help Epsilon, there is a guarantee they won't survive."

"I understand Sergeant, but sacrifice is a part of war."

Malum's face was emotionless, clearly dedicated only to the completion of his objective, whatever he seemed to feel it was. The stress on Boone's face was becoming clear. While he obviously knew Malum treated his soldiers like this, the feeling of losing Epsilon had no doubt intruded his mind.

"Now get movin'," Malum instructed, signaling his pilot with his hand.

The Corsair began to rise back into the sky, leaving Boone staring up at it.

Boone sighed before looking back at us.

"I really hoped he had died," he said quietly, looking nervously over his shoulder.

"Well, chain of command just shifted. Now we all have someone to take orders from. I've heard good things about Malum... I'm a little less impressed in person," Ryan stated.

Chapter 16
Revelation

We proceeded on toward the large ramp that led into the capital. As we stepped within view of the base of the ramp, I felt a bullet ping off my armor, and immediately I dove to the ground. Slowly and carefully rising back up, I could see that the UED had established a chokepoint at the base. Around a dozen men seemed to be holed up behind various crates and metal barricades. Using the SF-42 I took several precise shots at the soldiers as they poked their heads above their cover. Each shot landed exactly where I wanted, resulting in clean kills.

Then I saw a bright flash as one of the troopers fired an RPG. The explosive seemed to be flying toward me and time seemed to slow. I hurriedly tried to catapult myself backwards to avert the rocket, thinking about the damage such a weapon could do, even with my armor.

Suddenly everything was normal again as I felt my impact with the snow and ground behind me. The rocket flew past my face and into the snowy sky. As I climbed back up I saw the Paladin was aiming its twin-barreled 100mm cannons into the pit. An earsplitting bang burst forth from the first cannon as it fired downrange. It was followed shortly by the second cannon. I returned to a crouching position for a better view, only to find the entire position was now covered in blood, bodies, and damaged metal. Two craters were left in the stone flooring.

"We're clear," Ryan said, starting the walk

down the ramp.

Our team formed up on Ryan as Boone and Alpha prepared themselves behind us. Malum seemed expectant of more friendlies. I knew better than to expect that. We moved slowly down the ramp, taking our time to examine the walls around us. There were two passageways that could be taken up ahead. When we reached the split, Ryan split us up. We divided into our usual teams of three. Nevin, Cassidy, and myself would be going with Boone and Hood. The rest were taking the left door with Boone's other two troopers.

"This isn't right. We ought to be using our resources to save every life. We should be rescuing House and the rest of Epsilon," Boone said, looking straight at me.

I simply nodded, unsure how best to respond. At the end of our path was a turn, heading the same direction that the ramp had gone. After only a few meters in that direction however, it then turned back the way we had been walking. At the end of this last hallway was what appeared to be an elevator.

We moved closer to it, watching out for additional UED forces. I could hear the faint sounds of gunfire echoing below. The UED was fighting something below us… that much was for sure. We piled into the elevator and I took a look at the unusual control panel. It appeared to be a touch-pad screen displaying two characters.

"Well, this is more advanced than any Tredecim tech I've seen so far. Prior to this was all wooden ladders," I pointed out.

"Yeah, I've noticed the same thing," Hood said as he examined the touch-pad.

"I believe its function is fairly obvious, Hood," Boone stated.

He then reached out and tapped the lower symbol, causing it to change from green to red, then swell slightly. After a brief second of being larger, it returned to normal and the doorway before us closed.

"First Sergeant, when should we try to get more information out of this laptop?" Hood asked.

"After we've made Malum happy enough to go save Epsilon," Boone replied coolly.

Abruptly the elevator jerked, then I starting having the sensation of falling. It felt like we were moving at incredible speeds, pressing deeper into the planet. After nearly a minute the elevator slowed down, coming to a complete halt with a loud thud.

"This thing better work on our way out," Cassidy murmured softly.

The doorway slid open and I felt myself fly backwards, slamming into the wall. A sizable amount of gunfire ensued, bullets pinging off the metallic walls. I rolled out of the way of incoming fire, taking cover behind the front wall of the elevator. I took a quick evaluation, finding Boone and Hood using the other side as cover, Nevin behind me, and Cassidy up against the control panel. Boone stuck his shotgun out into the line of fire and took a shot blindly. The cry of pain marked his accuracy.

I prepared myself to move out of the elevator when I saw a single grenade roll into the compact space. We would all be KIA if it detonated where it was. I rapidly crouched down, scooping the grenade with my left hand. With my right hand firmly placed on the handle and trigger of my SF-42, I opened fire into the swarm of UED soldiers that had set the ambush. As fast as I could, I brought my left hand forward, giving the grenade a toss straight back into the heart of the enemy squad. There was a flash, followed by the pinging sound of shrapnel hitting my armor.

Fortunately, my armor was not the only thing to be hit by the metal fragments. A majority of the UED formation had been impacted by the position of the grenade at its point of detonation. Capitalizing on the opportunity, I darted forward, fully out of the elevator and leaped over the nearest cover point, landing on top of a dead UED trooper. I fired a pair of bullets across the room at a now exposed target, when I heard someone behind me. I spun with incredible speed, bringing my left hand to bear on the neck of a UED soldier, knocking him off his feet. Only then, as I put the kill shot into the downed soldier, did Nevin emerge from the safety of the elevator, opening fire on the last pocket of resistance.

"Clear," I said, glad to have made it through the rough spot. "Ryan, this is James. We had an encounter with some UED troops, anything on your end?" I asked, this time over the COM.

"Blood. Just a lotta blood," he said, his insinuation of Tredecim responsibility being clear.

"Alright, we'll be on the lookout for UED or Tredecim," I replied, acknowledging my understanding.

Everyone had now exited the elevator and were looking around the vast chamber that we stood in. The ceiling rose at least thirty meters over our head, creating an empty feeling in the expanse of space.

"What do you think this room was used for?" Cassidy asked.

"Based off of the fact that it seems to be one of only two destinations that elevator has, I'd say it's where everyone lined up before going outside," Nevin said, a faint smile on his face to mask the fear of what may actually be there.

We moved quickly across the immense room to a single doorway on the other side. Tapping the single button on the touch-pad beside it caused the metal door to slide upward. Behind the door was a darkened hallway made of the same stone material that the towers were. Again I heard distant gunfire.

"Ryan here, we've got some Tredecim guarding somethin'. Trying to get through enough of them to figure out what."

"It's not going down!" I heard Max scream into the COM.

"Roger that, we've got nothin'," I replied to Ryan.

"It doesn't sound good," Cassidy said.

"They're Rangers, they'll be fine," Nevin stated, assuring himself as much as anyone else.

At the end of the narrow hallway was a T-shaped split, giving us two choices. I looked over at Boone, who seemed to be thinking the same thing that I was.

Alex Pennington

"We'll take this way," he said, jerking his thumb over his shoulder down the hall as he backed into it.

Hood followed close behind him, rifle raised. Nevin, Cassidy, and myself made our way cautiously down the other path, which turned several times without any apparent reason.

"James, we've... something. It's... Not sure who..." I heard Ryan's voice say over the crackle of static.

"Repeat that, there's interference," I replied.

"James... Are you... You read?" he returned, seemingly having not heard my prior statement.

"Yeah, we're here. You aren't coming through clearly," I repeated.

A silence ensued, making it clear that Ryan had given up.

"Well, they found something. The question is... what?" I said.

The other two looked at me, neither putting forth any guesses.

"Let's keep moving," Cassidy suggested.

After the contact from Ryan, it wasn't long before we found a likely candidate for what he had found. We entered a narrow room, extending nearly forty meters. Along both walls were rows of tubes containing strange beings that I did not recognize. They certainly weren't Tredecim, though they seemed plenty tall, standing a full two meters in height. Their skin was silvery, almost white in coloration. Its eyes were yellow and were located near the back of its elongated head. Two small pincers were located at the tip of their face, likely surrounding a mouth. They were angled backwards in the pods at a forty-five degree angle. The pods seemed to be holding the creatures in a cryogenic stasis.

"Definitely... not Tredecim," Nevin said, observing the nearest pod.

"Then what are they?" Cassidy asked, running her hand over a tube.

"If this is what Ryan found, Phil's got to be in heaven right now," Nevin said, a true smile coming over his face.

Maintaining a serious tone, I replied, "I say we keep moving. We have to be close to the Beholder. That should answer all of our questions."

"How do you think these things open?" Cassidy asked, searching the surface for any sort of interface.

"I'm not so sure we want it open. Like I said, we should concentrate on the Beholder," I repeated, wanting to get away from the creatures.

They nodded, at last acknowledging my suggestion. The two rows of pods continued down the entire length of the hallway until a large doorway. As it opened I thought I saw a shadow move across the room. I entered slowly, gun raised to my shoulder. This room was far darker than the one before it, illuminated only by a dim blue light on either wall. It was only then that I realized one thing the SF-42 was missing was an under-barrel flashlight like that of the H-81. I snapped the 42 onto my pack and drew my pistol, clicking on its light. Running the light across the room I could see a heavy doorway positioned right where the shadow had disappeared. Across from that was yet another door. I immediately moved to the first door. I reached down and touched the pad, though instead of opening the door, the pad merely flashed red once. I repeated to the same result.

"I think it's locked. Nev, try the other one," I ordered. Nevin placed his finger on the opposite door's interface, resulting in the door slowly opening.

Unlike the other doors, this one appeared to be dual layered, the first layer rising while the second split in the center and slid to either side. Inside was yet another surprise. A bright light flooded out of the room, a stark contrast to the prior darkness. As I entered the room I realized it was far different than any other room or region I had been in since landing on Marzoc. The room overflowed with plant life, trees and shrubs distributed throughout. Some of the trees even seemed to bear small fruits of some sort. I could only make assumptions that the temperature and air quality had changed as well, though through my armor it was unclear.

"Whoa..." Nevin said in awe as he looked around the large room.

"I bet we could eat these," Cassidy said, plucking a round purple fruit from one of the trees. "We haven't had food since arriving in-system."

"But what if we can't? What if they are harmful to us?" I asked, feeling a slight pain in my stomach from over a day without food.

"We'll die eventually if we don't eat somethin'," she replied.

"You both make good points," Nevin interjected. "But I'm leaning towards Cassie's argument."

I sighed, giving a long gaze at the fruit in Cassidy's hand.

"Maybe we should get a go-ahead from Phil first," I finally said, completely unaware of how our bodies would react to the fruit.

"Phil this, Phil that. Phil's always the answer! What does he know about a random fruit in an underground city?" Cassidy said, sarcasm lining her tone. "Alright, I'm throwin' some in my pack."

"Go ahead. We have to be close though," I said, a hint of excitement in my voice.

Nevin and I approached the only other door in the room, a straight walk from the first one, while Cassidy gathered more fruits. Dropping my guard a bit after the pleasant surprise of the present room, I tapped the button. The door opened in the same complex manner as the one before, revealing a pitch-black hallway. Only the light from the bio room illuminated the entrance, though the entrance was all I needed to see. Multiple Tredecim were piled up against the door, some leaning against the walls in a sitting position, others sprawled in the center of the hallway. I brought my pistol up to a shooting stance immediately, but held my fire. Many of them looked at us longingly, some rising slowly to their feet. None of them showed any signs of aggression.

"Hold," I murmured softly to Nevin, careful not to move much.

The group of Tredecim continued to rise, then

began to meander into the bio room. As they came nearer, I backed up, keeping my pace slow and deliberate. The first Tredecim to emerge began to make a series of noises.

"What are you doing?" Nevin asked in a hushed tone.

Not responding, I slowly took one hand off my gun and reached out carefully toward the beast. In response, it lifted one of its arms and cautiously touched my gauntlet with its massive claw. My heart rate began to elevate as I considered how fast everything could go wrong. Its face had a large scar across its right eye, which did little to reassure me that it was friendly.

"I'm James," I said in a friendly tone, unsure why I even dared to pursue communication.

The Tredecim grumbled a return, though I was still clueless to its meaning.

"Friend," I offered, placing my pistol back at my side.

"James who are you..." Cassidy said loudly before pausing. "What are... uh..."

"It's okay," I said to both her and the Tredecim.

The creature said something else. Several of the Tredecim behind it began to push by, entering the bio room. They reached for plants and trees, taking down fruits and eating them by the handful. At last the one before me lowered its arm, nudging past me into the room. I stood in place, amazed that this was happening.

"May we enter?" I asked, trying to sign my

question to them by pointing at us, then down the dark hallway.

Only the lead Tredecim watched me as I spoke, though it had no reaction to my question other than casually looking back at the fruits it was picking. Cassidy's face still showed clear signs of shock, but we were still alive, and so were the Tredecim. I silently motioned for us to enter the hall, and the three of us moved in. After we entered the hallway, I redrew my pistol to make use of its light.

"I hope Boone doesn't find them. He and Hood will probably open fire," I said after escaping earshot of the bio room.

"Okay, yeah, but why are they friendly?" Nevin asked.

"I... I don't know," I said, realizing it just didn't seem to make sense.

The incredible darkness made traversing the area particularly difficult, especially due to the small stairwells and abrupt turns that littered the path. Though the environment did its part to slow us down, it wasn't long before we stumbled upon something incredible.

We exited the darker tunnel, entering a tremendous room. The room had several points along the walls lit with an ominous blue light. The source of the light couldn't be seen, but it reminded me of the ones I had seen beneath the first Observation Post. In the center of the room stood an enormous column that protruded from the floor to the ceiling. Upon the column was a screen of some sort displaying an unusual picture. A single yellow eye, perfectly symmetrical stared down at us. Though at first I believed it to be unmoving, it seemed to have adjusted to view our entry.

"Whoa," Nevin murmured, taking in the surroundings.

Excitedly, I glanced over my shoulder at the other two, then took a cautious approach toward the screen. It was then that it began to speak in a voice that seemed both deep and mono-toned.

"The Beholder recognizes three entrants. All human. Origin... Eli," the voice stated calmly. "To what end do they enter the Bastion?"

"We are the Rangers. We are here to attempt to learn more about... you. And this planet," I said, slightly unnerved by the eye's penetrating gaze.

"The Beholder has access to all knowledge provided by the Praetorians. Any questions in pertinence to Marzoc, its native population, or the Beholder's Mission can be answered."

"The Praetorians? Are they the ones from the tubes?" I immediately inquired.

"The Praetorians are the masters of all. They forged this world into what it is today. They forged the Beholder. They now rest in a prolonged slumber, until their triumphant return."

I looked over at Nevin, figuring we both had the same thought.

"So they are here? In this facility?" I asked.

"Yes. The Praetorians are here. Should they need to be awakened to defend their creations, they shall."

"Can you explain what the Praetorians have

done?"

"The Praetorians discovered this world when they first expanded into the vastness of space. This planet was one of three that made up their colonies. Corzam, Marzoc, and Zormac each acted as a gate to their homeworld. Each of these planets were considered unique anomalies, as each was without a star. In response, the Praetorians constructed the Facticius Phoebus Platforms. These Platforms provided heat and light for the planet below. It was after this construction that the Tredecim were discovered. The Praetorians were not the first species to live on Marzoc. With light and heat, the Tredecim rose from their caves and onto the surface of the world, making contact with Praetorian scouts. The Tredecim were developed; small villages populated the deeper caves, leadership existed, and they had developed a language of their own. Technological superiority by the Praetorians caused awe among the Tredecim. Though communication was challenging at first, the Tredecim eventually accepted Praetorian leadership. The Bastion was once a major center of Tredecim culture. At the time it was merely a cavern, unfortified and unprepared for war. After the clearing, the Tredecim had a greater understanding of their place. They believed the Praetorians to be god-like creatures sent to cleanse them of their sins," the Beholder explained.

"If the Tredecim viewed the Praetorians as gods, why did they create you?" I inquired.

"As the Tredecim developed sight, they spoke of the "All-Seeing Eye" of the Praetorians. It was this superstition that resulted in the Beholder's design. The Beholder was meant to serve as their God. A figure beyond even the Praetorians themselves. Though the design served as a target for Tredecim mythos, its true purpose was to serve as a both a governor and a databank for the planet. Praetorian population was low, numbering barely over one hundred, while the Tredecim were several thousand strong. Should the Tredecim ever have banded together in rebellion, the Praetorians knew they would be overrun. The Beholder represented the Tredecim's greatest fears, and those who witnessed it spread those fears among their people. Prior to the Beholder's creation, Tredecim population was heavily concentrated near their old capital, but outliers dotted the planet. Many were moved to stone facilities crafted by the Praetorians for the Tredecim. This move allowed for greater control of the population, and exposed the Tredecim to both the generosity and the control of the Praetorians."

"The observation posts?" I whispered to Nevin.

"I'd say so," he replied quietly.

"These reservations provided limited room for the Tredecim, though provided efficient shelter and warmth, coupled with light. This combination was the Praetorians' first attempt to give the Tredecim sight. Through generations, evolution and adaptation gave the Tredecim the sight they needed to witness the Beholder's form as the incarnation of their fears."

"Earlier, some of the Tredecim we encountered weren't violent toward us... but before that they all had been. Why is this?" Nevin asked.

"The Tredecim who were left to the wild after the Praetorians entered their slumber grew volatile. Once fired upon by Earth-born humans, they prepared to fight against all humans. Those within the walls of the Bastion have no qualms with humanity," the Beholder responded.

"How long have the Praetorians been here?" Cassidy said, breaking her long-held silence.

"The Praetorians reign came to its closure a short time before the humans of Eli were planted," The Beholder answered.

"Planted? What do you mean?" I said with confusion.

"By Them."

I glanced at Cassidy and she shrugged.

"Them?"

"The Beholder's final purpose. When the Praetorians learned that They were coming, they prepared stasis pods on their colonies. Though each colony held only a miniscule fraction of the Praetorian population, this allowed some to remain hidden, giving the race another chance. The Beholder was tasked with maintaining order in their absence, and to judge when they shall make their return."

"But who are they?"

"They are the only thing the Praetorians ever truly feared."

Giving up on the question, I thought hard about anything else I could ask. Having so many answers open to me was overwhelming in itself. My mind kept bringing me back to the word *Planted*. It seemed to serve as the start for understanding our similarity with the UED.

"What do you know about the UED?" I asked.

"Information is unavailable. Topic Unknown."

"Uh, the United Earth Defense... the other humans here," I tried, hoping the explanation might trigger something.

"Humans. Origin... Earth. The first group They established. Given only a single habitable world, the people of Earth were intended for warfare. Known Praetorian hypotheses state that They intended to use Earth people as an extension of their military, a force of experienced, though expendable, troops willing to serve loyally. Final results are unknown. Additional information could be attained should one present itself to the Beholder."

"So, if we bring one here, you can help us understand our connection? Why we are so alike?"

"Given an Earth-born human within the inner chamber of the Bastion would provide a link to relevant information."

I looked again at Nevin and Cass.

"I say we try to get one here. I want to know why we're the same," I said, again running the word *planted* through my brain.

Nevin nodded silently.

"There may still be more to learn now," Cassidy stated. "We should try to understand the planet before we go too deep into our connection with the UED."

"Anything in particular?" I asked.

Looking up at the Beholder she presented her question. "When will the Praetorians be awakened? You said you make the choice... but what causes you to make the decision?"

"The Beholder will trigger the release of the Praetorians should they be threatened or upon manual override by the Homeworld."

"Wait... so you have connections clear to the Praetorians' homeworld?" I inquired.

"No."

"Then what do you mean?"

"Should Praetorians return to awaken their sleeping brothers after They have swept the galaxy, they shall be awakened without the need of threat."

"What constitutes a threat?" I asked.

"They do."

The Beholder seemed to be very ambiguous about *Them*.

"Okay, come on Cass, let's go find a UED Trooper," I said, figuring our information was limited until he had one.

She looked over at me and sighed.

"Alright James, we'll keep movin'," she said.

We walked away down another nearby hallway, maneuvering through the dark carefully. The thoughts continued to plague my mind, *Who could They be? What was meant by the word "Planted"?* I just kept thinking that when we found the enemy we could learn the truth.

Alex Pennington

Chapter 17
Fear the Reaper

We traveled a fair distance through the dark, winding tunnels before we found another door. We opened it, revealing another bright room, more like the Bio Room we had been in before. Inside, computers were set up on several desks and military sleeping bags had been deployed on the floor. Within many of them were what appeared to be UED Scientists, asleep and unaware of our presence.

"Should we take 'em loud or quiet?" Nevin asked quietly.

I thought about it as I gazed around the room containing nearly ten scientists.

"Let's hold our stealth while we can," I murmured as I seized the nearest man, placing my hand over his mouth.

He attempted to scream, but his voice couldn't escape my gloved hand. He had a small frame and wore thin glasses. Resisting his squirms, I backed out of the room, pistol still held in one hand. We closed the door as we exited, and made our way down the dark halls again before I released his mouth.

"What do you want with me? I'm just a scientist!" he immediately called out.

"We are the Elonian Rangers, and so far your kind haven't been too nice to us. We need you for something," I said plainly.

"Is that why you haven't killed me yet?" he asked, his voice sounding irritated.

"It's a good part of it, yeah," I answered,

continuing to usher him down the hall.

When we arrived in the Bastion once more, the Beholder's gaze shifted slightly, seeming again to observe us as we approached it.

"The Beholder recognizes four entrants. All Human. Origins… Eli and Earth."

"Wait… the Beholder? You mean we were this close?" the scientist questioned in excitement. "We were right there?"

"Alright Beholder, we've brought you what you needed. How are we connected?" I asked, ready to learn the truth behind our similarity.

"They created you. They planted you. They wanted subjects, slaves, soldiers. Then They left you to grow. Someday They will collect their creations. The Humans of Earth, planted first, were purely soldiers. The singular planet and lack of room for expansion made for a breeding ground of war and infighting. The Humans of Eli were meant to be softer, given a multitude of planets in which to expand and develop. After They left you, They disappeared, waiting for their chance to remove the Praetorians from existence."

"When will They be back? When will they reclaim us?" I asked, pondering what I was being told.

"Data unavailable. The Praetorians were never aware of Their final agenda. Though they knew that They were unstoppable, thus they took to hiding underground in facilities such as this. Their safety was beautiful," the Beholder explained.

"Beautiful?" Cassidy asked, questioning the

word choice.

"The measure of Beauty is whatever one desires most. Though the determination of Beauty is in the eye of the beholder," it reasoned.

The mention of desire reminded me our true purpose here. We had to find Robert and Rigel and bring them both to their ends.

"There is a third group of humans here... not Earth-born... well they are more like us," I said, unsure how to explain the Vorgians to the ancient machine.

"The Beholder possesses no data on this group."

"Gah, Um..." my mind raced, trying to think of a cue.

"Threat Detected. Unintended detonation in secondary stasis chamber. Releasing Praetorians," the Beholder interjected suddenly.

"Wait, no, what?" I stuttered, having no desire to meet a Praetorian in person.

"Messor, Commander of the Praetorian Cadre, is ranking officer. He shall preside over Praetorian response to aggression."

"What aggression?" I asked, then giving the COM another go I continued. "Ryan? Ryan, you read? We might have a problem."

Still no response came through.

"So, suggestions?" I asked the other two.

"I say we get out of here," Nevin said.

"Maybe the Praetorians weren't released due to us. Maybe they will help us against the UED," Cassidy suggested.

"An optimistic thought, but I'm doubting it. Oftentimes pessimism is realism, and I think this is one of those times Cass," I stated.

"But what if… well, alright. Aversion will keep us alive either way the Praetorians fall," Cassidy admitted.

"What of the scientist?" Nevin asked.

I thought, considering our choices, considering the situation at hand. I wanted to simply shoot him and be done with it, but so far he'd been at least moderately cooperative.

"Please… don't kill me! I've only helped you!" he begged.

On one hand, he was the enemy. On the other, he was innocent. The choice weighed heavy on my mind.

"You're free. See us again and I can't guarantee the same fate," I said solemnly.

He sprinted away down the route we had taken to get him and we turned and made our way toward the path from which we had originally entered the Bastion. As we reached the doorway, I felt the urge to thank the Beholder, despite it being an AI. Succumbing, I turned around before leaving the room.

"Thanks… for the information," I said simply, before moving on with the other two down the dark hallways.

I kept my pistol up, light shining, unsure when the Praetorians might show up. We had a ways to backtrack, and we had to be quick. We barreled through the halls until we were nearly to the Bio

Room. Though as we approached it, my heart sank. Boone and Hood were there, beating on the closed door into the room. It was the same one that the Tredecim had been trapped behind for so long.

"Boone," I said.

"James, uh… what the heck did you guys do in there?" he asked aggressively.

"We found it Boone, we found the Beholder. But we have other issues now. The Beholder was not created by the Tredecim… it, the light stations… everything advanced was created by a race known as the Praetorians who claimed this world as theirs!"

"So where are they? We saw some tubes on the way over… creatures inside… that them?" Boone asked.

"That's my guess, and according to the Beholder, they've been released to neutralize the 'threat'," I stated intensely.

"How long ago?" he asked, something clearly clicking in his mind.

"Maybe a minute, at most," Nevin replied.

"Same time the door closed, this Beholder seems to not want us getting out."

"Any other ways out?" Hood chimed in.

"We saw one… UED guarding it. We can take 'em," Cass announced.

"Then let's roll," Boone said as we turned around and made our way back again.

It was entirely possible the way would be barred as well, denying any escape. Still tired, still hungry, and still without hope of ever returning home, we put all of our effort into our sprint. When we reached the Beholder, we were not treated with its usual dialogue.

"The humans have sinned. They shall be smitten for their transgressions," it stated, void of emotion or feeling, though clear in intent.

I glanced back at Hood as I ran, unable to help but notice his interest in the machine. We no longer had time however, we had to keep moving.

"We can take the UED, maybe we could take the Praetorians too," Boone thought aloud.

"Maybe, maybe not. They've got size on us, that's for sure," I pointed out.

Soon we were back at the door from before. He breathed in, hoping it wasn't locked. I softly placed my hand onto the panel. The doorway slid open, revealing the scientists' encampment, though it was abandoned. The computers had been hastily gathered and removed, and most of the heavier equipment had been simply left behind. The brightness of the room was a nice change of scenery, but as we opened the door leading on, there was nothing but darkness.

"The UED was here, they might have soldiers nearby. And we don't know when the Praetorians are gonna show up," I said.

"We just need to stay sharp," Boone commanded.

"I almost wish they'd just show up, I'm tired of the suspense… I'd rather just start shooting," Cassidy said, pulling ahead to the front of our unit.

As a whole, we slowed down, assuming a more tactical approach down the hall, Cass on point.

Alex Pennington

As we ran, I heard gunfire. It was brief, then footsteps. We were nearing a corner in the nearly pitch black hallway, only our flashlights giving us any line of sight. We slowed, nearly to a stop. I saw Cassidy steadying her gun. A figure appeared around the corner and a burst rang out from Cassidy's rifle. The helmetless figure seemed to be in power armor. Then another power-armored soldier came around the bend. Staring at me, face pale, was Ryan. I glanced to the ground and back up. Phil appeared.

Cassidy's rifle slumped, then it fell to her side, barely holding onto it with one hand. I walked closer, lowering my weapon as well. I heard Cassidy whisper something under her breath, then drop her rifle entirely, it clanging on the ground. She dropped to her knees, eyes fixated on the lifeless body several meters before her.

"Cass…" I said softly, also observing the man.

"I… I killed him…" she said, her voice broken.

The man's sandy blonde hair was dripping with blood as I finally took my light off of him.

"I killed Max."

"Gah, Cass… I… you…" Nevin stuttered.

"What the hell were you thinking Cass?" Philip yelled. "Identify your targets!"

"I… I don't know Phil, okay? I don't freakin' know!" Cassidy responded, pounding her fist onto the ground.

"As if the UED and Tredecim… and now these silver skinned freaks weren't enough, we have YOU killing our troops!" Phil continued, his fury causing him to speak without his usual intellectual forethought.

"Phil, calm down, we need to stay calm," I said, raising my arms slightly, pistol gripped tightly in one hand.

"James, Max survived the *Procyon*'s explosion, he waited in that armory for hours until by some miracle we found him! And now—"

"Phil! Enough. He's dead," Ryan said, speaking for the first time since the incident. "People die. Get over it, and let's get moving."

Phil ceased his tirade, his face red with rage. Cassidy slowly rose, once more grabbing her AR-27. She said nothing, though her body language spoke volumes for her emotional state.

I wanted to tell her it was alright, that it wasn't her fault. But neither of those things were true. The stress, the unusual conditions of the mission... it had gotten to her. She reacted too quickly, by instinct. The first member of the Rangers had fallen. With all the advantages we had always had, it had gotten to seem impossible. Our own power had weakened us. While physically adept and mentally acute, we weren't emotionally prepared for loss. Not of one of our own, hardly of an Elonian soldier at all. Without my family, the bonds I had with the Rangers had come to replace them. They *were* my family.

I approached Cassidy and wrapped one arm around her. She returned the embrace, clearly near tears.

"We're gonna make it. We'll make it home

Cass," I said softly.

She backed up, composing herself.

"I'm sorry. I'm so sorry. We're soldiers..." she paused, still holding back her emotion. "Okay. Alright. Let's keep... let's keep going."

I shined my light on Max one final time, three bullet holes oozing blood from his skull. Cass had made a mistake, and any mistake could cost us dearly. Each of us cast our final glances before we started walking in the direction that Ryan's team had come from. I took a look at Boone's face, though it was blank and expressionless. I wondered if he was thinking about when he shot Phil, how if Phil hadn't had his helmet, he would have done the same thing as Cassidy had.

"If we backtrack our steps, we're going to encounter the tube-monsters again," Ryan warned as we kept moving, trying anything to put distance between ourselves and the body.

"Those are the Praetorians, Ryan, we found the Beholder," I said.

A glimmer of hope showed up in Ryan's eyes.

"What'd ya learn?"

"It's a lot, it's complicated... the Praetorians built most of the infrastructure on this planet, as well as the light stations. They took in the Tredecim as a vassal species, basically. Though there is a threat even greater than the Praetorians, and apparently we are their creation. Just as the UED are."

Phil was listening intently, trying to refocus and continue the mission. As I explained everything I had learned, I allowed myself to forget the hurry and the pain. I even mentioned the friendly Tredecim, and my hopes that they could be of use.

"James… you've done good work. I hate to say it, but if your end was locked, our only choice is to fight through the Praetorians… and they're no easy fight."

"I understand."

We each checked and readied our weapons. Our only choice was to blast our way out against an advanced and unknown foe. We traversed the hall as fast we could, coming upon a lighted room, it's door damaged, and many stasis pods lining the walls.

"This is it, here's where we fought them," Ryan said. "We took out one pod over there, trying to open it," he continued, pointing toward a darkened portion of the wall and mangled remains of a pod.

"You were the threat? The Beholder only released the Praetorians because it detected a threat! Might you have been that threat?" I asked, putting together the pieces.

"Unfortunately James, that sounds about right. They started opening up right after we popped the Eupholium."

"Why did you want in so bad? We found some and kept goi—" I started when several violet projectiles soared past me.

They greatly resembled fusion rounds, like those deployed for infantry suppression by the Elonian Marines. Looking toward the end of the hall, their source became clear. A Praetorian stood, pistol in hand, aiming toward our unit. Instinctively I raised my pistol and opened fire, hearing others do the same.

Alex Pennington

To my shock, the Praetorian held out its left hand, maintaining the pistol in the right, and abruptly, our bullets slowed to a stop in midair before him. The air rippled ominously in front of his left hand.

I stopped shooting, lowering my gun just slightly to get a clearer picture. The ripples stopped, the bullets falling idly to the ground and immediately I snapped back into position and fired again. Once more the Praetorian activated its defenses, this time resuming its pistol barrage. I finally backed up a few steps and stepped back behind the frame of the door.

"Okay, so what is that?" I asked.

"You don't know? You're the one who talked to the Beholder!" Ryan countered.

"We need to overwhelm it, but we're channeled down this corridor," I pointed out.

"If we all head down the hall together, we should be able to close the gap," Nevin suggested.

"I agree," I said, fusion rounds still searing through the doorway.

"Then we go for it," Boone said.

I gave the four Marines a brief look, worried for their lack of heavy armor.

"We've got point. Marines, you fall in behind us," I ordered.

"Will do Sergeant," Boone said, offering no protest.

Ryan lifted his hand, three fingers lifted.

Then two.

One.

We charged, Ryan first, then me. The rest of the team moved in behind us, all of us opening fire as we fanned out into the hallway, pushing as near to the tubes as we could. The Praetorian kept its arm extended, preventing us from having any great effect, but we crept nearer and nearer.

One of its shots nailed Phil in the chest, causing him to stumble. Two more rounds soared by, over his head. I heard a scream of pain. We kept moving, we had to.

Another few seconds and our line had reached the end of the hall. I broke rank and sprinted into the Praetorian, sliding under his field and tripping him from below. As he fell I heard numerous shots go off, my team finishing the job. I slowly returned to my feet, looking back down the hall. Lying on the ground, writhing with pain, was Hood. He had a terrible scorch on his shoulder and neck, the clothing and skin melted away. Boone approached him, then helped him to a sitting position, leaning him against one of the now empty Praetorian tubes.

"Sir, leave me. I've done my part… I've seen enough. Go save Epsilon," Hood pleaded, though the damage to his neck caused his voice to be rough and unclear.

"We have enough dead soldiers, hang in there," Phil said, kneeling down beside his fellow tech specialist.

"Daniel, you're a good man. You've fought hard. It's been appreciated," Boone said to Hood, a solemn look adorning his face. "But you're right. House and Epsilon are probably all dead by now, but every second we lose is another chance that they really are."

"Boone, we can't just—" Cassidy started.

"We can. He's my man, and he's made a request. Let's keep moving," Boone said, reaching down and taking the UED laptop from Hood's pack and adding it to his own.

"I can try to patch him up, he can pull through," Phil added, trying to change Boone's mind.

Hood's wound looked severe, and without medical treatment he wouldn't live any more than an hour at best. Even with medical treatment, his situation was critical.

"Just go," Hood said, his voice strained.

Only Boone turned to walk away.

In a surprisingly fast action, Hood reached into his holster and removed his H-81, placed it to his head, and fired the gun, his blood splattering onto the clear material of the stasis tube.

"Gah, why!?" Phil called out. "We could have…" his voice trailed off.

Boone knew. Ryan knew. They understood that war had casualties. They experienced it. Now if only the rest of us could grasp it. The ability for any one loss to tear apart the squad was perhaps our greatest weakness. It was one thing that could be used by our foes to stop us.

I turned away, focusing on what was left to be done. Our unit moved on down the hallway, pushing ever closer to escape from this capital that we had worked so hard to find. Soon though, we found opposition. A group of at least ten Praetorians had secured a position near the elevator. As we first came within line of sight of them, they failed to notice us, and I ducked back behind the corner.

"How are we gonna take down this many if a single one was so hard?" I inquired.

"They don't all have those… gauntlet things that stopped our bullets. We killed a few before reuniting with you guys, none of them used one," Ryan stated quietly.

"Alright, let's make our opening count," I said, scoping in with my SF-42.

I peered around the corner from a crouching stance, while Nevin assumed a prone position beside me. I sighted in on my target and waited a few seconds more for everyone to ready themselves. Hoping they were ready, I took the shot, a single round soaring through the air and tearing into the Praetorian's skull. Upon hearing my round, the rest of our team opened fire on the sizable unit. Three or four went down in our opening attack, but two of them extended their arms, once more catching incoming fire. The others moved for cover throughout the room. I moved my rifle quickly between targets, trying to put more fire down on any of the Praetorians who had yet to take cover. Several of them had already begun to return fire, forcing me to time my shots between taking full cover.

It was then that I noticed one of the Praetorians seemed to have more elaborate armor and be absorbing many of our rounds using both hands to catch them. Perhaps it was some sort of leadership figure.

"Ryan, I think that one's the leader," I said, popping off a few rounds at the Praetorian in question.

"Might that be... Messor?" Nevin proposed, looking up from his firing position.

"The one the Beholder mentioned? I guess it'd make sense. Let's bring him down and maybe we can put a halt to the Praetorian escape," I returned.

Many of us shifted our targets to Messor in an attempt to bring him down, though with incredible skill and agility he kept us from securing many hits. To make matters worse, the few hits we could get were unable to pierce his powerful armor.

"Prex," I heard Nevin mumble as we continued to barrage him to no avail.

"This guy is certainly good, if nothing else," Ryan called out over the constant sounds of gunfire.

I paused, my rifle empty, dropped a mag, then reached down for another. As I did so, I saw two Praetorians moving in from the side, crouched down, weapons raised. In a rush I pulled the new magazine up quickly, missing the slot and fumbling it to the ground. Thinking fast, I drew my pistol with my left hand and fired a few loosely aimed rounds in their direction, trying to prevent them from closing in. The one in front took a bullet to the chest, but the other dove to a prone position in response. From there it immediately opened fire on me, so I pulled back behind my cover.

I holstered my pistol and scooped up the fallen magazine. I then locked it nicely into the gun before peeking out again. The Praetorian I had been firing at was dead, one of my teammates having nailed it in the head. A quick glance at Messor confirmed that he still wasn't down.

"I don't think we can take this guy!" Nevin yelled.

"Let's board the elevator, we can evade him if we're fast," Phil suggested.

Ryan looked back at Boone, who nodded. Four of the Praetorians were left, two of them armed with the defense mechanism.

"I've got point," I said, hoping to use my superior speed to dodge incoming fire, while still drawing as much as possible from my allies.

I then bailed from my cover point, sprinting across the open room toward the elevator. Messor and the remaining Praetorians were close to the far wall, giving us some space to get in and activate it before they boarded as well. Behind me I heard Nevin and Ryan, all three of us firing rounds toward the Praetorians to minimize their ability to fire at us.

I reached the elevator first, swinging in and taking cover behind the edge. Within a second however I was exposed again, laying down a blanket of SF-42 fire by rapidly pulling the trigger. In a quick motion I switched it to full-auto, allowing a devastating flurry of bullets to be unleashed. One of the Praetorians went down as the final group, the Marines, made their way into the elevator.

Messor released the tremendous amount of bullets he had amassed and removed a sizable rifle from his back. With only one hand on it, he opened fire with a mighty stream of fusion rounds, multiple striking the Marine in the back of the formation.

Out of instinct I stepped forward to help, but

then Boone appeared in front of me, slapping the elevator's activation. Without delay a doorway sealed us in, several light taps being heard as the fusion rounds melted into the other side. The elevator began its ascent.

"It had to be done," Boone stated, perhaps as much to himself as to us.

No one said a word, each of us truly exhausted of the sorrows of war. I didn't even know the name of the soldier left behind, but still it bothered me that he had been lost. I shook my head lightly, trying to clear my thoughts before we arrived at the top. We were nearly out of the Capital, just a little further to go.

It wasn't long before the elevator reached the top, opening its doorway. No sooner had the doorway opened than we heard gunfire. Moving forward slowly, guns raised, we neared the sound of the gunfire. The light swish of fusion rounds could be heard amongst the hard cracks of rifles. When we reached the bend in the U-shaped hallway we encountered the rear of a UED unit. It was a mix of soldiers and scientists, possibly some of the men from the encampment we had found near the Bastion.

They were exposed and with little cover from our direction, so our entire team opened fire. Men ducked and rolled, trying anything to escape our hail of lead. The purple glint of fusion rounds could be seen soaring by at high speeds from the other direction, indicating that the UED forces were completely surrounded.

"We need to punch through these guys, we

only have so long before Messor and his team get up the elevator behind us!" Nevin called out.

His statement reminded me of the pressure of the situation. While we had the upper hand over the UED here, we would still have to get through more Praetorians quickly, or else we'd be pinned in with no cover, just like the hapless UED were at present. Two of the scientists, apparently unarmed, sprinted toward the Praetorian fire and out of sight, perhaps attempting to simply run the gauntlet.

Then the last visible soldier dropped and immediately we began our advance, well aware of our limited time. As we turned the corner, we could see the light and snow pouring into the large opening. We were so close. Unfortunately, I also saw at least fifteen Praetorians in firing positions on the far side of the hall, having come from the direction in which my team had initially descended. I emptied the mag on my SF-42 before clicking it to semi-auto once more, and loading my last magazine. Now each shot had to count. I crouched and slowly took shots at the line of Praetorians, enemy fire missing me by mere centimeters at times.

As I lined up a shot for my third Praetorian kill of the engagement, I felt an impact on my left arm, near the shoulder, knocking me back. I then felt two more across my chest, stumbling me from my crouched position onto my back. I had been hit three times, the incredible heat of the rounds melting away parts of my armor. While I did have an incredibly warm sensation in the affected areas, I realized they didn't get through, and I wasn't hurt.

"TREDECIM!" Phil exclaimed, pointing toward the Praetorians.

I rose again to see a sizable force of Tredecim smashing through the Praetorian line, slashing them apart as they moved.

"Now's our chance, let's move!" Ryan ordered.

I took off running toward the Tredecim with the rest of the team behind me. When I reached the light I immediately swerved to finally escape the catacombs of the Capital. As I turned though, I saw a single Tredecim, quite tall in stature, and a large scar across its right eye. I paused for a moment, realizing it was the one I had met earlier, also making its escape from the capital that had so long held it prisoner.

"Thanks!" I called out, seemingly at random to the others in my squad.

Then I carried on past the metal barricades and crates left over from the UED's earlier chokepoint. Upon reaching the top of the ramp I saw the Paladin tank in view of the ramp, as well as the two Corsairs, both having landed a short distance from the entrance. All of us darted toward the two Corsairs, presuming it to be Malum's location. When we reached one, we knocked twice on the back hatch and it lowered, revealing Captain Malum leaned back in one of the seats, his usual stern, uncaring look about him.

"Sir," Ryan said plainly. "We've searched the facility. No Korth, no Elonians. Just some UED, Tredecim, and now a whole new enemy in the

Praetorians."

"The who? Is this more of your detective mumbo-jumbo or is this something I can actually work with?" Malum asked.

"It is a real threat. They've been released and now their leader, Messor, is on his way out. I advise we bug out before we have to fight him again," Ryan suggested.

"Again? You mean you lost against him?"

"Sir, with all due respect, we lost more than just the fight. We lost several good soldiers down there. We lost a Ranger. We cannot stay here."

"Sounds like we have a challenge. If these Praetorians are a real threat, we shouldn't merely flee. Let's stop them here before they intrude our mission later. Perhaps if you did your job you wouldn't be losing all of these soldiers. Look Lieutenant, leave the big jobs to the professionals. We're stopping this… 'Messor' before he even gets started," Malum said, finality in his voice.

"Captain, we finished your objective," Boone started, stepping up. "May we send at least ONE Corsair to get Epsilon?"

"Boone, Boone, Boone… You said it yourself… Epsilon is already dead. We need to stick together and kill Messor."

Boone surged forward, appearing as if he was about to strike Malum, though Ryan's arm shot up in a second and seized Boone's. Slowly Ryan lowered Boone's arm.

"Soon," Ryan said plainly, trying to soothe Boone's anger.

"Now, let's get focused and stop Messor from escaping this place," Malum said.

"What about Korth? Should we break off to go try to finish the real mission?" Ryan inquired.

"No. No, no, no, no, no. We are killing Messor, THEN we'll finish the mission," Malum replied bluntly.

I then looked back toward the Capital's entrance nervously. Messor could be there any minute. When I saw movement I mentally braced myself, but then saw that it was not the lanky, silver-skinned Praetorians emerging, but rather large, brown creatures. The Tredecim were making a run for it themselves. Several of Malum's Marine's opened fire on the Tredecim.

Without a thought I ran toward them, hoping to stop the bloodshed.

"Stop! Wait, hold you fire! They are friendly!" I yelled out.

The troops stopped, looking toward me. Then I heard another voice.

"Don't listen to him! Kill them all! No monsters leave here!" Malum screamed.

An earsplitting roar followed as the tank began gunning them down as well. I ran toward them again, wanting to place myself in the line of fire. I grew nearer to the stampede, bullets and tank shells flying past me.

"They are on OUR SIDE!" I screamed, my throat dry from watching them be massacred.

I then saw what appeared to be the scarred Tredecim. I moved near it, but as I was closing in, within meters, a tank shell collided with its torso. The explosion was great enough to knock me back over, Tredecim blood spattered over my visor. I eased myself back up out of the snow only to see a massive cavity dug into the chest of the scarred Tredecim who had represented to me all that was civilized about their species. He expressed their true beauty and ability to be more than mere savages. And yet it was us who ruthlessly killed them unprovoked.

"He killed them," I murmured to myself as I brushed the snow off my armor.

Gazing around the desolate field of snow, I saw blood and bodies strewn from the Capital's entrance nearly to the broken hole in the wall. Not a single Tredecim was standing. I could hardly believe what Malum had done.

Disgusted by Malum's actions, as well as the soldiers around me who had blindly followed his lead, I walked back toward our group. When I once again neared the group, Ryan raised his hand and called out.

"Rangers, on me."

We obliged, all four of us following his lead as he walked outside of earshot of Malum. When he stopped, he turned around sharply, a grim look on his face.

"James, Nev, Phil, Cass… I… I wanted to say that it has been an honor to serve alongside every one of you. We've been through thick and thin, and through it all we've always been a team… inseparable. Invincible. These conditions we've been faced with here on… Marzoc… they are beyond anything we've experienced before. They have cost us one of our own. I know you're all tired. I know you're all hungry. I know you are all ready for this mission to end..." Ryan paused, looking each one of us in the eye before continuing. "But just like that first mission on Enphuerzo, we can't bug out whenever we want. We are stranded, and we have to earn our way out. We did it then, most of you untrained and unprepared for the situation we were in. This time we are as ready as we can be. Malum hasn't made this easy on us, but we're going to follow his command. We're going to stop Messor."

"Those Tredecim were on our side... they could have still helped us," I said quietly.

"I know James. As soon as I saw them I knew they had to be the ones. But we can do this," Ryan responded.

We all nodded, acknowledging what had to be done. Cassidy still looked distressed, holding her gun loosely and having yet to say a word since the incident.

"Check your ammo and let's make it count," Ryan said in conclusion, walking off toward the entrance to the Capital.

Phil and Nevin both reloaded their weapons, and I simply checked on how many clips I had for the H-81 and SR-4, knowing my supply of SF-42 rounds was drained. Then we each followed suit behind Ryan to await the engagement. Though we didn't have long to wait. No sooner had we reached the Paladin I saw Messor and another team of Praetorians making their way up the ramp. I heard the roar of

Malum's Corsair taking off behind me to prepare for the fight. The supporting Praetorians opened up, tearing into Malum's Marine support. Messor had his weapon on his back once more and his arms raised slightly from his sides.

Then I heard the distinctive sound of the Paladin's 100mm cannon firing. A second later the sound repeated. What I then witnessed left me in awe. Messor's arms, now fully extended, had each caught one of the tank shells, holding the sizable warheads in midair in front of him. As he did so his unit charged forward, quickly gaining ground on us. I rapidly regained my senses and swung my rifle to take a few shots, trying to drop a few of the Praetorians before they reached the tank. Messor casually dropped the two tank shells, neither having struck a target with sufficient speed to trigger their detonation. Several Praetorians were already to the tank and had jumped onto it, some firing toward us while one or two concentrated fire on the cockpit.

I tried desperately to pick them off, but to no avail. A hole was melted into the hatch and some sort of object was tossed inside. The Praetorians dove off as I fired my last round into the head of the one on the hatch. Seconds later an immense explosion blinded me. Even through my armor my ears were left ringing. When the smoke cleared, the Paladin was little more than a burning hull.

Snow erupted rapidly around the Praetorians who were still near the tank as both Corsairs opened fire with their chin-mounted guns. Messor then appeared at the top of the ramp, ascending onto the snow for the first time in ages. His weapon in one hand he opened up a spray toward one of the Corsairs, which after taking several glancing blows to the belly began to veer off, as if it were leaving the fight. I took this as a chance to drop Messor, while he was distracted.

I removed my SR-4 as quickly as I could and then crouched. I placed the Oracle scope over his head and squeezed the trigger as fast as I could. In a flash his hand shot up, activating its force field, and catching my bullet. His reflexes were clearly far superior to that of a human. I looked around, trying to get a read on everyone's locations. Only a few Praetorians remained, though the ground was littered with the black-clad Elonian Marines. Only one seemed to remain standing. It was Boone, presently engaged in a hand-to-hand brawl with one of the Praetorians. I took the opportunity to help him, firing a 12.7mm round from the SR-4 through the Praetorian's chest, causing Boone to spin from the sudden impact. He regained his balance and shot me a thumbs up.

Resuming my search I saw Nevin and Phil laying down fire on a few of the remaining Praetorians. Then I saw Ryan charging across the snow, his rifle held in one hand. Mere seconds passed and he dropped the rifle, then I realized what he was doing. He was repeating the tactic that I had used during my first Praetorian encounter.

He leaped forward, arms extended and tackled Messor, both him and Messor doing a complete roll across the ground. Ryan punched him twice before he drew his pistol. Messor's arm shot up and activated the force field, sending Ryan's arm flying upward and disarming him of his pistol.

I readied my SR-4 and fired a shot to try to assist Ryan, though Messor's insane reflexes caught the bullet in the field. It seemed as if there was no way to beat him.

Ryan brought his fist back into Messor's face once again before being knocked to the side by the creature. Messor returned to his feet swiftly, and then approached Ryan who tried to do the same. Ryan then pulled out his combat knife and moved in a quick thrusting motion toward Messor. The Praetorian grabbed hold of Ryan's arm, twisted it back, then grabbed the combat knife. In a quick action, it shoved the knife through Ryan's stomach with incredible force.

In response, Ryan head-butted Messor, then seized both of his arms tightly. In an instant I realized the opening. I peered back down my sight, calming myself as best I could. I lined up the silver skinned head, aiming for a spot not guarded by the helmet on his head. I breathed in, then held it. Slowly I squeezed the trigger. The crack of the gun was followed by a splatter of Praetorian blood from Messor's skull.

Ryan stumbled back, both of his hands coming in toward his stomach as Messor's body fell limply to the ground. I lowered my rifle and sprinted toward him. When I reached him, his gauntlets were covered with blood, and the knife was still inside of him.

Alex Pennington

"Ryan? You alright? Hang in there," I said encouragingly, reaching for the knife.

Ryan placed one of his arms around me, leaning heavily on me. I eased him toward the ground slowly. I observed the wound, the knife thrust clear through the softer, more flexible portion of the power armor. I looked over toward the rest of the team, though they all seemed to be relaxing their guns. We had won.

"Nev! Guys! Get over here!" I called out. "Ryan's hurt!"

The group reconvened from their various places on the battlefield to Ryan and I's position. Observing Ryan's face, he was growing pale, we had to do something.

"Phil, patch him up!" I ordered.

"10-4," he replied, slinging off his pack with great haste.

Phil then knelt down, immediately gauging the wound, trying to conclude the damage as he pulled bandages from the pack. Already Ryan was looking bad, and I began to grow incredibly concerned for him.

"C'mon Phil, you've got him right? He'll be good?" I asked hurriedly.

"Yeah, yeah… well, Gah, I do not know. Give me a few James," he replied.

Phil slowly pulled out the knife, blood gushing out rapidly as he slipped it from the incision in the armor.

"Curse it! The Praetorian had to have nailed a fairly significant artery. He's hemorrhaging real bad," Phil said.

I knelt down beside the two. Ryan had yet to say anything.

"Ryan, you're a Ranger. Remember. Inseparable, invincible, we can finish the mission!" I said intensely, my own face becoming strained to see Ryan this way.

"James…" Ryan mumbled, coughing blood onto the inside of his helmet. "You know… what needs to be done… It is up to you to finish the mission."

"Ryan, hang in there," I said, frantically glancing back at Phil, whose hands were moving as quick as he could to try to limit the bleeding.

"James… this is real war," Ryan said, his eyes closing.

"Ryan, hey, listen… we're doin' this together. C'mon! Ryan?" I spat, moving his head slightly side to side.

I looked back over my shoulder at Nevin and Cass, both of whom looked as stricken by grief as I was. He was gone. Our most experienced soldier, our only pilot, our explosives expert, our jack-of-all-trades… our leader… was dead.

We were all silent, Phil taking his hands off the wound. There was no way to try to revive him in time, the armor over his chest was too thick. I remained there, kneeling, for quite some time, everyone staying in their positions. When I at last stood up, I looked back at our team. Three others stood in power armor, each damaged in its own way. Phil's visor had been shot out, Nevin's remained clawed up, and Cassidy has numerous marks across her armor from UED and Praetorians alike. My own visor still had claw marks of its own impairing some of my vision.

"Let's go... We all suffer losses. We... we need to move on."

"We should take his body... for proper burial," Phil suggested quietly.

"No. We need to leave it. James is right, we all suffer losses, we just have to move on," Nevin said, stepping up.

I gave a glance at Cass, thinking about what had happened to Max. Then I added more to Nevin's point.

"I know what it is like to lose family. I know we are all family here, in our own way. As our numbers may dwindle, we still have those who are left, and we always have the families of others to fight for. Then there are always those who might still be out there, perhaps alive, perhaps dead... but that hope can always live on," I said, my thoughts drifting to my sister, Amanda, who I hadn't seen or heard from in the revolutions after that fateful day.

Phil finally rose as well, leaving the body of our commander in the cool snow. He waved his arms toward the Corsair, and I took it as a symbol he was ready. I too joined in, and soon the Corsair moved over, parking itself beside our small team. Boone slowly approached us, having been watching from afar, avoiding any interference with our moment.

The Corsair lowered its back ramp, revealing that it was Malum's Corsair that had abandoned the fight. We each stepped up and took seats in the back of the Corsair. We remained there for another minute, uncertain what to do next, when I decided to speak to the pilot. I rose and approached the doorway to the cockpit. With a simple knock, I proceeded to open the door. The pilot turned around, his face mostly obscured by his flight helmet.

"I've had no contact with Malum, he didn't even say where he was going," the pilot said.

"Boone, come here," I said, waving Boone over from his seat.

"Yeah?" he asked casually.

"We need a plan. We haven't heard anything from Malum, which for the moment means we're in charge. I propo—"

"We? I'm in charge Ross," Boone replied coolly.

"Right, uh, okay. But I was going to suggest that we take advantage of this time to try to save Epsilon, or to find the Vorgians and finish this."

"This is our one chance to go back for Epsilon without that loathsome rat Malum barring our path. We're taking it," he replied.

"All right, then let's roll," I said, looking at the pilot.

He nodded and assumed the controls, sealing the back hatch and starting the Corsair's ascent. The cockpit was tight, so I stepped out to let Boone in. He watched out the window in search of the structure that they had taken shelter in. We only had a general idea of its direction, and locating the structure could be difficult. Equipment on board the Corsair would certainly play its part though. As I looked around the hold of the aircraft, so few soldiers were still there. With Boone now up front, only the Rangers remained in the back. Nevin seemed to be in deep thought while Phil and Cass were using the time to try to catch up on some sleep, an understandable activity considering it had been well over a day since the last time we had slept. I too found myself thinking though, about everything we had been through and all the lives we had seen lost, and those we had taken ourselves.

The War Across the Stars

Chapter 18
A Man In Armor Is His Armor's Slave

As we scoured the wastes from above, I heard the COM crackle on up front. I moved closer, wanting to see what Malum had to say.

"Gamma Two, you read? This is Captain Malum."

"Figured sir," the pilot replied, almost sarcastically.

"Soldier, we are taking anti-air fire from what appear to be Vorgian flak cannons. I am led to believe we have located the—Shoot! Steady! Steady! We have been hit, get your rear over here and give us some support Gamma Two!"

"Uh, sir, we're presently on a SAR mission under 1st Sergeant Boone's orders."

"I don't care! Scrap the op and get over here! We are losing control of this bird!"

I heard a pause as no voices spoke.

"Stay the course," Boone's voice uttered.

My heart beat faster as I pondered what the pilot would do. If he sided with Malum, Boone was liable to shoot him on the spot and take the controls himself. If he sided with Boone, Malum could be all nature of furious when we did choose to go save him.

"Uh… copy that sir, inbound," the pilot said, cutting the COM. "Sergeant, let's find Epsilon."

I smiled briefly at the display of wits by the pilot. He now had Malum believing we were inbound to rescue him, while still sticking with Boone to find Epsilon. Fortunately, it wasn't long before we stumbled upon something.

"That's it. That has to be it," Boone said.

I felt the Corsair descend, landing softly on the snow. The back hatch opened, though Cass and Phil didn't seem to realize. The door to the cockpit opened and Boone moved out in a rushed speed walk. As he exited the aircraft he pulled his shotgun off his pack and held it ready. Nevin and I followed him, noticing several dead UED bodies that weren't there before. They had been mostly covered by snow already, and all of our original footprints were gone. I wasn't entirely convinced we had found the right one, but the dead bodies had to come from somewhere. We entered the building and looked up the spiraling stairwell. Boone on point, we ascended, the stream of bodies as endless as the stairs.

As we neared the top, Boone began to yell.

"House! Sergeant House! Wells? Epsilon, status report!" Boone cried out.

Boone was first to have his head emerge, just as Phil's had when we first encountered the two refugee Elonian squads. I saw Boone's speed go from hasty to a very slow trudge as he witnessed the room. My heart sank. When I reached the top as well, I saw blood spattered everywhere, adorned with the bodies of both UED and Elonian Marines. Boone's face held a firm frown, though he showed no other sign of emotion. Against the wall, in the same location he was when we first passed through, was Sergeant House.

"Malum," Boone said through clenched teeth.

He walked over to House, kneeling down and

securing his tags. He then proceeded to collect the tags of every soldier who lay dead on the floor. Next he approached Nevin and I, gave one last look toward Sergeant House, then began down the stairs again.

"We're done here," he said plainly.

As I looked around the room, I noticed that the naval personnel did not appear to be amongst the dead. I dismissed him as a prisoner for the UED nearly immediately however, then carried on with Nevin and Boone back to the Corsair. As we stepped out into the snow once more, I heard voices talking. One sounded like Phil's, though I didn't recognize the other. We hurried over to the back hatch to see the swabbie sitting directly beside Phil in the Corsair.

"Missed someone," Phil said, looking toward me.

Boone said nothing and simply walked back to the front. Nevin and I took our seats as the aircraft once more took to the skies.

"So what's your name and rank?" I asked inquisitively.

"Ensign Lowell."

I paused, realizing that the swabbie actually was an officer, higher ranked than either Boone or myself. Despite this he hadn't seemed to make any effort to take charge.

"Sir," I stated, saluting him plainly.

"No, no. That's not necessary. Uh, I'm really not trained for this. I was a back up for Navigation on board the *Procyon*. I don't mind you guys runnin' the show," he stated, his face nearly expressionless.

"Um, alright. May I ask how you survived the

UED attack?" I asked, surprised that he wasn't using his power.

"I… When we were attacked we took out the first wave… then I ran. I left the team behind and journeyed out into the cold. I laid down in the snow and waited. I heard the gunfire, I knew what must have happened… They didn't make it did they?" he asked, his face showing signs of distress.

Perhaps he actually didn't know they were all dead. Maybe he had yet to muster the courage to go find his team dead.

"Sir… Uh…" I started.

"Please, just call me Jeremy," the ensign requested.

"Okay, Jeremy, the UED did kill them. All of Epsilon are dead. You're the last one," I said.

His face became even more troubled, and then he looked toward the floor, making no comment. The ride was silent for a while before Boone returned from the front.

"Ross, we're off to save Malum's hide, or better yet, eliminate the Vorgian targets near him. This might be it, we may almost be through this," Boone said.

"I hope so," Nevin said. "I've had enough of this planet."

"Likewise. Our experiences here are universally despondent… I'm ready for some solace," Phil added.

Cassidy said nothing, maintaining her veil of near-silence that she had held since Max's death. Her bright blue eyes were just barely open and her face remained solemn. Several strands of her brown, shoulder-length hair had come loose from their bindings and were draped across her face. It was evident that she had taken the deaths the hardest.

None of us spoke for the remainder of the trip as we pursued Malum's downed Corsair's transponder. As we drew near, the pilot brought us in low, as to help avoid falling into the anti air fire. Then I heard him speaking.

"Sergeant? I've got a visual on a large structure… appears to be native in design, but definitely has some human mods on it. I'd call this as the place," the pilot said.

"COM Malum. He should at least be able to watch how a real soldier does his job," Boone said menacingly.

"Uh… I've got no response. His Corsair's COM system must be down."

"Then set us down, we've got a war to win," Boone returned.

As the Corsair landed in the snow and the hatch began to drop, I approached Cassidy.

"Cass, listen," I said, placing my hand on her shoulder. "I know it's rough. But hang in there. We are almost through it all. I need you focused on the mission. We'll have time to remember the dead later. And trust me, remember them we will."

She nodded quietly, keeping eye contact with me. I took a step back, then made my way out of the hatch.

"I'm with you James. Let's finish this," she said, finally snapping back into shape.

Alex Pennington

The four Rangers and Boone made our way toward the large structure, it's design more akin to the Capital's than to any of the observation posts. Vorgian anti-air turrets adorned the top, in several places, as well as some nature of missile battery. I hoped to myself that within that structure we could finally end this wretched mission and prepare ourselves to leave the forsaken world of Marzoc. I held my SR-4, the same one I had been issued so long ago. Nevin had his SMG-56, also having essentially emptied his SF. Boone and Phil both had their SG-13's at the ready, and Cassidy's assault rifle was once more held in a combat stance. We approached the structure ready for anything, though even the greatest of preparation is prone to failure.

A series of cracks was heard from somewhere near the building, and immediately I searched for the source of the gunfire. Several rounds pelted the snow around me, others hitting my squad mates' armor. I quickly pondered how we could perform without the armor. Our dependence on it had grown so great, we were unaccustomed to warfare without it.

Breaking from my distraction I found one of the gunmen, lying prone near one of the AA turrets. I lined up a shot and fired, the 12.7mm round soaring through the air and splitting into his head. I lowered my scope and began a sprint toward the structure as more gunmen arose. Phil held his shotgun in one hand as he raised his pistol with the other to return fire from a range.

We pressed forward quickly, downing multiple hostiles on the approach. As we reached the structure's outer walls, I heard another mix of gunfire apart from our own. It sounded as if it was coming from the other side of the structure, which may have been where Malum's Corsair went down.

"We should flank around the structure and try to save Malum," I suggested.

"Is he worth the time?" Boone questioned.

"Yes, I think so," I stated.

Without another word Boone led the way along the wall until the corner, making a swift turn. We followed along behind him, moving hastily. When we reached the next corner, we had a clear view of Malum's Corsair, its nose plunged into the ground. Two Marines and Malum himself were firing toward the roof of the structure. We approached them, keeping our eyes toward the roof until we could get clear shots. In short time the heavy increase in firepower brought down the Vorgian defense. The ringing of gunfire finally was silenced.

"Boone! Where the heck were you!? We already lost two, and the pilot! Much longer and we'd all be dead," Malum scolded.

"Oh, what was that? A rescue attempt being too late? Sounds so familiar… but where? Oh right, Captain. Epsilon. They are all dead. And it is all because of you," Boone retorted, anger seeping through his voice.

"First Sergeant! You're out of line! You need to unders—"

"Shut up Captain. I saved your rear, and without us, you'd be dead now," Boone interrupted.

"How dare you—"

"Shut. Up. Am I clear, Captain?" Boone stated intensely.

"Are you all just going to stand for this?" he asked us, waving his arms about.

None of us replied, simple silence filled the air. Malum looked as if he was about to give further protest, then lowered his arms, admitting defeat to Boone. Even the two Marines who stood behind Malum offered him no aid.

"When we get home Sergeant, there will be consequences. For now… lead the way," Malum stated.

"If… you make it home," Boone replied dryly.

Our group retraced our steps toward the front of the building, where a doorway had been seen. When we arrived, we stacked up, preparing our entrance. Phil and I were the first man on either side of the doorway, which appeared to be some nature of bulkhead placed there by the Vorgians. In place of Ryan I held my hand and counted down from three, eventually displaying the okay, then swiveling around to open the hatch. As I grabbed the circular handle and tried to spin it, I found it locked in place. To make matters worse, our stores of Eupholium remained in Ryan's pack, which we had foolishly left behind. We were making mistakes, and time after time it was costing us.

"It's locked. What do we do?" I asked the group, looking back at them.

It was far too strong to be kicked in, and our options were limited. So long as they wanted us on the outside, it seemed there was nothing we could do.

The War Across the Stars

"The Corsair," Cassidy said, at last speaking again. "We could have the Corsair unload its missiles on the door."

The simple genius of the idea hit me in an instant. Chances were high that once we had breached the exterior, the rest would be easy.

"You're right," I agreed.

The rest of the group nodded, though Malum didn't seem too pleased.

"I'll tell the pilot," Nevin called out before sprinting off toward the parked Corsair.

It wasn't long before I saw the Corsair lifting upward, Nevin making his way back toward us. We all cleared the area around the hatch in preparation for the breach. A few seconds later a volley of missiles released from beneath the Corsair's wings, pummeling the door with explosive force. As the smoke cleared, the hatch had been dented and scorched, as well as blown out of its position and lying several meters inside the building.

"Let's go Rangers! It's time to end this," I stated as I led the charge toward the building.

I found myself again forced to swap for my pistol for the close quarters interior. Ammo was scarce, but we were almost out of this mess.

We proceeded down the thin hallway, stepping carefully over the door that lay damaged in the path. Soon it opened up into a wider room with some nature of electronics and wires hanging across all of the walls. We all filed into the room and I began to examine one of the larger pieces of equipment that resembled some sort of radio dish. Then looking back I saw a camera.

"Something's wrong guys, this doesn't feel right," Cassidy said cautiously.

Then I saw a flash, heard a strange buzzing noise, then felt my body go numb. I lost my balance and fell backwards onto the hard, stone floor. I couldn't hear anything but a strange ringing, and I couldn't see anything but the ceiling above me. I tried to move but just couldn't. I started to regain my hearing, the sounds of rushed footsteps clattering nearby. Soon I started to feel my body again as well, but when I tried to lift my arm, it felt incredibly heavy. I was just barely able to lift my arm before it fell back hard onto the floor.

"What just happened?" I asked, finally able to compose words.

I heard a mumbling, then I heard Phil's voice.

"Some sort of energy pulse. I think... I think our armor has been disabled."

"We haven't ever worn it without power before," Nevin stated. "It's so heavy, why did they make it this heavy?" he continued in a slight panic.

The footsteps were drawing nearer.

The helmet was light enough I could now turn my head, looking to see Phil sprawled nearby. Then I saw Boone, back on his feet. His lighter Marine armor was actually proving advantageous.

"It's heavy to bring us closer to invincible. Unfortunately even that wasn't enough," Phil said, a tint of sadness in his voice.

I heard Boone grunt before looking over at me, holding his shoulder that had been hurt earlier.

"You need to dump the armor, I need you guys on your feet."

The thought rushed through my mind. Removing the armor that had so long protected us. We'd all be exposed just like any other soldier. The realities of war grew ever-clearer as every hour on this planet passed.

"Alright, alright, help me out," I said, trying to lean upwards, though to little success.

Boone ran toward me, then I heard the sound of more gunfire in the room. Boone stumbled, but caught himself without falling. He then turned around and fired his shotgun at an enemy outside my line of sight. Pumping the shotgun, he fired again. It seemed a whole firefight had erupted around us, though for once the Rangers were all helpless. I saw my pistol lying just out of reach of my right hand. With great effort I scooted closer, my fingers struggling to seize the gun's grip.

"Clear!" I heard a Marine call out.

Then I saw Boone crouch down beside me, removing my helmet and gaining access to the two clips that would loosen the armor. I heard them snap into the open position, and the armor felt looser. I was able to slip my arms out of the suit's arms, then began to loosen the waist. Boone moved down to unfasten the boots so I could remove my feet. As the suit's pressure eased up, I began to feel the incredible cold of the planet.

With enough of the suit loose, I slipped off the cuirass, then up and out of the legs. My standard black BDU was all that covered me from the cold.

Alex Pennington

The pants and shirt seemed like so little compared to the armor that had adorned me for over a day. This also marked the first instance that I had been in a combat scenario without the safety of the armor since the Vorgian War.

I removed the backpack from the armor, then shouldered it myself. I also picked my H-81 up from the ground, the armored gauntlet so close to its grip. My feet, covered only by socks, needed some nature of protection, so I began to equip the boots from the armor as a stand-alone pair. As I did so I saw Boone and the other Marines helping the rest of us to do as I did.

Chapter 19
The Eye of the Beholder

Those of us who could kept the Vorgian SAS at bay while the rest of us removed their armor. Removing the armor took a considerable amount of time, but we held firm. The suits were never meant to be removed while powered down, arguably a flaw in design. Though I still had no concrete explanation for what had happened to us. The Vorgians must have designed some sort of trap expecting a power armor team such as ourselves to walk into it.

"Alright, I'm good," Cassidy said as Boone helped her out of the suit.

With the team prepared, it was time to continue the search for Korth. We could only hope our delays hadn't given him time to escape the facility.

"Let's move," I said, beginning down the hallway now littered with Vorgian bodies.

It felt strange, every step feeling so loose without the firm armor guiding it. I was exposed, vulnerable. Any wrong move could have me killed like every one of those Vorgians now scattered in the hall.

But regardless, we pressed forward. We searched room-by-room, facing little resistance at first. Then we found a doorway blocked by several large crates.

"This might be it. They may consider this a defense," I warned as we approached it.

"Not for long," Boone said, walking up and

giving the upper crate a powerful straight kick.

The crate slid back, but its top corner caught on the ceiling and it didn't fall through. He repeated the action, knocking it to the floor and immediately gunfire was heard. I ducked, using the lower steel crate as cover. I could hear the bullets pinging off of the crate, much as they had my armor before. I took several deep breaths, thinking back to the Vorgian War. I popped my head up, pistol firmly gripped between my hands, and sighted in on my first target. I placed several rounds downrange, nailing him twice through the skull. Moving to my next target I fired once through the shoulder before I heard a round tear by my ear. It served as a grim reminder that I was no longer unstoppable.

In response I ducked down, resuming full cover behind the box. Phil and Boone were each blind firing from either side of the doorway, the hail of shotgun pellets no doubt shredding the SAS. I peered back over to see the room still crawling with Vorgians, many in cover behind a line of crates.

"Someone get a grenade in there!" I said in a strong, but hushed voice.

Without a word Boone pulled the pin and tossed a frag grenade into the room. Seconds later the explosion was heard, shrapnel bouncing around the room. The screams of the Vorgian soldiers filled my ears over the sound of gunfire, though only for a moment.

Suddenly, I saw Cassidy pass by me, leaping over the crate that I had used for cover. The bold move looked more like an action we'd do in power armor than in BDU's. She fired quickly and precisely. I attempted to provide support from cover, unwilling to take such a risk as she had. She continued into the room, bounding over their cover as if it were nothing and gunning them down. Then it appeared her AR-27 ran dry, she swung it as a club into the nearest Vorgian before dropping it and pulling out her pistol. She proceeded to fire two rounds into a target obscured from my view before stopping, at last ceasing her river of fluid motion.

"Clear," she said calmly.

I vaulted over the crate in the doorway and looked around the room myself. The best the Vorgians had lay dead across the floor. More SAS had escaped the Jerico system than I had imagined, their black and gray uniforms stained with blood.

"That was… impressive, Cass," I complimented, after pondering between impressive and risky.

"That was my job, James. But thanks," she replied.

"Right… It's just that without the armor…"

"We're still Rangers. We're still the same soldiers. Let's prove it," she said, a new confidence in her voice unlike I had heard since before Max's death.

"Let's," I said in response.

Looking back, the others had moved the crate out of the doorway and were searching the room. It seemed to be the most heavily guarded, and no other location had showed any signs of being Korth's hideaway. The room seemed elaborate however.

Across one wall was a large image of the Beholder, scrawled across the stone. The other walls had decorative columns lining them, indicating some significance to the room.

"Where are they?" Malum asked. "Where are the leaders? Korth! Show yourself!" he then yelled.

I continued to look around the room. We had killed every Vorgian we'd seen, we had no prisoners to interrogate, no soldiers to break. I glanced back at the drawing of the Beholder, the golden form of the eye surrounded by red and yellow rays. On either side were two more of the columns that adorned the other walls.

"Next room?" Phil asked.

"This one's a dead end, we'll have a ways to backtrack to get to the last turn," Nevin stated.

The sketch kept drawing my attention, pulling me in. Something was there. I thought about the Beholder, the super computer we had worked so hard to find. It had been what we desired most. It was…

"Beautiful," I murmured, walking closer to the wall. "The measure of Beauty is whatever one desires most. Though the determination of Beauty is in the eye of the beholder."

The words left my mouth softly, my mind almost in a trance as I felt pieces come together. I stood before the wall, my hand slowly outstretched. I placed my palm calmly on the cool surface of the wall, directly across the eye of the Beholder. I pressed in, feeling the stone give. As I released it, I heard some nature of power source activate. Then the stone wall before me, adorned with the image of the

Beholder, sank into a socket beneath it, revealing a hallway.

"Guys… I found something."

"Clearly. Now do you care to share precisely what?" Malum said rudely.

Ignoring the statement I entered the hallway, my pistol raised. It was cold and the hallway was dark. My mind flashed back to the day Nevin and I were escorted through the dark Vorgian corridors alongside the soldier from Beta Squad. I thought I saw a shadow dart across the darkness, but no room existed on either side. The end of the hall was lighted however. I looked back over my shoulder to see Nevin directly behind me. He nodded solemnly.

Then I entered the light. Before me stood the two men that our mission revolved around. The two men whose death was our sole objective. I raised my pistol.

"James! Nice to see you again!" Robert said, a surprising smile coming across his face.

My instincts said to shoot him immediately, though instead I paused, staring down my sights at his face. His dark hair had lengthened since our encounter on Sontonos. A thin beard had appeared on his face around the devious smile.

"Don't you feel the same? I mean, how's your family been? They enjoy their date with my friends?" he continued.

"Your… your what?" I asked, flashbacks of the pirates now flooding my mind.

"Oh? You didn't know? You seemed to care about your parents so much. Honestly, I got tired of hearing about it. And after your stunt in the hangar on Sontonos… I couldn't just leave you be! You shot me!"

My parents, dead in my arms, soared through my mind. Unwilling to listen to him any more I squeezed the trigger. The bullet went off, but as it did something pushed my arms upward. An SAS had intervened, causing my bullet to strike the stone ceiling, powdered rock floating down from the impact.

I brought my knee into the stomach of the soldier, then brought my elbow back down onto his head. He might have been strong, but Cassidy made a point. We were Rangers, with or without the armor. He tried to counter with a swing of his fist, but I dodged it and followed up with a strike to his face. Bloodied, he stumbled backwards. I raised my pistol and fired, striking his shoulder as I felt myself fall to the ground. Robert had tackled me, pinning me to the floor. My mind raced, but still it couldn't keep out the flow of memories. When Robert had tackled Nevin in training, it allowed for me to have my first victory. This day I would have another victory.

I punched his face three times, then rolled him off of me. As I began to rise he used his leg to sweep mine, dropping me back down. In a quick motion he was back up and kicking me. On the fourth kick I seized his leg with my hand and pulled it out from under him. He fell and I attempted to pin his shoulders. He reacted by grabbing my own shoulders and rolling us. He remained on top of me, bashing my head into the ground when he was abruptly thrown off. Looking up, my vision blurred, I saw Nevin standing above me. Behind him was a scene all too familiar. Just as I'd seen that night in Ebony, the night when my life changed forever, Rigel stood behind Nevin with a knife. I didn't think, and I didn't process… I just did. I reached over for my dropped pistol, sliding it into my grasp in an instant, then fired at Rigel. A blood splatter burst out from behind his head. The man who had started a war fell backwards, his lifeless body toppling to the cold floor. The knife clattered to the ground beside him. I had never seen him before in person. He represented all that was Vorgian, the instrument of their will. Revolutions ago when the Treaty of Paix was signed… that was not the end of the war. This marked the end of the war.

I stood up, Nevin seizing Robert and holding him to the floor. Phil and Cass had just gunned down the last SAS in the room. Robert was all that remained. I turned and faced Robert. The others came over beside me, and as a team we stood united around him.

"Robert. It's over. Your game is up. Nevin, get off him," I ordered.

Nevin gave a final blow to Robert's head before rising up beside us. Robert remained, sprawled on the floor, his face bloody.

"The time has come for you to answer for your actions, Robert. We all trusted you. We had the simple camaraderie that you would be there if we needed you. When you offered us a way off of Sontonos, we followed, trusting that you were leading us to safety. Instead you killed our ally and would have killed us too! Each one of us felt that loss, that betrayal. And the role you claim in the attack on Ebony! It disgusts me Robert. It disgusts me…" I said, my voice filled with a flurry of emotions.

"James," Cassidy said, placing her hand on my shoulder and turning me slightly. "What if we offer him redemption? Something to repair what he's done to you, to all of you."

"Our objective is to kill him Cass, you know this," Phil stated. "And every second that man lives is a second too many."

"But listen," she said, backing up to gain audience to everyone. "He is an administrative figure in the Vorgian caste. The Vorgians clearly have a pact with the UED. We are stranded on this planet with no ship capable of getting us home. He has access to one."

I looked down at the broken remains of the once cocky Robert.

"How do you propose?" I asked.

"We can have him contact his UED buddies to bring a transport within range, then take them out and nab the transport."

"James, remember last time we let him live. Shoot him now," Nevin said quietly.

I looked between the two, Nevin's eyes burning with anger, while Cassidy's glistened with hope.

"Cass is right. We can use him. But Robert I want you to understand something. You will die. This does not make up for what you've done to us."

"I understand James… Gah, you guys are

right. I was merely serving my people, you can't blame me for that, but maybe I took it too far," Robert admitted, his face showing signs of pain. "I'll do whatever it takes to repent for the mistakes I've made."

"We'll see about that," Nevin said, disbelief evident in his voice.

"Prove it," Phil said angrily. "Call the UED, get us our ship.

"I'll get better. I'll bring you the admiral of the entire UED Fleet. You can take him out while you secure yourselves a transport. That prove enough?" Robert said, a hint of his usual tone slipping back into his voice.

"If it's true," Nevin said. "Then it's a start."

Robert slowly picked himself up, none of us offering him our hand. When he rose he walked toward a table with a COM unit on it, likely salvaged from one of the *Hornet*'s vehicles. He reached for the activation, and I held my breath. He could use it to give our location to the UED and make his last big bang before we kill him.

"*Odyssey* Actual, what's the matter Korth?" a voice said from the COM.

"It's Washington. We need to talk. In person. Now."

"What about?" the voice replied.

"We've got a few problems, I need to discuss the details with you, and I can't afford to be monitored by these newcomers."

"From what I hear Marzoc isn't the safest of destinations right now Washington. Why do you require my presence?"

"Admiral, you said you would do anything to ensure our safety, so long as we led you to the Beholder. As long as we never gave you reason to distrust us," Robert protested.

"And yet we have yet to find the Beholder Washington."

"Korth is dead. That important enough? I need to see you. You promised protection, and these infiltrators are compromising that."

"He's… dead? The situation is indeed more grave than I had anticipated. You know Camp Echo?"

"Yes sir."

"That shall be my LZ. Get there. You'll get your talk," the Admiral responded.

"Yes sir. Right away sir," Robert said, cutting the COM. "You guys happy yet?"

"Looked pretty legit," Cassidy said optimistically.

"Looks can be deceiving," Phil countered.

"Okay, you guys need to understand what I've just given you! You kill Admiral Cope and their whole freakin' fleet tumbles into disarray! You guys can get out of here unnoticed!" Robert defended angrily.

"Robert, shut up," I ordered.

He scowled, but ceased to run his mouth. We opened up our circle, letting Malum, Boone, and the two Marines in. Every survivor excluding our Corsair pilot and Lowell was present. We were nearing our escape, all we needed was the clearance to access the *Hornet* and a distraction so the rest of the fleet wouldn't see us.

"So we're killing their leader? Excellent. I suggest explosives," Malum stated.

"We already had this problem sir, our explosives are with…" I paused, sighing deeply. "With Ryan sir."

"Then we go get them. I don't want the enemy knowing we are there. It will allow you to capture the transport easier."

"But sir, we could snipe them just as easily… it's what snipers do!" I protest.

"Enough excuses. A dead soldier is a dead soldier. Just because you can't get over it doesn't mean I will let it hinder my mission plans."

I looked around at my team, Malum clearly not making sense. Every fiber of my being wanted to strike him across the face and let Boone lead the way. But the thought of Ryan catching Boone's attempt played back in my head. Ryan had expected us to follow Malum's orders, regardless of whether or not we agreed with them.

"Okay, how do we use explosives?" I asked.

"We strap them to your friend."

"There's no way he'll—" I started.

"I'll do it. Strap the Eupholium to me," Robert said, the devilish grin on his face frustrating me.

His smile was no doubt the result of him piecing together that Ryan was dead. The satisfaction he received from it disturbed me.

"At least let us act as a failsafe, what if the

explosives don't go off?" I proposed.

"Fine, two of you may go. I need our presence there to be small, nearly undetectable. You will NOT engage the enemy unless you are certain the explosives failed to activate. Do you understand that soldier?" Malum inquired intensely.

"Yes sir."

"Now, let's go get our explosives," Malum concluded, walking from the secret room back into the dark hallway.

Chapter 20
Endgame

The Corsair slowly eased itself to the ground near the Tredecim capital. The dead still littered the ground, though many were half-buried by the endless snow. I alone stepped out of the warmth of the Corsair and approached the site where my life had been changed dramatically, just as it had in Ebony. Rising partially from the snow was the helmet of a warrior. The helmet of a leader and a friend. I walked toward it, the cold biting away at me. When I reached it, I brushed off some snow, revealing the body of Ryan.

Emotions once more flooded through me, but I had a mission, and I would complete it. I removed enough of the snow to slip off the backpack that was still strapped around his arms. Inside it was a sizable portion of Eupholium, Ryan's favorite explosive ordinance. I slipped the pack over one of my shoulders, then carefully removed the helmet from Ryan's head. I reached down and pulled his tags from his neck, and then placed the helmet back. I slipped the tags into my pocket before proceeding back to the Corsair.

When I reached it I silently climbed back aboard, letting the pack slip to the metal floor with a clank. Without a word Malum nodded his approval, and we soared toward the location provided by Robert.

As we flew, Phil and Boone did what they could to strap the Eupholium to Robert without giving any sign that it was there from the outside. When they finished, they had done a fair job, nicely securing it to his chest and thighs without any exterior bulges.

"We're close enough. Land the ship," Robert instructed as he watched from the door to the cockpit.

The pilot nodded and the Corsair sank down toward the snow. A soft thud was heard as it touched down on the solid ground, pressing into the deep snow. The hatch dropped and I looked around at those who survived. My team, my friends, each knew how close we were. Boone rose from his seat and approached me. He extended his hand. I took it, and shook it once, looking Boone in the eye, despite them still be obscured by his shades.

"It's been an honor James. Good luck out there," he said softly.

"We'll be back Boone, and we're all getting off this rock together."

I then turned my head to Cassidy and Phil, who would be staying behind as we went out to capture the transport. It seemed so foreign to see them without their armor and know we were in a combat zone. While the sight itself wasn't so unusual, considering we lived together on base, the danger of the environment and the notion that any one of them could die at any time was haunting.

"You two get us that ship," Cassidy said, her eyes sad and her tone tired.

"Will do," Nevin chuckled.

"You stay safe Cass," I said, stepping down from the Corsair.

"You too James… You too," she replied.

I turned slowly, hoping Nevin and I could survive one final trial.

"Uh, James?" Cassidy's voice asked.

I paused, turning back toward the Corsair.

"I wanted to tell you… Um… Thank you. I appreciate what you've done for us… for me."

At first I was unsure how to respond, but I pondered a response briefly.

"Yeah, it's been… this mission is rough. But we all just needed some hope. We're going to make it through Cass," I finally answered.

Without a response, we continued into the snowy wastes. As we proceeded away Malum finally spoke.

"Don't get caught."

Nevin and I both opted not to respond to his parting comment, and as we had done on Sontonos, followed Robert to our destination. We pressed on through the snow for a good twenty minutes before reaching the peak of a massive hill. From the hill we could see a sprawling UED camp, tents scattered in tight clusters and soldiers ambling about.

"This is it. And look guys, I'm sorry for what I did. I'm sorry for your family, for your soldiers, for everything. I know it'll never make up for it, but my life is all I have to offer… My life and Admiral Cope's," Robert stated smoothly, seemingly unfazed by his eminent death.

I opened my mouth to respond, but Nevin replied first.

"I don't believe a word that comes out of your

mouth anymore Rob, but at this point I don't really care. Go 'redeem yourself' and get out of our lives," he said angrily, his face red with fury.

I looked up to see a silhouette in the sky, likely an approaching ship. Cope was here.

"Light me up," Robert said.

With the timer on the Eupholium preset by Phil and Boone, I tapped the activation button and concealed the explosive again. Five minutes. Robert would be dead in five minutes. He smiled slyly at me, and then took off in a sprint toward the camp.

Nevin and I assumed prone positions overlooking the camp. I passed him my SF-42, equipped with a scope, and he loaded it with his last mag. I peered through my Oracle scope briefly, then watched carefully as some sort of UED gunship landed on the far edge of the encampment. I breathed in carefully, keeping a steady eye on the transport. Robert reached the base and walked toward the center.

We were watching, waiting in the cold, harsh weather of Marzoc. Nevin was to my right. Our fingers were on the triggers, despite them being numbed by the cold. Admiral Cope was in our scopes. We could have fired but instead we held our fire. We followed orders and waited.

The man in charge of the entire UED fleet marched from his gunship toward a larger tent in the center of the camp. Admiral Cope entered the central command tent. Robert followed him in. We waited for the explosion. It didn't come.

"Hasn't it been five?" Nevin asked in a

hushed tone.

"It has to have been. Or the adrenaline has severely slowed our time perception."

"Gah, C'mon!" Nevin called out, though still not loud enough to be heard from more than a few meters away.

The main tent, larger than the others, had two guards standing near the door, and several more patrolling nearby. If the Eupholium would detonate, it'd easily kill them all. But still the only sound was the heavy wind that blew the snow across the surface of the planet. My eyes began to feel heavy as I watched, and I felt my focus begin to slip away.

The tent flap ruffled suddenly, and then Robert appeared.

"What's he doing?" I whispered.

"Living."

His finger pointed toward us, my scope identifying the details of his second betrayal.

"Shoot, he's busting us! He must have disabled the Eupholium!" I said, my crosshairs dancing around his head.

As I steadied the rifle, I heard the crackle of gunfire and soon the sound of bullets pelting the ground around me. Snow began bursting up as the bullets tore into the ground.

"They're headin' for the gunship!" Nevin said, the sound of his rifle firing overwhelming that of the enemy MG.

"Keep them off it, we need that ship!" I said, frustration setting in as Robert turned around, about to reenter the command tent.

I breathed slow, processing the situation.

"Ross, you need to work on your aim," Colonel Miller's voice boomed in my head.

I was tired. I was hungry. I was cold. But above all, I was a Ranger.

My crosshair moved, as if in slow motion across the front of the tent, then across Robert's back. I lifted, the to bars marking an X across the back of his head.

I fired.

The singular 12.7mm round soared through the air, freed from its prison within my SR-4. The same SR-4 I had used on Enphuerzo, the same one I'd killed my first man with on Sontonos, the same one that had been by my side to do my bidding for every mission that it could be used.

A burst of blood and a fragment of skull raced from Robert as his body fell into the tent's flap. His head remained exposed, as the tent's flap was pushed aside by his arm. He may have been dead, but I couldn't be sure. I fired again, once more striking the head of my former squadmate. He could not have survived. Looking back toward the gunship, too many troops were closing in on it. They had to be preparing for Cope's escape. We needed to be there.

"Nevin, let's go!" I screamed, leaping up and charging down the hill.

Without another thought he was on his feet sprinting beside me. I watched as round after round rippled past me, though left me untouched. The freezing snow fell from my body in large chunks as I continued the sprint. All I could think about was taking that gunship and getting home. Everyone was depending on us. Toward the end of the hill I slipped, sliding down the slick hill until I tumbled at the bottom. Though like Nevin at the Cover Point during training I gracefully somersaulted, once more on my feet and running. The tents were directly beside us as we tore alongside the camp. I saw a man nearing the gunship's side entrance and quickly pulled out my pistol.

With my SR-4 held with its stock beneath my shoulder, I raised my pistol left-handed and fired two shots. The man nearest the gunship dropped and I picked a new target, still moving nearer the ship. He dropped. Another target. Two rounds to the chest. Then I saw Cope. He was close, just a few meters away. From the essentially un-aimed position beneath my shoulder, I fired a round of the SR-4, the kick stumbling me due to the awkward stance. Against the odds, the round struck Cope's leg, splintering the bone and instantly bringing him to the ground.

I holstered my pistol and made a final dash to the gunship. When I reached it, I leaped through its open hatch in a single swift move. Not even a second later, Nevin had done the same, slamming the hatch behind him. I checked the other side hatch, which was sealed, and then quickly entered the cockpit. Gazing down at the controls, I realized that Ryan was our only experienced pilot. We had made it this far, but how were we to fly the gunship away?

To my surprise, Nevin seized the controls and began punching buttons. I heard the engine engage and just as I heard something slam into the hatch I also felt a strong jerk upward. We were airborne. I backed up, grabbing the controls for the gun mounted directly beside the port hatch. The digital interface provided me line of sight for the gun, and I squeezed its trigger. The minigun's rounds unleashed a hail of lead onto the UED forces, shredding anything that couldn't retreat, including Admiral Cope's body.

Soon Nevin had pulled away and the ship was returning the direction we had come. We had done it. The gunship was ours, Robert and Cope both dead in the cold, unforgiving snow.

"Nev, we… we did it! How did we just… how are you flying that?" I asked, exhausted, though jubilant.

"I'm improvising James. I'm no pro, but I'm doing the best I can," he said, the gunship rocking uneasily for a moment.

"We are going to make it Nevin, we're going home."

He nodded, his hands shaking has he held the controls. We had all picked up the roles that Ryan had left behind, filled the void of his absence. Nevin ran the controls of a gunship. Phil had set up explosives. Cass filled the same combat role, wielding an assault rifle. And lastly, I was the leader. My team looked up to me to guide them through this mission.

The sound of a few final bullets pinging off the exterior of the gunship faded away as we soared toward our team. Within a few minutes, we had traversed a distance that had taken twenty to walk.

The War Across the Stars

"There they are," Nevin said, pointing with his head, unwilling to remove a hand from the controls to show me.

I smiled, knowing what it meant. We were in the final stage of our escape. We were in the endgame.

Alex Pennington

Chapter 21
Into the Hornet's Nest

Nevin eased the gunship to the ground, slowly resting it on the snowy plains. He exhaled loudly as he disabled the engines and leaned back. Together we opened the starboard hatch and dismounted the gunship. Despite the gray, angular metal, the gunship truly was a beautiful sight. Stepping into the snow, I once more could feel the omnipresent cold. We each approached the Corsair, and the back hatch opened, as if on cue. Within the team was eating the fruit that Cassidy had picked from inside the Tredecim capital. She smiled and tossed one to me.

"Phil said they're safe. I say they're good," she said.

Though hesitant, I took a bite from the fruit and was satisfied by the mere feel of food in my mouth. Without delay I consumed the remainder of the fruit, wishing only that there was more to go around.

"Thanks. Good idea to grab 'em Cass," I said, stepping into the relative warmth of the Corsair.

"Congratulations Ross. You survived. Washington and the Admiral are dead, I presume?" Malum inquired, his face plain.

"Yes sir. We're done here. I suggest we take the *Hornet* before the UED can reorganize."

"Agreed," Boone pitched in.

"Anyone else a pilot, I can't say I'm the best," Nevin admitted.

"Uh, I can," the ensign, Jeremy announced. "I

was trained in basic dropship flight before I went to be a Nav officer."

"That's more than I've had, controls are yours," Nevin said, pointing to the gunship.

"How should we split?" I asked.

"I'd advise—," Phil started, before being cut off by Malum.

"Rangers, you shall take the UED Gunship. Ensign Lowell will be your pilot. My pilot, two Marines, and Boone shall take the Corsair."

Not seeing anything wrong with the plan, aside from what was likely to be shaky piloting of our craft, I nodded. Everyone loaded onto their respective ships, and we took off, ascending from the horrid planet for the last time. I extracted Ryan's tags and twirled them slowly between my fingers for a few minutes, reflecting on how Operation UNKNOWN had been in so many ways, a disaster. Though our mission was accomplished, and it was nearly time to head home.

I used the digital screen of the port gun to watch the icy planet slip away, fading into an ever-smaller entity. We began our approach on the massive UED fleet, though due to their disarray, and our UED IFF, we were not fired upon. We smoothly approached the one ship of Vorgian design, the title *Hornet* emblazoned across the starboard side of the bow.

We glided effortlessly to the aft of the ship, slowly lowering toward the open hangar bay. Its gate was hung ajar, though it appeared the pressure field remained active. We passed through it, our ship first, followed seconds later by Malum's Corsair. We touched down with a clank, and I braced myself. If any Vorgians were left, they would all be on this ship.

I slipped in the final magazine of 9mm rounds for my H-81. Nevin readied his SMG, and Phil did a double check on his shotgun. Cass slowly ran her fingers over her AR-27 before checking the magazine.

"Let's finish this," I said, opening a hatch and sliding out of the craft.

My team followed suit, Jeremy taking up the rear.

"Take this, keep it safe," Nevin said, slipping Jeremy his H-44.

The higher caliber round seemed an odd fit for the naval officer, but he accepted it graciously and tried to mimic our stance.

We advanced through the dark hangar bay, old Wildcat dropships and Preston-Class Tanks lined the walls. When we reached the doorway out of the hangar, I looked back, confirming Malum and his team were with us. I entered the hallway right behind Phil, who had assumed point.

It seemed as if the entire ship was trying to preserve power, almost all lighting disabled. The light from our gun-mounted flashlights was our only dependable source of luminance. In a way, it reminded me of the pirate base we had destroyed on our last mission before Operation UNKNOWN. But then they had been confused, untrained. They were hardly a threat. Here the Vorgians could be waiting for us, having set a trap. We had no way of knowing how much Robert had told Cope, or whether any of the exchange had left that tent via COM.

Phil turned a corner. Still nothing.

We were en route to the bridge, there we could gain lights and hole up as we departed the planet's orbit. Passing by another corner, only darkness treated us.

"Is it… is it empty?" I asked, barely able to believe it.

"Surely not, they'd have had to leave some nature of sentinel, would they not?" Phil countered.

"One would think… but… Not seeing anyone," Cass murmured in response.

Several more minutes of the nerve-racking travel resulted in no hostile encounter. Though we did find the bridge.

Exiting the dark hallway, we stepped into the dimly lit command room of the *Hornet*. It was a wonderful sight, several consoles scattered about, a large port providing a view into space.

"Let's lock down the entrance to the bridge. If anything is alive on this ship, I don't want it in here until we're back in the Jerico system," I said, an air of command in my tone.

"Roger that," Phil said, closing the lone bulkhead into the bridge.

"Ensign, take the Nav station, get us moving," I requested.

"On it sir, uh, Sergeant," he replied, still submissive as usual.

Each of us split up amongst the room, assuming positions on stations and consoles that we knew little about. But somehow, some way, we would make it work. It took every person on the bridge, but we filled every necessary slot. Our skeleton crew was prepared for launch.

"Ensign, take us away. Engage Ultradrive and plot our course for Euphola," I said.

"Right away," Jeremy's chipper response echoed.

It seemed everyone was smiling, taking in the fact we may actually survive. Only Boone and Malum seemed to hold their stern postures.

"Good work back there, James," Cassidy complimented.

"This has been a lot for all of us, but we're home bound now," I sighed.

"The war is finally over," Nevin added. "When we reach home we can rest easy."

"While we head home, I think I'll crack open that ol' laptop and see what I can learn about the UED. We might be hearing from them again sooner than we'd all like to think," Phil stated.

Thinking about our experiences, I sat down in the captain's chair. Mysteries still remained, unsolved, and perhaps forever doomed to remain that way. Might my sister still be alive? Who are They? Might we ever contact the UED again? But as we soared through Ultraspace, our course set to home, I couldn't help but push the questions from my mind. We still might not make it through the Black Hole Belt, we may still fail to reach home. But if we die, we can know we died having completed our mission and having done everything we could to survive against the odds. In real war, you have to.

The War Across the Stars

Observing the adjacent console, I opened the log. At the time the unlimited access to the information stored within the Vorgian captain's log meant little to me. With the mission complete, it all seemed so far away. Though what did matter to me, was remembering every soldier that fought alongside us on Marzoc. Giving every one a chance to be remembered for what they did. I scrolled to the bottom before appending my best guess at the date. I then began to type.

```
In Memory of the Soldiers who Gave
      Their Lives on Marzoc.
unknown Soldier- Killed by UED Sniper
 Cpl Rush- Killed by UED Explosive
  Cpl Hood- Killed by Praetorian
Marines of Alpha- Killed by Praetorians
 Marines of Epsilon- Killed by UED
 Paladin Tank Crew- Killed by Messor
Corsair Pilot- Killed by Vorgian AA
  Cpl Max Pippin- Death Unknown
 Lt Ryan Dunkelman- Died a Hero
```

Alex Pennington

Note from the Author

Five years in the making and the tale of the War Across the Stars has finally come to its conclusion. The project has meant a lot to me and served as a creative outlet for the entirety of my High School career. I am proud to have started it in 2007 and to have remained dedicated to it for the years following. It is hard to fully comprehend that it is all over, but I appreciate everyone who's been a part of helping to fulfill this achievement.

Special Thanks

James D. Pennington
Kristi McNary
Falisa Calhoun
Coree Rogers
Kerry Beach
Davion Bowens
Troy Pennington
Genna Pennington
Jasmine Miller

Alex Pennington

About the Author

I was born on 13 October 1993 to Troy and Marquita Pennington. We have lived in the city of El Dorado, Kansas for my entire life, and as such it really represents home to me.

I've always had an interest in writing, ever since I was a little kid, but it wasn't until 6th grade that I set out to write a book. The result, wasn't too great, and I dropped the project for a while. Then in 2007, after just starting my 8th grade year, I was inspired to give it another go. With a brand new story set in a science fiction universe, I set off to create what later become The War Across the Stars.

In addition to my writing, I've always put my academics as a priority, seeking to go above and beyond when I can, and ensure that I maintained my 4.0 Grade Point Average throughout my entire education. I participated in the school's Scholar's Bowl team as well as the City's Youth Commission, on which I served as Chairman for my final two years. In 2012 I was awarded the Dean's Scholars' Scholarship to attend Wichita State University, which I will be doing in Fall.

The War Across the Stars